The Gambler's Last Chance

One Night in Blackhaven
Book 4

MARY LANCASTER

DRAGONBLADE PUBLISHING, INC.

ARE YOU SIGNED UP FOR DRAGONBLADE'S BLOG?

You'll get the latest news and information on exclusive giveaways, exclusive excerpts, coming releases, sales, free books, cover reveals and more.

Check out our complete list of authors, too!

No spam, no junk. That's a promise!

Sign Up Here

www.dragonbladepublishing.com

Dearest Reader;

Thank you for your support of a small press. At Dragonblade Publishing, we strive to bring you the highest quality Historical Romance from some of the best authors in the business. Without your support, there is no 'us', so we sincerely hope you adore these stories and find some new favorite authors along the way.

Happy Reading!

CEO, Dragonblade Publishing

Additional Dragonblade books by Author Mary Lancaster

One Night in Blackhaven Series
The Captain's Old Love (Book 1)
The Earl's Promised Bride (Book 2)
The Soldier's Impossible Love (Book 3)
The Gambler's Last Chance (Book 4)

The Duel Series
Entangled (Book 1)
Captured (Book 2)
Deserted (Book 3)
Beloved (Book 4)

Last Flame of Alba Series
Rebellion's Fire (Book 1)
A Constant Blaze (Book 2)
Burning Embers (Book 3)

Gentlemen of Pleasure Series
The Devil and the Viscount (Book 1)
Temptation and the Artist (Book 2)
Sin and the Soldier (Book 3)
Debauchery and the Earl (Book 4)
Blue Skies (Novella)

Pleasure Garden Series
Unmasking the Hero (Book 1)
Unmasking Deception (Book 2)
Unmasking Sin (Book 3)
Unmasking the Duke (Book 4)
Unmasking the Thief (Book 5)

Crime & Passion Series
Mysterious Lover (Book 1)
Letters to a Lover (Book 2)
Dangerous Lover (Book 3)
Lost Lover (Book 4)
Merry Lover (Novella)
Ghostly Lover (Novella)

The Husband Dilemma Series
How to Fool a Duke (Book 1)

Season of Scandal Series
Pursued by the Rake (Book 1)
Abandoned to the Prodigal (Book 2)
Married to the Rogue (Book 3)
Unmasked by her Lover (Book 4)
Her Star from the East (Novella)

Imperial Season Series
Vienna Waltz (Book 1)
Vienna Woods (Book 2)
Vienna Dawn (Book 3)

Blackhaven Brides Series
The Wicked Baron (Book 1)
The Wicked Lady (Book 2)
The Wicked Rebel (Book 3)
The Wicked Husband (Book 4)
The Wicked Marquis (Book 5)
The Wicked Governess (Book 6)
The Wicked Spy (Book 7)
The Wicked Gypsy (Book 8)
The Wicked Wife (Book 9)
Wicked Christmas (Book 10)
The Wicked Waif (Book 11)
The Wicked Heir (Book 12)
The Wicked Captain (Book 13)
The Wicked Sister (Book 14)

Prologue

THE VALE TWINS, Leona and Lawrence, sat on the stairs of Black Hill House, as they often did late in the evening when they were supposed to be in bed. Their older siblings rarely told them off for it—they were fifteen years old, after all, and no longer children. It was all part of their intelligence gathering, very necessary in their self-appointed task of looking after their troubled siblings. They learned a lot from who stayed up late and what state they were in when they went to bed.

Usually, Roderick was the last to retire. But tonight was different. The twins had called their family meeting, during which they had set their brothers and sisters on the path most likely to get them all to the Blackhaven ball and forward to greater enjoyment, if not happiness, in life.

Although the house was silent, there was still a light beneath the drawing room door. The twins waited patiently, but it was not Roderick who emerged with the solitary candle to light himself up to bed. It was Felicia, their widowed sister.

In the glow of her own candle and the one Lawrence had placed on the step above him, Felicia's beauty was almost wraithlike. Fairer than her siblings', her hair glinted with hints of silver, and the skin seemed to be drawn too tightly over the delicate bones of her lovely face. Exhaustion, grief, and anxiety had made her too thin, but recently her eyes had begun to shine once more with vitality. Even her pale skin had developed a touch of healthy rosiness. Leona thought of that as the natural effect of Blackhaven, and was delighted. But it was time for a slightly less natural nudge.

Felicia stopped and eyed the twins with the mixture of humor and annoyance that was quite familiar to them. Even at her lowest, Felicia had always smiled. And she had always looked after them.

"Well?" she demanded. "Why are you not in bed at this hour?"

"Why aren't you?" Leona countered.

"I fell asleep in my chair."

Lawrence smiled. "No, you didn't. You never do that."

"Well, I was thinking," Felicia amended, "about what you said earlier. You are very perceptive twins and, I think, quite right. It is a good beginning. Come on, up to bed with you."

Lawrence picked up the candle and led the way up the staircase.

"We were thinking, too," Leona said. "It just struck us that so much of this depends on you. We don't want you to be so busy at the ball that you forget to enjoy it on your own account."

"Oh, I am quite the social butterfly," Felicia said lightly. "I have missed that part of my life since Nick died. I shall enjoy making friends and introducing dance partners to all my siblings. Including Delilah."

"But you must dance, too," Lawrence said.

"I shall. With all the handsomest and most dangerous gentlemen. And I shall drink champagne—if they have such wines out here in the wilderness—and play cards for money. In short, I shall be *wicked*."

The twins beamed upon her, and she laughed.

"You are not supposed to be pleased by my misbehavior!"

"You deserve it," Leona said generously. She did not expand, but the brief look she exchanged with Lawrence confirmed that he thought the same.

The world knew that Felicia, who never wore her heart on her sleeve, had been devastated by her husband's death. In her own understated and yet lively way, she had also provided the twins stability since their father's death, and even before. She had survived a difficult marriage and a harder widowhood, but was ready, at last, for fun.

And the beauty of it was, she knew she was helping her siblings at the same time and so would not resist. The twins had managed that very well indeed.

Chapter One

FELICIA MAITLAND, NÉE Vale, twirled down the line of the country dance with Lord Linfield. He was a tall, graceful man of pleasant conversation and understated wit. She liked him, and so as the music came to a close, she smiled warmly as she curtseyed, and happily took his proffered arm.

"Allow me to escort you back to your family," he said.

Perfect, Felicia thought, until she realized a very slight change of direction would bring them straight into the speeding path of her elder sister Delilah. Delilah may have been in pursuit of their mischievous sister Lucy, or of simple escape, but either way, Felicia was happy to thwart her.

She had promised not to drag gentlemen across the room to Delilah, but a chance encounter was entirely different.

"Oh, Delly, have you been dancing?" Felicia said as though surprised to run into her. "So have I. This is Lord Linfield, who is visiting the town with his sister for the benefits of the waters. My lord, my sister, Miss Vale."

Delilah responded with a curtsey but absolutely no intention of keeping Lord Linfield from more enjoyable pursuits. At thirty years old, Delilah was convinced she was on the shelf and a mere annoyance to anyone but her family. The twins were not alone in their determination to rectify that. Delilah was much more than beautiful and funny, she was strong and loyal and brave, and she deserved every happiness life had to offer.

Felicia barely gave Delilah and Linfield time to murmur, "How do you do?" to each other before she excused herself as though taking over the pursuit of Lucy.

Lucy, however, had far stricter duennas in her brothers, and Felicia's goal was, in reality, the card room. A great deal, both serious and trivial, depended on it.

Felicia had already observed that this was not a gentlemen-only kind of card room. A group of ladies of indeterminate years played whist at a table near the door. A younger lady seemed to be watching the gentlemen playing faro.

Felicia moved further into the room. The ladies were playing whist for farthings. Another table full of gentlemen played macao for higher though not outrageous stakes. Regarding them with more interest, Felicia realized she knew one of them. The Honorable Waller Harlaw had been a friend of her husband Nick's.

Well, Nick had called him a friend, but it always seemed to be Nick's vowels that ended up in Harlaw's pockets, never the other way around. She had only just redeemed the last of those vowels before leaving London for Blackhaven.

Judging by the pile of coins and vowels at his elbow this evening, he was winning again, although another player had a pile almost as large. A young man in his early twenties, dark-haired, willowy, handsome in a fine-featured way that somehow looked more masculine than the deliberately Corinthian style favored by Harlaw. But what intrigued Felicia was the young stranger's concentration on the game. He watched the cards, he watched his opponents' faces, and he placed bets with quick, calm civility, but he paid no attention to his surroundings. A much more experienced player, she deduced, than his years might suggest.

And yet he did not have the dissipated looks of the hard-gaming, hard-drinking, womanizing rakehell that she knew all too well. She wondered who he was.

Harlaw won again. Then, as the game began to break up, he

caught sight of Felicia with astonishment. He sprang to his feet with rather less than his usual elegance and bowed.

"Mrs. Maitland! What a pleasant surprise. I did not know you were in Blackhaven."

"I did not know you were here either," she replied, keeping her voice light. "But then, there is no reason why we should."

He looked slightly taken aback. "Indeed not." Then he smiled as though just struck by a delightful idea. "Perhaps a hand of piquet later?"

It was an odd request at a ball. Should he not rather invite her to dance? On the other hand, perhaps he understood that she would rather play cards with him.

"Perhaps," she agreed, and was about to turn away when she caught the intense gaze of the handsome younger man she had noticed before. He was scooping up his winnings and cramming them into his pocket, but mechanically, distractedly, for all his attention was fixed on Felicia.

It was a long time since a man had looked at her like that, with the unselfconscious admiration that wanted nothing in return except, perhaps, a smile. A hint of color even seeped along the fine line of his cheekbones. Felicia was enchanted.

"But where are my manners?" Harlaw said, glancing from her to the young man and then back to her. The other gamers at the table had wandered off. "Do you know Mr. Muir, ma'am?"

"I do not," Felicia said, though she vaguely recalled the name.

"Then allow me to present Mr. Bernard Muir. Of Blackhaven, although his sister is Lady Wickenden. Muir, Mrs. Maitland, the widow of a dear friend of mine. Will you excuse me?"

"Of course," Felicia said, and Harlaw strolled away, very well aware of being the great man of fashion among all the rural nobodies.

Perhaps for that reason, Felicia gave Mr. Muir her hand, which he bowed over with perfect grace. He was not wearing gloves, and she liked the shape of his long fingers, their cool, brief clasp. Her other goal of the evening, naughtier and only half acknowledged, nudged her memory.

"How do you do?" She smiled. "So you are Gillie Wick-enden's brother?"

"You know Gillie?"

"Only slightly. I was widowed shortly after her marriage, so I have not been out and about much recently."

"I'm sorry," Mr. Muir said, with a sincerity that took her by surprise.

He had kind eyes. She could not remember when she last noticed a man had kind eyes. "Oh, it was more than two years ago now..."

The strains of a waltz introduction drifted through from the main ballroom.

Mr. Muir gave a quick, self-deprecating smile. "You came to play cards, I must assume. I don't suppose you would care to dance instead?"

Apart from an elderly gentleman dozing comfortably in the corner, only the whist-playing ladies remained in the card room. No doubt it would fill up again in a few moments and she would find a way to play. On the other hand, a handsome young man with kind, admiring eyes, and the sort of smile that turned one's knees to jelly, had just asked her to waltz.

"I believe I would," she replied. Well, it would have been rude to refuse.

Mr. Muir offered his arm, and she laid her hand on his sleeve. They were a few seconds late for the beginning of the dance, but with unexpected aplomb, he merely led her onto the floor and into the waltz.

How strange to feel a man's arm at her waist again, to sense the warmth of his fingers through her glove as she followed his steps around and back and forward. The waltz craze had really only begun around the time of Nick's death, and she had never danced it with him—one did not dance with one's own husband! But she had found the experience exhilarating. Although, if she was honest, she had enjoyed being just a little fast more than the actual closeness of the dance.

Mr. Muir danced naturally, gracefully. He did not grab or try to haul her too close or catch her out by stepping forward too quickly and trying to brush against her hips. Intriguingly, he held her gaze as they danced and yet always seemed to find the space they needed. She felt no urge to rush into conversation, merely let herself *feel*, absorbing the very physical sensations of the waltz.

It was he who spoke first. "Will you stay long in Blackhaven, Mrs. Maitland?"

"Oh, I am quite fixed here for the time being. I am staying with my brother at Black Hill House."

His eyebrows flew up. "Black Hill? Then you are Sir Julius Vale's sister?"

"One of them. Do you know Julius?"

"We met him on the way in this evening. With another brother and two sisters. Apparently, my aunt was acquainted with your late father."

"That almost makes us old friends," she said lightly. "And neighbors, of course. Where is it you live?"

She had not met all the surrounding landowners yet.

"In the town. Cliff Crescent. My father was an officer of the Forty-Fourth and was stationed here for years. Gillie and I grew up in Blackhaven."

"I stayed here as a child sometimes, but I don't remember it very clearly. My father was always dragging us with him on his travels."

"Did you mind?"

"I never considered it. Looking back, I realize how lucky I was, seeing so many different and beautiful places."

"You sound quite wistful."

She smiled self-consciously. For some reason, she did not want this young man to see her as a whiner. "I am, a little. I have been trapped in London too long. But I am enjoying Blackhaven. It is good to be back."

He nodded, as if he understood that, but did not enlarge. He seemed flatteringly content just to watch her face. Well, she rather liked looking at his. It caused a pleasant little tingle somewhere in her stomach. And yet he seemed so young, unmarked by life, let alone vice. And she was a widow, free of the constraining bonds of both married and unmarried ladies...

"Have you traveled much?" she asked, mostly to redirect her wayward thoughts.

"No further than Paris for a fortnight," he replied with apparent regret. "I mean to go back as soon as I can. And further afield."

"Why?" she asked.

He blinked, and she laughed.

"Am I too blunt? You may tell me to go to the devil—I shan't take offense. I merely wondered whether you are drawn to Paris, or simply away from home. And if the former, what is it that attracts you? Art? Theatre? A love affair?"

He gave another of those quick, devastating smiles that lit up his face like a lightning flash. It seemed to strike somewhere beneath her stomach. He was a very attractive man.

"You *are* blunt," he agreed. "Refreshingly so. Let me just say I have ambitions that cannot really be achieved at home. Or anywhere, if luck does not favor me."

She was conscious of disappointment, quite out of proportion to the length of their acquaintance. "You are a gambler?"

"Aren't you?"

She raised her brows. "Why would you think so?"

"Why else would you come alone into the card room?"

"I might have been looking for someone."

"Did you find him?"

She smiled. Once she had flirted as naturally as breathing and enjoyed it. "I might have."

Gratifyingly, he caught his breath. But his smile was rueful. "I hope you do not mean Mr. Harlaw."

She laughed. "No."

"Good." He bent his head closer, and this time it was she who had trouble with breathing. He smelled of clean, spiced soap, and his mouth looked sensitive and wildly seductive. "He may be a friend of yours, but I would not play piquet with him."

It was hardly what she expected, so her voice was a little sharp. "Why not?"

"I would hate you to lose."

"One of us would have to. It is the nature of the game."

"And yet he always wins." There was an accusation there, unspoken but unmistakable. His head dipped closer yet, until his breath caressed her lips. "Es—" He broke off. His lips curved in apology as he straightened. "You could always play with me."

She tilted her chin. "Are we still talking about piquet, Mr. Muir?"

"About anything you wish. We could certainly *begin* with piquet."

She laughed, mostly because she had expected to make him blush again and failed. "And I should play with you because you do *not* always win?"

"I always try to."

"So I might expect no favors?"

"Not in cards."

She met the humorous challenge in his eyes, and the veiled warmth of something that was surely desire. "Exactly where I need none. What a fortunate beginning. How well you waltz, Mr. Muir."

"Only because of how well you do."

"Also an expert in flattery, I perceive."

"Hardly. I decided against it when I was nineteen years old."

"I doubt that," she murmured.

"You do not believe me?"

"My dear sir, you play macao far too well to be believed."

"Hoist with my own petard," he said with a sigh.

"Not entirely. I still look forward to our game."

Having thus dealt effectively, she felt, with any impulse to cozen her, she was gratified to see the gleam in his eye. Pleasure, she thought with growing excitement, and gave herself up to the dance.

There was something very intimate about the waltz, something she had not noticed when she was younger. It was more than the physical closeness—it was following his lead, learning the subtle signals of where he would go next. Like a really good card game, only...more. On top of which was the relentless rhythm and melody of the music. She could not remember noticing that before either.

She had been too blind in her youth. Too obsessed by Nick, his attention, his love, his infidelity. But she refused to think of Nick now. Mr. Muir was an attractive stranger, a clean slate, a little well-earned excitement that might mean nothing, or... But no, this was not about the past or the future. It was the present, and she was happy.

When the dance ended, of course, reality intruded. It was time to round up her brothers and introduce them to prospective partners for the next dance, to track down Lucy and make sure Delilah was not lurking out of sight.

Mr. Muir, she realized, would make a fine partner for Lucy, only not until Felicia had played a hand of piquet with him...

"Are you looking for someone in particular?" he asked.

"All my siblings," she replied, "apart from the twins. Lucy has vanished, but so has Roderick, so they might be together. Cornelius—ah, there he is with a young lady whose face I cannot see, and Aubrey is naturally with the most beautiful girl in the room. Julius... Where is Julius? And Delilah?"

"Is it your duty to chaperone them all?" he asked, apparently amused.

"I want them to have fun."

"They seem to have found it on their own," Mr. Muir said mildly.

She regarded him, unsure whether to be amused or offended. "Meaning I should stop clucking about them like a mother hen?"

"I think when you appeared in the card room, you were

having at least *some* fun escaping them. What makes you think they are so different?"

She closed her mouth. "A promise to the twins," she said wryly. "But even they would not expect me to supervise the entire evening. Are we playing piquet, sir?"

"If you are so minded, it will be my pleasure."

She took his offered arm, and they strolled into the card room once more. He held the chair for her at one of two unoccupied piquet tables, called a footman by name, and asked him to bring two glasses of wine.

Felicia's hands itched to pick up the waiting pack of cards and shuffle it, but she forced herself to wait for her opponent, learning something of his skill and experience from the way he did it. They cut the cards and she won. Mr. Muir dealt.

The wine appeared, but neither of them paid much attention. Mr. Muir took occasional sips, without looking at his glass. His attention was all on the cards or on her. Occasionally, his quick smile flashed across his face and vanished, but it seemed to have little to do with winning, more to do with her surprising him, or perhaps with learning something of her skill.

She certainly learned about his. He played well, not recklessly, though with occasional sparks of brilliance.

"You are good," she said after the first partie.

"So are you. Who taught you?"

"My father. I was something of a prodigy. He used to invite senior diplomats and even a few princes to play me. I usually won."

"Are you trying to frighten me?" he asked, passing her the cards to deal.

"No. I am waiting to learn your story."

He shrugged. "I played with my father and his friends—army officers at a loose end before they were sent to the Peninsula. After he died, my sister and I held card parties in the house to try to make ends meet."

"Did it work?"

"Up to a point. Although we were too naïve to realize that it could have ruined Gillie socially. But then she met Wickenden, who has been everything that is generous."

She paused in her dealing to look at him more closely. He was not entirely happy with the situation, she guessed. Like most men, he would have rather stood on his own feet than be beholden to his brother-in-law.

"Did you never want to follow your father's footsteps into the army?" she asked lightly.

"At one time. He would not countenance it, and then, after he died, if I had gone, who would have been here for Gillie and my aunt? Besides, I would be a terrible soldier. My father always said my only signs of intelligence were my palate and my card playing."

"Very gentlemanly skills," she approved, which made him grin.

"What of you?" he asked. "Did you play cards with your husband?"

She shook her head. "Nick only played to win," she said. "And playing his wife, he would lose either way."

She laid down the talon between them and picked up her cards, just as a lady swept up to them, clearly in a hurry. She was dark and eye-catchingly beautiful.

"Bernard, I go home now," she said, her voice breathless and exotically accented. "Arthur will need me."

Mr. Muir began to rise immediately, but the lady placed one familiar hand on his shoulder and pushed him back down into the chair. "No, you stay with Aunt Margaret. Mr. Harlaw will escort me."

Mr. Muir did not seem to like that, for a frown tugged at his brow before he could smooth it. And with a jolt, Felicia realized why.

He is jealous... Dear God, she is his wife. And Arthur is his child.

Chapter Two

M RS. MAITLAND WAS breathtaking. Willowy, elegant, and graceful, she possessed the kind of rare beauty that consisted of as much character as regular features. Her pale, almost-blonde hair shone with silver lights that reflected in her eyes—large, expressive eyes so ready to smile. Yet her amusement tended toward the cynical, and behind her heart-stopping smiles he was sure he sensed suffering. Felicia Maitland was no sheltered, pampered lady of fashion. She was a strong and lovely woman.

Bernard Muir was dazzled by everything she did—speaking, smiling, dancing, teasing, playing cards. He lost track of time completely, so that when Isabella interrupted them, he was more irritated by that than by the fact she was allowing Harlaw to escort her.

He contented himself by saying only, "Is that wise?"

"Don't be silly. Danny will be there. Goodnight, Bernard." And she swept off again without even noticing his companion.

Presumably Harlaw was impatient, damn his impertinence.

Meaning to apologize for Isabella's apparent rudeness, Bernard glanced at Mrs. Maitland and found her staring almost blindly toward the door. "Mrs. Maitland? Isabella did not mean to be rude. She is just single-minded about the boy."

"As mothers are," she said with strange brittleness, making

him wonder if she had wanted children of her own. But then, she could have birthed the makings of a cricket team already and he would not know. He knew nothing about her except for her beauty, her allure, and her stunning skill at piquet.

She laid down her cards. "You should go with her."

"I don't like Harlaw," he agreed, "but Isabella doesn't want me there playing gooseberry."

"*Gooseberry!*" She stared at him. "Is the lady not your wife?"

He blinked once and let out a crack of laughter. "No, thank God! She is my stepmother."

A breath of laughter shook her, but he could not quite read her expression.

"I thought you would know," he said. "Blackhaven gossip was full of it a few years ago. No one here knew my father had married again in Spain, until Isabella appeared at our door threatening to evict us."

Mrs. Maitland's eyes widened. Every change of expression made her more fascinating. "And yet you seem comfortable now."

"That was Gillie. She took pity on her when she realized Isabella was with child and had no money. Isabella only wanted to evict us because she thought the card parties showed no respect to my father. Gillie brought her home just before our little brother was born. We all rub along pretty well now. Are you giving up because your hand is so poor you know I must win?"

She returned to the game. He had never encountered a woman who played with such focus. Although she conversed at the same time, her mind clearly never left the cards altogether. Neither did her gaze, except, rarely, to glance at him.

What did she see? The green, unsophisticated boy everyone in Blackhaven still thought him? Did she compare him to his handsome, self-confident brother-in-law and find him wanting, but at least worthy of a game of cards?

But then she had agreed also to play with Harlaw. Another man from her own world, far from Blackhaven.

Why had she come north?

Concentrate, Bernard. She's beating you…

At last, she threw down her cards and regarded him, her beautiful blue-green eyes gleaming. "Still think I should not play with Mr. Harlaw?"

"Yes."

She smiled and rose to her feet. "Thank you for the game, Mr. Muir. I have thoroughly enjoyed it."

He stood at once and bowed. He wanted to dance with her again, but he had already monopolized her for too long. "So have I. I hope we may play again."

"So do I," she said cordially, and, with a quick curtsey, hurried out.

"Bereft, Bernard?" a male voice asked lightly beside him.

Bernard glanced up at the Earl of Braithwaite. Despite their difference in rank, they had known each other most of their lives. Although the earl had learned haughtiness as a means to repel both toadies and cozeners, Bernard liked him and even thought of him as a friend.

The card room was largely clearing out for the supper dance, so they had a little privacy.

"Are you acquainted with the Vale family?" Bernard asked.

"I have met a couple of them. Cornelius Vale is very knowledgeable about the land. Forward-looking fellow. My wife knows your Mrs. Maitland."

Of course Braithwaite had seen them together. It was an unusual enough piquet pairing to have caught most people's attention.

"Did you know Maitland?" Bernard asked.

"Only by repute." Braithwaite held his gaze. "Bit of a loose screw. Left his widow with massive debts and little means to pay."

"Then that is why she came back to Blackhaven," Bernard murmured. "A repairing lease, as they say."

"Well, all the Vales are here. I believe Eleanor said the sisters and the children were living in the Maitland house, so if they had to sell it, they would all have been homeless."

"That bad?" Bernard said, frowning.

Braithwaite shrugged. "Town gossip, my friend, and delivered thirdhand and probably inaccurately. I don't pay much attention."

Together, they began to walk toward the door to the main ballroom. Bernard's frown deepened. "But Black Hill is a bit of a mess, is it not? Old Barton neglected it for years, to call his behavior no worse."

"I think the estate will probably come right in the end. Cornelius Vale will see to that if no one else does. The trouble is that with this summer's weather, *all* the harvests are likely to be poor, which does not give the Vales much of a start." Braithwaite glanced beyond Bernard. "But speak of repairing leases, there is a man requiring one. I saw him leave with your stepmother not half an hour ago."

Harlaw. Bernard scowled. "What is he doing back? Isabella made it sound as if he was the one in a hurry to leave." Perhaps before Mrs. Maitland could fleece him at piquet! But he had definitely returned.

"His attentions to Mrs. Muir have grown marked," Braithwaite said. "Is she aware of his gambling proclivities?"

"I can't imagine so," Bernard said, although he had an unpleasant suspicion that it was not his stepmother's good looks and character that had drawn Harlaw to Isabella. "But she will be. Who is he, exactly?"

"The Honorable Waller Harlaw? Younger brother of Viscount Denny. Fancies himself as a bit of a sportsman but likes the high life too much. Inherited some money and a town house from some uncle or other, but rumor says he doesn't pay his tailor."

"Living on his expectations?" Bernard suggested.

"Don't believe he has any. Denny has three thriving sons to inherit the title, and the family wealth and rumor says the brothers don't get on."

Then he was hanging out for a rich wife…

"He was a crony of Nicholas Maitland," Braithwaite said casually. "I expect they encouraged each other in their folly. Maitland died owing him money. Apparently, he let the widow off with most of it." He caught Bernard's gaze. "And yet he does not seem to me to be the chivalrous sort."

"No," Bernard agreed bleakly. "He does not."

WALLER HARLAW WAS delighted with his progress as he had walked the short distance to the Muirs' house by Isabella's side. Though she was not his motivation for journeying all the way to Blackhaven, she was certainly the reason he was still here, the reason all his plans had changed.

And she was not ill-looking. In a dark, foreign kind of way. Her English was almost perfect, and she was so proper that he was very glad she had never been to London. He just hoped no one would enlighten her about his own past before he managed to marry her.

"I so admire your motherly devotion," he told her warmly. "But you must go out to enjoy yourself occasionally."

"A couple of hours is quite enough for me. But Margaret and Bernard, it is good for them to stay longer. And good of you to escort me."

"I would allow no one else," Harlaw assured her. "Did you enjoy the evening?"

"Very much. Did you?" Her glance was shy.

He smiled. "Of course. My favorite part was dancing with you."

"You did not dance with anyone else?"

"Why would I?"

She blushed under the street light, and they walked in blissful silence the rest of the way to her front door. She turned but did not give him her hand.

Instead, she blurted, "Would you care for a glass of brandy, or some other refreshment, before you leave me?"

It was a triumph—the first time she had invited him in more than general terms. But the house was full of protective servants, one of whom, a retired soldier, was already glaring from the front doorway. He would have accepted just to annoy the man, but Harlaw had, he recalled with glee, other fish to fry.

"I will not risk waking your dear son," he said after a moment for dramatic hesitation. "But if I may, I shall call tomorrow?"

"Please do," she said warmly, giving him her hand.

He thought of kissing it but decided it would be more productive merely to bow over it and give it an extra, meaningful squeeze that the servant would never see.

"Goodnight, Mr. Harlaw."

"Goodnight, Mrs. Muir." He tipped his hat and sauntered back the way he had come. Only when he heard the door close behind him did he speed up, striding back around Cliff Terrace, past the church and the vicarage and onto the high street and the assembly rooms, in time to pursue Felicia Maitland.

His pulse quickened at the very thought of her. Nick Maitland had been a damned dog-in-the-manger. Neglected his beautiful wife and bedded anything in skirts, yet growled at any man who dared look twice at Felicia. Well, Harlaw had looked more than twice, but, unfortunately, he had never found a way to get close enough to do anything else.

Even when Maitland had died. He had nurtured hopes of her when she acknowledged Maitland's considerable debt to him, but the money had all been paid via solicitors without any meeting between them at all. Not that he wasn't glad to get the blunt, but the widow with it would have been best. He would even have sacrificed some of the former for the latter.

And yet here she was in Blackhaven of all rural backwaters, at the same time as Harlaw. It had to be fate.

He all but strutted back into the assembly rooms and, as luck would have it, encountered Felicia almost immediately.

She smiled at him as she had never done before. "Perhaps that hand of piquet, sir?"

Oh yes. His world was almost perfect.

IT WAS SOME time after supper, toward the end of the ball, before Bernard again encountered Mrs. Maitland. He had glimpsed her dancing once, and then, with anxiety, he had seen her in the card room, playing piquet with Waller Harlaw.

His every instinct was to rush over and protect her. But he had no right. He had warned her, and she understood. She played with almost supernatural skill, but what could anyone do against a cheat? Unless they were prepared to denounce him with witnesses and cause a scandal.

Even so, Bernard had made an involuntary movement toward her table before his aunt's hand jerked him in the other direction. He was very fond of Aunt Margaret, who had more or less brought him and Gillie up. She was kind and funny and more perceptive than she looked. But right now, her wittering was giving him a headache.

Patiently, he guided her back to the ballroom, to a huddle of her gossiping friends, and stood beside her chair, chatting with them all—or at least smiling—for several minutes.

Harlaw emerged from the card room with a face like thunder. Did he realize Mrs. Maitland could not pay? She and Bernard had agreed to play only for the points, but Harlaw would always play for money.

Mrs. Maitland strolled out only a little later, with her younger brother, the one Bernard had met outside the assembly rooms. Neither looked concerned. In fact, both were gazing around the ballroom as though in search of further amusement. Deliberately,

Bernard kept his gaze on her, just to see what she would do when she noticed him. Pretend she had not? Bow very slightly? Smile?

Stop being pathetic, Muir.

Their eyes met. Bernard bowed acknowledgement, and she smiled graciously. She did indeed look quickly away, so quickly that he followed her gaze to the open balcony doors. She kept walking.

Bernard's heart galloped. Was he the biggest coxcomb who ever lived, or had she just invited him to an assignation on the balcony?

Bernard was no stranger to amorous intrigue—even in Black-haven, before he had discovered the revelations of London fashionable Society when he had accompanied Gillie and Wickenden there. To him intrigue had always been an adventure, a welcome, intense bout of fun given and received with careless affection.

But this woman was different. He had not quite worked out how, unless it was the vulnerability he recognized mixed up with all the sophistication. He certainly had not expected an invitation to dally on the balcony.

Does she truly like me so much? he wondered, as he deliberately returned his attention to his aunt and her companions. Hope warred with doubt, for it did not seem *right*.

Even if she was attracted to him, her pride would never allow her to summon him so boldly when he had barely flirted with her. But she wanted—or needed—something from him.

He eased out of the conversation with the skill of much practice and excused himself, strolling toward the balcony as though for some fresh air. A couple stepped through the doors, and he stood aside to allow them to pass back into the ballroom before he went outside.

The fresh, cool air hit him at the same moment as Mrs. Maitland's presence. Mrs. Maitland's beauty. For a moment, he could not speak.

It was she who turned toward him. "Sadly, it is not a night to admire the stars."

"What stars?" Bernard asked, looking only at her.

She laughed, a delightfully husky sound of genuine amusement. She would never fall for flattery, but he doubted she believed in his genuine admiration either.

"He cheats," she said, turning her back on the door to look out over the town.

He knew exactly whom she meant. He joined her at the balustrade, glad that, for at least this moment, they were alone. "I know. Did he fleece you?"

For answer, she placed her reticule on top of the balustrade and opened it wide, revealing a couple of folded banknotes and several golden guineas. Even as he raised his startled gaze to hers, she closed the reticule and let it dangle from her wrist once more.

"How?" he demanded. "Did you accuse him?"

"Lord, no, I think we can milk him for a lot more before we need to do that. You were winning at macao. You held all the cards, and yet somehow, he always pipped you."

"How do you know I held all the cards?"

"I watched. The point is, *you* won. He cheated. I have won your money back for you, though it might be indiscreet to return it here."

He frowned. "You won it back for me? How?"

"I avoided spades. He has them up his sleeve or somewhere similar. I never saw him put them there or retrieve them."

Bernard closed his mouth and swallowed. "Then how do you know he did?"

"There were too many spades when he played macao with you. Mr. Muir, where can one play cards in Blackhaven for truly high stakes? Is there anywhere? Or just at private houses?"

"The gaming club? They hold it once a month or so at the hotel. Why?"

"I am proposing an alliance with you, sir. But we cannot discuss it here. If you are interested, you may call at Black Hill tomorrow. If you don't come, I'll send your money by a servant."

"Mrs. Maitland, the money is not mine. *You* won it."

"You lost it unfairly. But we can quarrel over it later. Not here."

Bernard drew in his breath. "No, not here. I'd much rather dance with you."

For some reason, that seemed to surprise her. She cast him a quick, clear look, and he was sure she flushed in the lanterns' glow.

"Now?" she asked uncertainly.

For answer, he offered his arm, and heard again that soft, husky laugh that turned him inside out. But she laid her gloved hand sedately on his arm, and they re-entered the ballroom in time for the last waltz of the evening.

FELICIA, DELIGHTING IN the freedom of widowhood, warmed by her budding friendship with Bernard Muir, and cock-a-hoop over defeating Waller Harlaw at cards, still knew, somewhat guiltily, that she had left her family rather too much to their own devices.

She would have felt worse, except that none of them seemed unhappy. Apart from Julius, who had vanished at some point before supper. But at least he had come, and as the rest of them gathered in the foyer to await their carriages home, she thought they were all pleasantly distracted, even Roderick.

"Where the devil is Lucy?" Cornelius fumed.

"You need not wait for her," Felicia reminded him. "I'll bring her in the second carriage." On the other hand, she had been in there for some time. "I'll fetch her."

At the cloakroom door, she met not Lucy but the sweet-faced, middle-aged lady she had previously seen with Mr. Muir— no doubt his aunt—on her way out with her evening cloak flapping. She stumbled slightly, and one of her gloves floated to the floor.

Felicia picked it up. "Your glove, ma'am," she said politely.

"Oh, bless you!" The lady beamed at her. "You are one of the Vale girls, are you not?"

"I was. Now I am the Maitland widow."

Miss Muir peered at her a little more closely, perhaps to see if she was joking or offended. Which was when Felicia realized the lady had imbibed a little more than was wise.

"I did not know your husband," Miss Muir said, her face falling. "Though I am sorry for his passing." She brightened. "I knew your papa, though. We were great friends at one time. In fact, you know, he was my first love. I might even have been his."

Papa, bless his rakish old heart, had had many loves, which was one reason the nine Vale siblings had five mothers between them.

"He was a little too charming," Felicia said tactfully. "Are you quite well, ma'am? It has been a long evening, has it not? Take my arm, and we shall find Mr. Muir."

"Bernard is a good boy. He should not—" Whatever she had been about to say vanished into the ether as Bernard himself strode up to them.

"There you are, Aunt," he said in relief. "Mrs. Maitland." Over his aunt's head, he mouthed, *Thank you.*

Clearly, Felicia did not have to tell him that his aunt was tipsy. He took her arm from Felicia's and placed it firmly through his.

"This is Mrs. Maitland," Miss Muir said, beaming upon her nephew. "One of George—*Sir* George—Vale's daughters. I remember her as such a pretty, lively child, rushing everywhere at a fast trot…! You must call on us, Mrs. Maitland, whenever you are next in Blackhaven."

"I will, ma'am. Thank you," Felicia said.

Bernard cast her one more grateful smile and, without comment or scold, escorted his aunt outside.

"Good fellow, Muir," Aubrey said, apparently having watched this by-play. "Plays a devilish hand of macao."

"And piquet," Felicia murmured.

"And loo," Aubrey said. "Haven't tried him at faro."

"You can't afford to try anyone at faro," Roderick pointed out. "And here is Lucy at last. Shall we go?"

Chapter Three

FELICIA WOKE LATE the following morning, her head spinning with possibilities, both amorous and financial. Approaching the ball, the former had been very much in the background, a mere awareness that her life was not over because she had buried a husband whom she might have loved but who had, frankly, made her miserable. She missed the physical closeness of marriage, those few moments of a man's utter devotion.

With all the grief of Nick's death and then dealing with his debts and moving up to Black Hill, there had been no time to dwell on the trivia of dalliance.

Only with talk of the ball had she begun to realize the possibilities. She could discreetly take a lover, banish the loneliness just for a little, without the pain of caring or the bonds, the ownership, of marriage.

Felicia could have fun.

All the same, apart from ensuring her siblings' safety and potential happiness, her main aim had been financial. Nick's debts of honor were paid—unless more appeared out of the woodwork—but there was still money owed to tradesmen and other, more shadowy figures dealt with by Julius or the lawyers. She still needed money for those expenses, to pay Julius and her other siblings back and find some way of not sponging off him forever.

She wanted independence, personal and financial. And the

ball was as good a place as any to begin, to test the waters, the possibilities, and her own skill at cards, which Nick had always derided.

Well, Bernard Muir had not derided them. And she doubted Waller Harlaw did either, although he had made a point of congratulating her on her "beginner's luck."

Bernard Muir... She smiled into her pillow. He was young, strong, handsome...and he played cards with intelligence. What more could she want in a prospective lover? A little affection, and a lot of physical desire. She had seen the latter in his eyes as they had danced. Even on the balcony when she had made her alliance proposal. He had not been certain what kind of alliance she meant, but then, neither had she. Both, if the truth be told. He made her heart beat as it only ever had for Nick before. And she liked him.

He was a likeable man. He looked after his family, squiring his spinster aunt and his widowed stepmother to local events that may well have bored him to tears. He was on good terms with everyone from the assembly room staff to the Braithwaite family. She had seen him conversing with the earl and with the earl's pretty young sisters, who seemed to treat him like a brother.

An unusually decent young man. But that was not what aroused her. It was the wicked side of his character that she had occasionally glimpsed in his eyes, the feel of his arm around her, his warmth and strength. She had almost forgotten the pleasure of butterflies in the stomach, the racing pulse... She wondered how he kissed, how it would make her feel. She wanted to see him helpless in the storm of passion and know she had brought him there.

Wicked thoughts, wicked desires...with a warm coating because she liked him and because they could help each other.

Would he come today?

He would not come to collect the money she had offered him. But he might call to hear her proposal. Or just because he liked her.

Of course, there was danger in pursuing any such involvement, but she ignored the nagging, sensible voice that tried to tell her so. *He is a gambler. Like Nick.*

She rose at last and dressed in her favorite morning gown. She supposed it was no longer fashionable, having been bought before Nick's death, but she was glad to have saved it from the fate of its fellows, which had been largely dyed black. She brushed her hair until it shone. It was paler than her siblings', almost blonde in the sunshine. She twisted, scooped, and pinned it into a deceptively casual style that she knew became her.

Is it enough?

Enough for what? she challenged herself.

The truth was, she had never really been enough for anyone or anything. But she was only five and twenty, and with her new freedom, new possibilities beckoned. She smiled at her reflection in the glass and decided to enjoy herself.

Most of her siblings were out and about. Cornelius would be somewhere on the estate, trying to deal with drainage—all this summer's rain was damaging to the crops. Roderick walked for miles every day, escaping his own demons. Julius had gone into Blackhaven, no doubt taking Aubrey with him. Delilah and the twins were invisible.

Only Lucy haunted the drawing room, as though she too were expecting—or hoping—to be called upon. Felicia wished her well. Lucy's infamous betrothal, made in childhood to a stranger, should be broken sooner rather than later. Felicia would not have her tied to any man, however rich, who did not love her. And at least Lucy's judgment of character could be trusted.

Felicia wondered if she would like Bernard Muir. But then, if Lucy lurked in the drawing room, she could not speak privately to him.

Ah, the summer house…

Ensuring that Delilah was at home to play chaperone if necessary, she abandoned Lucy and instructed Betsy the parlor maid, "If Mr. Bernard Muir calls, show him to the summer house."

"Yes, ma'am," said Betsy, trained well enough to hide whatever surprise or disapproval she felt.

Between them, the siblings had made the neglected summer house casually welcoming and comfortable. Unfortunately, the weather had never made it an attractive place to linger so far, but it had a little stove ready to be lit, plenty of cushions and blankets, a table, and, most of all, a new, untouched pack of cards.

Having lit the stove and put a kettle of water to boil, she went to the kitchen to find some sandwiches and honey cakes, which she brought back to the summer house. She left the untouched cards and settled to wait with an old pack from the house, playing a complicated version of patience.

Had she known he would come?

When the knock sounded on the door, a smile formed involuntarily on her lips and lingered as she called, "Come in."

Betsy opened the door. "Mr. Muir, ma'am."

"Thank you, Betsy." She rose as Bernard walked in with his quick, graceful stride.

He looked half amused, half admiring, and her heart beat too quickly. Was that relief she felt that he still moved her in the clear, prosaic light of day? Or anxiety?

She gave him her hand with studied carelessness. "Mr. Muir."

He took her fingers and bowed over them. He kept one of his own hands behind his back, and the gesture was peculiarly elegant. This time, he wore gloves and she did not.

"Mrs. Maitland." He glanced around the summer house. "I am impressed. Gillie and I did something similar with our garden shed—much to the gardener's annoyance—but this is on quite a different scale."

"We tried to make it comfortable for adults as well as children. Tea?"

"Thank you," he said gravely, releasing her hand.

She felt his eyes follow her as she went to the stove, pushed the kettle back on to the heat, and got out the box of tea.

"Were you so sure I would come for your money?" he asked,

his tone oddly expressionless.

"I was fairly sure you would *not* come for that," she replied. "But I hoped my proposal would intrigue you enough." She cast him a quick smile over her shoulder, aware she was flirting, but who could resist? He was just so handsome with his broad shoulders and fine-boned face, so...*flirtable.*

"Your proposal of alliance," he said as she placed the teapot, cups, and saucers on a tray. "Or was it a partnership?"

His last words were spoken close behind her, almost making her jump. Her neck prickled with awareness. His breath stirred her hair like the lightest breeze, and then he reached around her, almost touching her, to lay something on the tray. A posy of red rosebuds.

He must have held them behind his back since he came in.

"For me?" she managed as heat suffused her face. "Thank you."

He reached fully across her, and this time he did brush against her as he picked up the tray.

"Where shall I put it?" he asked, glancing from the table with its two chairs to the pile of cushions on the rug surrounding the lower table.

"Here," she said, slipping ahead of him to the cushions, carrying the plates of sandwiches and cakes, which she placed on the low table. "We went with my father to Constantinople, once, and to other Ottoman lands. We re-created some of that experience here. Make yourself comfortable."

In fact, he already looked quite at home, lounging gracefully among the cushions. She sank down in front of the tray, which was almost opposite him, and poured two cups of tea, offering cream and sugar. Then she passed him the plates of sandwiches and little honey cakes.

He took one of the former with a murmur of thanks. Then he caught and held her gaze.

"Tell me about this partnership," he said softly, "if you are now comfortable."

Suddenly, she was not comfortable at all. Did he expect a personal alliance? Did he imagine she was that desperate for a lover?

Aren't you?

"I am perfectly comfortable," she replied, rather more sharply than she intended. "And my proposal is to do with cards."

"Cards." To his credit, he betrayed neither surprise nor disbelief. But then he was a master of macao, a game of secrecy, pretense, and misdirection. "I am most happy to partner you at loo or whist whenever you wish. There is no need for discretion or fuss in the matter. At least, none that I can see."

Felicia sipped her tea and set the dainty cup down in its saucer. "That is because you do not yet understand the nature of my proposal. Ours would be a business partnership, with the vulgar aim of making money."

His eyes remained veiled, his voice light. "With respect, ma'am, I do not need your help playing cards for money."

"I have offended you," she observed. "Which was not my intention. I think we need to play cards for you to appreciate this proposal."

"What would you like to play?" he asked politely.

She passed him the new pack of cards. "You choose."

While he unsealed the cards, she reached behind her for the reticule and turned it upside down over the table. The coins and banknotes fell out.

"Since neither of us will accept this money, I propose we divide it evenly and use it to wager with."

Bernard raised his gaze from the money to her face. His eyes were cold, a little bitterness in the amusement she read there. "If this is your plan to give me the money by deliberately losing—"

"I shall not lose," she interrupted. "Begin."

His face expressionless once more, he quickly removed the lower cards from the pack and dealt a hand of piquet.

When they had played several parties, they reunited the pack and played loo, dealing two hands each and each playing as though with a partner. After that, they played faro. The afternoon passed in a blur. At the beginning of each game, she insisted he shuffle the cards, and each game started evenly. But Felicia always won in the end.

At last, he shoved the last of his share of the money across the table to her and sat back.

"Thank you for the demonstration. How are you doing it?"

"Doing what?"

"Cheating."

She smiled very faintly. "You think I am cheating because I am a woman and I have beaten you. It is what many men will say, which is why I need you."

His gaze was steady on hers. "My sense of gentlemanly conduct extends neither to cheating on my account nor covering up for yours."

"I never supposed it did," she said swiftly. "I have not cheated."

"You lost the odd hand, but to win quite so often is far against the odds. And even if it were not, you are worryingly confident of repeating that success whenever we are partners. Or have I misunderstood you?"

"Partly. I don't need a partner to win. I need him to take me places a lady does not go alone, to protect me and to vouch for me."

"I don't need a partner to win either. I certainly don't need to cheat."

Heat stung her cheeks. "I would be grateful if your manners remained gentlemanly and you refrained from using that word without proof."

He did not drop his gaze. "Show me," he said without apology. "Show me how you did it."

"I remember," she said. "I remember every card that is played and calculate the odds of every new card appearing."

"How?"

Her lips quirked. "In my head. All the time. I can do it very quickly. I was something of a prodigy in mathematics, too. I love the beauty of numbers and patterns that few people seem to see. But it is not a ladylike subject."

A frown tugged at his brow. She could not tell if he believed or discounted anything she had said. "Show me."

She recited every card they had turned in faro, with her calculations, and had gone over several hands of loo before he gestured to stop her.

"Enough," he said. "Enough." It seemed he still could not look away, but there was a hint of wonder, even awe, in his face. "You are indeed amazing."

No one had ever told her that before. Her father had thought it little more than a party trick. Her siblings barely noticed. Nick had derided it as lies and stalked off in such a temper that they had never played again. He did not even like her playing at parties, even though she could have won more than he lost—if he had ever allowed her the money to play with.

It was her gaze that fell. "Thank you." The emotion made her voice hoarse, and she hastily cleared her throat and summoned a smile. "So, that is the skill behind my proposal. Together, we would be irresistible at whist, loo, or macao. We can also play separately at other tables, and at the end of each night, pool and divide our winnings. Soon, we will be able to play for higher stakes, and the winnings will increase accordingly. What do you say?"

He stared at her. "You are not cheating," he said slowly. "But you do have an advantage."

"Because I use the brain that God gave me? You have an advantage over Waller Harlaw, who plays like a fool. That is considered perfectly fair. And yet he cheats."

"He does," Bernard agreed.

She took a deep breath. "My husband died owing him a great deal of money, gaming debts built up over years, loans that were never paid back because Nick's luck never turned. Harlaw was not the only debtor, but he was the biggest. I had to sell our house in London to pay him back. I made my little brothers and sisters homeless. Or I would have done, if Julius had not come home and remembered we had Black Hill."

"There is a rumor," Bernard said, "that Harlaw forgave most of what Maitland owed him."

It felt like a slap across the face. Only pride kept her voice steady. "A rumor begun, no doubt, by Harlaw himself. But if you believe it, you should go now."

"Of course I don't believe it," Bernard said impatiently. He rubbed his knuckles against his chin. "So Harlaw cheated your husband, and therefore you, out of a fortune. And so out of any security for your future."

"Julius and Roderick both used some of their prize money to help with my debts. We even had to use some of my parents' legacies to each of my siblings. I vowed to pay it back, and I still mean to."

Bernard's lips quirked up at the corners. His eyes began to gleam. "We take it back off Harlaw," he said softly. "I will happily aid you in that pursuit."

Felicia smiled back. "We aid each other, Mr. Muir. I am not proposing a chivalrous rescue."

"I am not in difficulty," he replied evenly. "I have not been wronged or cheated—or at least not very much—by Harlaw. I require nothing for any service I might do you."

"I know you do not require it. You are a good man and, I think, kind by nature. A little pride is a good thing—it has got me through some dark days—but don't be so proud that you reject opportunity just because it is offered by a woman."

He regarded her, head tilted to one side. "You will accept partnership but not service?"

"Exactly. I won't owe anyone else, sir. And neither will you. Think about it. You have ambitions to spread your wings, do you not? To go where you please and choose your own life. I don't doubt you will achieve your ambitions, but it will take years alone. Together, we can both achieve independence and quickly."

"Just by beating Waller Harlaw?" Bernard said in disbelief. "I'm happy to make the scoundrel sell his house to repay you for yours, but I doubt it will keep us both in the lap of luxury for the rest of our lives."

"Of course it won't. There are lots of wealthy people in Blackhaven who like to gamble."

"And you would fleece them all?"

"I would try to win. As would they. You make it sound as though I would cheat and steal from them."

"I know you would not," he said at once. "Your advantage merely...troubles me. And if we are partners, then I take advantage from your advantage."

"You think too much," she said impatiently, for her disappointment was profound. And she did not like that it made her uncomfortable. She wasn't even sure why it did. "No matter. Forget my proposal, since it offends your honor. You need worry about it no more. Shall we go back to the house? Julius has some very decent brandy."

Bernard glanced at his fob watch, and his eyebrows flew up in astonishment. "Lord, I must be going." He sprang to his feet. "Another time, I would be happy to call on Sir Julius. If he will see me after I have shut myself up in here with you all afternoon."

She rose more slowly and summoned a smile as she offered her hand. "Goodbye, Mr. Muir."

"I feel dismissed," he said, taking her hand. Neither of them wore gloves now, and a little thrill of awareness shot up her arm.

"You are. It is a lady's privilege, is it not? Though we both know we have dismissed each other." She tried to draw her hand free, but he held on to it, frowning.

"I could never dismiss you," he said. "Forgive me if I was ungracious."

"Forgiven and forgotten, Mr. Muir."

His rueful expression told her he felt that barb too. She would be sorry in a little. For now, she began to walk to the summer house door, forcing him to release her hand.

"My regards to your aunt," she said. "Is your horse in the stables?"

"I walked."

It was a long walk, but she would not feel guilty.

<hr />

IT WAS INDEED a long walk back to Blackhaven, which gave Bernard plenty of time to go over and over all the ways he had wrecked a promising friendship with the loveliest woman he had ever encountered.

In truth, he had not dismissed her ideas. He was indeed willing to help, just on his own terms. But he had been clumsy. She had taken him by surprise. More than that, he had been so comfortable with her that he had forgotten the vulnerability he'd sensed in her last night. She had been badly hurt—Bernard's money was on the late loose screw of a husband—and wrapped herself in pride and prickles and flirtation to make sure it never happened again.

Not that Bernard flattered himself that he could hurt her very deeply. But that he should have done it at all made him ashamed. After all, would *he* ask for help? Would he voluntarily be beholden to anyone, let alone a near stranger? He found it hard enough to accept what he did from Gillie's husband, and Wickenden had written that into their marriage contract.

And then there was her amazing gift that gave her such a huge advantage in games of chance and skill. He had tactlessly implied it was cheating. It was not. She brought no more to the table than herself. She did not spy on other people's cards. She did not mark the cards or hide them up her sleeves. She used her mind, like everyone else. Why should she be punished or reviled because hers was better?

He remembered all she had said about the cards, last night and today, and understood a little more. She came somewhere in the middle of a large, tumultuous family where she probably felt her gift of mathematics was all that made her stand out from her siblings. All that made her special. It was not, of course. But mathematical abilities were not valued in girls. If he had lessened her value in her own eyes, he deserved to be shot.

Badly managed, Muir, he castigated himself. *Damnably done.*

Could he make it right? Or at least better?

By the time he got home, he was both tired and hungry, and dinner had just begun. Worse, when Bernard stuck his head in the dining room door to apologize, he saw that they had a guest—Waller Harlaw.

"Good God," Bernard said. "Are you lodging with us now?"

"Bernard!" Isabella exclaimed, appalled by his manners.

"I cannot imagine why you would think so," Harlaw said haughtily.

"Really?" Bernard said. "I all but fell over you on my way out this morning, and look, you're still here."

Harlaw smiled very thinly. "I made a perfectly proper morning call upon Mrs. and Miss Muir. Your mama was kind enough to invite me to dine."

"My mama," Bernard uttered freezingly, *would not have allowed such a commoner over the door.* Perhaps fortunately, Aunt Margaret interrupted him before the rest of the words could escape from between his teeth.

"Go and change, Bernard," she said happily, as though she had not heard any of this conversation—which, of course, she had. "We shall hold the next course for you."

Bernard went without a word. By the time he had washed, changed, and returned with his belated apologies, he had himself much better in hand. Although hardly the welcoming host—he had the feeling Harlaw was trying to be that—he avoided being rude until their guest finally departed, and Isabella, with a reproachful glower at Bernard, went upstairs to look in on Arthur.

"Is that fellow really sniffing around Isabella?" Bernard demanded of his aunt.

"Why wouldn't he?" Margaret said in her vague way. "Isabella is still young and beautiful. The fact that she is widowed does not mean her life is over."

Bernard thought immediately of Felicia Maitland. Of course, the cases were not the same. Felicia's husband had been something of a gentlemanly scoundrel. Isabella's had been Bernard's own father, a gentleman of honor and integrity.

"But she can't be considering him," Bernard said, genuinely appalled.

"Why shouldn't she?" Margaret asked.

"Because he's a scoundrel and a cheat!"

"Oh dear," Margaret said. "Perhaps best not to say so to Isabella. She will dig her heels in all the harder. But truly, Bernie, he does not appear to threaten her virtue. He is very proper."

Bernard grunted, then suddenly swung away from the window to his aunt. "Wait! She didn't let slip about her good fortune, did she?"

"Of course not," Margaret said comfortably. "Isabella would never speak of anything as vulgar as money. Why do you find it so hard to believe that a man might genuinely esteem her and wish to court her?"

"I could believe it of another man," Bernard muttered. "*That* one is up to no good."

Chapter Four

F ELICIA DID NOT see Bernard Muir again until Sunday at church. Which was only two days, though for some reason it felt much longer. Perhaps because her brothers had involved themselves with stolen horses and were all behaving oddly. So were her sisters. Or perhaps it was just Felicia's mood.

Nearly everyone in Blackhaven went to church. This had as much to do with Mr. Grant, the vicar, as with virtue. Handsome, humorous, and a fine raconteur, he held the whole congregation's attention with apparent ease.

Felicia had been surprised, just at first, to discover that the vicar's wife was none other than "Wicked Kate Crowmore," who had vanished from the London scene under a cloud of scandal even before Nick's death. Felicia had been sorry for that scandal, for though she did not know Kate well, she liked her wit and had sensed no spite in her at all. Now she appeared to be one of the chief pillars of the Blackhaven community, deeply involved with good works and charity, and her husband's greatest support. And yet she had danced at the assembly room ball with all her old sense of fun.

No one in Blackhaven appeared to hold Kate's past against her, not even the prim and proper ladies one always found fawning over vicars. Felicia was glad of that. Blackhaven was not such a bad place to live, she thought, as she and her siblings filed into church. Julius had not come with them—he rarely did—but Roderick appeared to regard attendance like being on parade. Or perhaps he too found something in the service, or Mr. Grant's sermon, to bring him much-needed and even more deserved peace.

She caught sight of Bernard across the aisle, sandwiched between his aunt and his stepmother. And beside Mrs. Muir was Waller Harlaw. Only Harlaw noticed Felicia's scrutiny. He smiled and bowed.

She nodded curtly and faced the front for the first hymn.

In the churchyard after the service, she refused to avoid Mr. Muir. On the other hand, she had no desire to speak to Harlaw, who detached himself from Mrs. Muir to approach her. She grasped Cornelius's arm as though they were leaving, but Harlaw appeared to be oblivious.

"Mrs. Maitland, always a pleasure. This must be one of your famous brothers."

"No, I'm just the steward," Cornelius said sardonically.

"*And* my brother," Felicia corrected him. She would not allow anyone to think less of Cornel, least of all himself. "Mr. Cornelius Vale. This is Mr. Harlaw, Cornel. He was a friend of Nick's."

Cornelius had been away learning his profession and earning his living during most of Felicia's marriage.

He shook hands with Harlaw. "How do you do?"

"Considerably lighter in the pocket since your sister fleeced me at piquet the other night."

"Join the club," Cornelius said carelessly. "Fliss has all the skill. We learned early on not to play her for money."

"I was hoping she would allow me a rematch," Harlaw said.

"Your funeral," Cornelius murmured. "Ready, Fliss?"

Before they could move, Miss Muir fluttered in front of them, and had to be introduced to Cornelius too. Her eyes were very bright, her manner friendly. But her gaze was on Felicia as she said, "You will call on us, will you not? Here is my card. We are in Cliff Crescent, a mere step from here…"

Felicia took the card. "I should be happy to call." She wondered if Miss Muir recalled their last tipsy encounter and wished to apologize in private. She hoped not, but all she could do was smile reassuringly and finally walk to the carriage with Cornelius.

Bernard had made no effort to speak to her. It was probably as well. She would just have to manage without him. She let Cornelius hurry her into the carriage, although when the door had closed, she searched the churchyard and found Bernard looking directly at her, his expression unreadable.

Something in her heart began to ache.

"Is that the Miss Muir who was the old gentleman's flirt?" Cornelius asked, apparently amused.

"According to Julius," Felicia said thoughtfully. "Apparently, she was too respectable for him."

❦

SHE WAS STILL angry with him. Not that Bernard meant to take his dismissal lying down, but he had no intention of offending her further. And he was damned glad her brother was with her when Harlaw abandoned Isabella to go to her. What did he want with Felicia? After all, he appeared to be courting Isabella, devil take him.

Bernard could not help following Felicia with his eyes as she climbed into the carriage. He could see her beautiful face through the window, and just for an instant, she looked unbearably sad. Then her gaze met his, and the carriage swept her away.

"You look uncharacteristically bereft, Bernard," Kate Grant said, taking his arm.

Kate had been his first love, if one could elevate his boyish crush to such heights. He felt vaguely embarrassed to recall it now. He suspected she would too, if she had ever noticed.

"Not I," Bernard replied, moving a little away from the nearest group of gossipers. "But can I ask you something?"

MARY LANCASTER

"Of course."

"When you were in London and moved in tonish circles, did you ever come across a Nick Maitland?"

"Of course I did," she said dryly. "I was Wicked Kate."

"Did he...pursue you?"

"Inevitably. He was an inveterate womanizer." She met his gaze, and her eyes widened. "You want the full truth, Bernard? Then, strictly between you and me, he was one of the most selfish hedonists I've ever come across. He didn't just think all women were fair game. He felt *entitled*."

Bernard felt slightly sick. "How did you ward him off?"

"Thank you for not asking if I tried. I laughed at him. He didn't like that, so he left me alone."

"Did you know his wife?" Bernard asked with difficulty.

"Slightly. She was brave, never betrayed a moment of annoyance with him, or even any knowledge of his exploits. Even when he rattled through his entire fortune and started on her marriage portion, which he should not have been able to touch. I believe Sir Julius dismissed a few lawyers when he came home, but it was too late. The damage was done. Maitland died leaving her up to ears in debts and with no means of paying them."

"She told me that part."

Kate held his gaze. "For what it's worth, I admire her."

Bernard grinned. "Kate! Are you warning me off? I am hardly in her class."

Kate laughed and squeezed his arm. "You, Bernard Muir, may be in any class you choose to be. But Felicia Maitland needs respect. Not coddling."

"I know," he said, and was almost surprised to realize he did.

⁂

FELICIA CAME TO with a start, to discover herself in the drawing room armchair where she had clearly fallen asleep. The candles

42

were sputtering, about to go out. By their uneven light, Aubrey weaved in front of her to the brandy decanter. He was pouring himself a drink before he noticed her and paused.

"Fliss," he said in surprise. He scowled. "Did you wait up for me?"

"I didn't know you were out. But it's as well I'm here, if only to point out that the brandy is about to overspill your glass."

Hastily, Aubrey turned the decanter upright and stoppered it. "A larger nightcap than I had planned. Want some?"

"No, thank you. I am going to bed. Did you have a pleasant evening?"

Aubrey sat down with his very full glass. "Damned if I know. Beg your pardon."

"The novelty of debauchery wearing off?" she asked innocently.

She expected him to laugh, but instead he looked morose. "No debauchery. Just a trifle disguised. Met some fellows who've come north to rusticate."

"What fellows?" Felicia asked as pleasantly as she could.

No one knew better than she the dangers of being drawn into bad company. She could not bear for her brother to go down the same roads her husband had. Aubrey had an entirely different nature, of course, and a vastly less entitled start in life. He had endured long illnesses since childhood and somehow come out of it with his nature still sweet—behind the show of cynicism and determination to take nothing seriously. But he was certainly making the most of the health and strength he enjoyed now.

The boys—at least Julius and Roderick—seemed to think it was a harmless phase, but Felicia feared for his health and for his habits. She had no right to interfere in his company, but she asked anyway. "What fellows?"

Aubrey frowned, but not, apparently, with annoyance. Instead, he set down the brimming glass and rummaged in his pockets, from which he produced a card, like a street magician taking a coin from behind someone's ear.

He peered at it owlishly. "Do we need more candles in here, Fliss?"

"We will when they all go out," she said, rising to douse those still sputtering and turn up the lamp beside Aubrey.

"Tranmere," he said triumphantly. He flapped one vague arm. "Lodging at an inn away out in the country. Staying there with a party of other fellows." His lips curled. "Rich young bucks, ripe for trouble. Rollicking good fellows. Invited me to a card party there."

Felicia absorbed the mixed opinion and said, "Then you'll go?"

"Lord, no. They play too deep for me." He frowned at her. "Know what, Fliss?"

"No, what?"

"Think I'll go to bed," Aubrey said with the air of a man making a vital decision.

Felicia's lips twitched. "Good plan."

Aubrey heaved himself up and walked to the door. He didn't weave this time. Only the extra looseness of his limbs gave away his condition. He abandoned his brimming glass of brandy on the table. His invitation to young Tranmere's card party fluttered to the floor. Ignoring it, Aubrey concentrated on the staircase, which was, fortunately, still lit.

Always the good housekeeper, Felicia poured the brandy back into the bottle without spilling a drop and picked up the invitation card.

She knew Tranmere by repute. He was some peer's wastrel of a grandson, an heir with too much time and money on his hands. Aubrey was always up for a lark. He would take her with him if she asked...

Only she couldn't have it both ways. Aubrey had eschewed the event with unexpected good sense. Clearly, he only half liked the company, and he had never been very bothered about cards. Felicia wanted to keep it that way.

No, this was exactly the kind of event she had wanted Bernard Muir for. It would have been more fun with him, she thought wistfully, and then, annoyed with herself, turned down the lamp and went to bed.

After all, she had decided on the joys of independence a long time ago. She would do just as well alone.

⤚⤜

THE FOLLOWING DAY saw Felicia in Blackhaven to buy some fresh fish and vegetables from the market. Tonight was to be their first dinner party at Black Hill, and she was—nominally, at least—the hostess. Their guests were Lord Linfield, the diplomat, his sister Miss Talbot, and her friend Mrs. Macy.

It was Lucy who had invited them, largely because Julius had danced with Mrs. Macy at the ball, and, judging by Delilah's tight-lipped disapproval, they had a past together. Lucy had taken a shine to Mrs. Macy, and Julius had not put up a fight. Accordingly, Felicia summoned up her skills as a hostess, warned her brothers under pain of death that they were all expected to be present—"even you, Aubrey"—and went shopping.

It did not take her long, but she subsequently ran into Kate Grant, the vicar's wife, who gave her tea and fresh scones and a pleasant gossip. Several times, it was on the tip of Felicia's tongue to ask her about the Muirs in general and Bernard in particular, but she refrained and left the vicarage with a different plan.

Miss Muir, Bernard's aunt, bothered her, and she could not quite put her finger on why. She would not be the first middle-aged lady to over-imbibe at a party, but for some reason, Felicia had the feeling it was a rarity for Miss Muir. There had been a sadness in her eyes, along with all the eager friendliness of the wine. And the woman had invited her to call. Twice.

By Felicia's experience, it was now the time of day when gentlemen were either about whatever business they might have or off to their clubs for luncheon or an early dinner. Blackhaven, of course, did not have gentlemen's clubs of that nature, but she presumed the same principle applied. The hotel and the coffee house were both busy at this hour.

At any rate, Felicia turned not toward the high street, but toward Cliff Crescent, where she easily discovered the Haven, the Muirs' pleasant old house. Her heart beating far too fast for a morning call, she walked up the front steps and knocked.

She was taken upstairs at once to a rather delightfully cluttered drawing room, where Miss Muir sat alone amongst a positive mountain of mending.

At the maid's announcement, she bounced up, beaming. "Mrs. Maitland! How kind of you to call! Bring tea, Mattie."

Felicia wasn't sure she could manage any more tea, but she could hardly refuse. "If you're sure I am not disturbing you," she said as the maid hurried off to obey her mistress. "That does seem an ambitious amount of mending."

"Oh, most of it is for throwing out. I'm just seeing what is salvageable before I go north. Do sit down."

"Thank you." Felicia chose a chair close to the sofa where Miss Muir sat beside the mending and ignored it. "You are traveling soon?"

"Oh, not for a few weeks—after the castle ball, you know. My niece and her husband will stay for a fortnight or so, and I would not miss them for the world. But I do so enjoy my annual pilgrimages to Scotland."

"I have never been in Scotland," Felicia said. "My father swept us all over the world, but never those few miles northward."

Miss Muir's smile became a little fixed. "I suppose he had no reason. His work was in foreign countries, or at least with foreign dignitaries."

For some reason, the mood seemed to need lightening. "Do you stay with friends in Scotland?"

"Indeed, I do. They are so kind. How are things at Black Hill?"

Felicia told her about the state of the house, the neglect of the steward, and Cornelius's hard work to whip the land back into shape. "It will take years," she finished as the maid returned with a tea tray, which she set on a table before Miss Muir. The post had clearly just been delivered, for a letter was propped against the teapot. "But he and Julius are confident they can make it work."

"No one will have a good harvest this year," Miss Muir pointed out, picking up the letter with bright eyes and laying it on top of the mending. "Not enough sun and too much rain." She began to pour the tea.

"True. Many will suffer," Felicia said sadly. "But Cornelius has hopes of at least preserving us and our people from complete disaster. Thank you," she added, taking the cup and saucer from her hostess.

Miss Muir's eyes strayed again to her letter before she brought her gaze hastily back to Felicia and smiled. "We must all do what we can, especially with others depending on us."

Felicia nodded. "Please, read your letter, in case it is important. I shall be fine just admiring your pictures for a little."

Miss Muir, it seemed, could read and chatter at the same time. "The one over the fireplace was a gift from my niece, Lady Wickenden. It's by Lord Tamar, you know. And the small one by the window was given to us years ago by Lady Helen at the castle. She painted it herself—such a talented child! Although she is quite grown...now." Her words trailed off, a frown of consternation forming on her brow.

"Not bad news, I hope," Felicia said. "Shall I ring for someone?"

"No, oh no." Miss Muir beamed. "Actually, it is good news. It seems I shall have no need of my annual jaunt to Scotland, since the friend I visit is coming here to Blackhaven very soon."

"How lovely," Felica said. "Will they stay with you?"

Miss Muir's eyes seemed to jump with fright. "Oh dear me, no," she said, flustered. "We will have no room, what with Gillie and David and the children... Oh dear." She smiled again, with determination. "We shall sort something out. It is of no moment."

With a lot of blinking, she appeared to banish her logistics problems and returned to Felicia. "I'm so glad to have this chance to speak to you. We were such old friends, your father and I." She flushed slightly, perhaps remembering the cloakroom after the ball. "I think I told you that."

"Indeed. I am glad for him." Felicia spoke the truth, for there was something warm and appealing about the eccentric lady, and too often her father's friends were made for diplomatic reasons rather than genuine liking. It pleased her that he should have an old friend only for friendship's sake.

"Forgive me if I upset you," Miss Muir said in a rush. "And you must feel free not to answer for any reason, but I—I read about his death in the newspapers, of course, but there were no details. I don't know. I wanted to ask you—if you don't mind... How did your father die?"

Felicia swallowed. "Of a fever, ma'am. I regret I was not with him at the time for he was abroad. My sister Delilah was there, though, and my brother Aubrey and the twins, so he was not alone."

"Thank you," Miss Muir whispered, groping for a handkerchief. She blew her nose defiantly and gave a watery smile. "It is a comfort to me as it must be to you. I never expected him to die in bed, you know."

When the news had come, his irreverent children had just been grateful it was his own bed.

"I thought it might be in some much more dramatic way, a duel or battle of some kind... But there, no one can choose the manner any more than the time or place. But I am so very glad to see you all back at Black Hill. Was he happy in his later years?"

It was a surprisingly perceptive question, and Felicia was not sure of the answer. Her father had always been the life and soul of any party, and he certainly had his moments of contentment, but his had been a restless soul. Lucy had once told her that Papa was sad. The boys had laughed at the very idea. She had never asked the twins their opinion. Perhaps she had been afraid of their answer.

Now, she gave the only one she could, with honesty. "Mostly, I think. He loved us all, and we loved him." Her voice caught, and she cleared her throat.

Unfortunately, the door opened at that moment and Bernard strode into the room. "Aunt, are you ready to...?" He trailed off, his brows rising in surprise at the sight of Felicia.

What on earth would he think of her emotional state? Would he notice? Something certainly flared in his eyes, something too warm and much too exciting, but he merely bowed with perfect courtesy.

"Mrs. Maitland, how do you do? Sorry, Aunt, I didn't realize we had company. I only came to see if you were ready for your constitutional, but we can easily go later."

"Oh, I don't think I have time today after all," Miss Muir twittered. "Look at all this mending!"

Bernard blinked at it. "Dulcie and Mattie can do that. And Isabella will help."

"No, no, and I have an urgent letter to write, too. But perhaps Mrs. Maitland would care to accompany you? It is certainly a pleasant enough day for a walk."

"Alas," Felicia said lightly, rising to her feet, "I must take my provisions home or Cook will have no time to prepare them. Thank you for tea, Miss Muir."

"I'll walk with you to your carriage," Bernard offered, following her from the room. He swiped his hat from the stand in the hall, opened the front door, and bowed her out. "You need not avoid me, you know. I don't mean to be either offensive or offended."

"I never imagined you did. Nor do I wish to be the only person in Blackhaven at outs with Bernard Muir."

His nostrils flared slightly, as though this did not quite please him, but he said only, "Not quite the only one. But I would certainly rather we were not at outs."

"Then we are not."

His smile was boyish, and yet when she took his proffered arm, it did not feel boyish at all, but muscular and strong.

"I have been thinking about card parties," he said. "I could organize something at the hotel. Or the inn—the King's Head— might be better. We could have tables for low-stakes games and others for higher. I could ask Gillie or Kate Grant to be hostess, which would make everything respectable. We could even charge an entrance fee or a percentage of winnings for charity."

"It would be an excellent beginning," Felicia agreed. Inside, she rejoiced, and had no intention of raising difficulties, such as their own stakes and winnings, or future enterprises. "What about the gaming club you mentioned?"

"Lord, no, you can't go there! It is not remotely respectable."

"They cheat?"

"Oh no, the tables and the cards are straight enough, but those who play are not necessarily clean potatoes. And ladies most definitely do *not* attend."

"What, no females at all?" she said, disappointed.

"No *respectable* females. Trust me, you would not be comfortable there. Your brothers would be rightly outraged to discover you at such a gathering, and frankly, so would I."

His voice was quite firm, causing a funny little frisson up her spine. Which made no sense. She hated people laying down the law for her. However, she did not want to quarrel with Bernard again. She had ways of attending the events she wished to without troubling him.

And she would have to. She had almost told him about Tranmere's card party. But there was no way he would take her to that. He would consider it out of his league, and besides, he had made it clear he would never take her to a male-only party. Not even in disguise.

Chapter Five

WITH TYPICAL DRAMA, the Wickendens arrived in Black-haven in the midst of a storm. Wickenden swept his wife and child straight into the house while Bernard and Danny, the Muirs' fierce manservant, helped the visiting servants drag in the luggage. Without instruction, Danny climbed up on the box of the lead coach to guide them to the livery stable.

Gratefully, Bernard shut the door on the storm and was ruthlessly hugged by his sister. Everyone was talking at once. Gillie's two-year-old son, the Honorable Davie—named for his father—was jumping excitedly up and down, hand in hand with his three-year-old Uncle Arthur.

Bernard grinned as he shook hands warmly with his brother-in-law, of whom he had grown fond over the years since Gillie's marriage. Gillie had relinquished Isabella to Wickenden, who gallantly kissed her hand and her cheek, when Waller Harlaw descended the stairs at a leisurely pace.

Bernard swore under his breath. He had forgotten the man was here—again—and he was damnably *de trop*.

"Oh yes," twittered Aunt Margaret unhelpfully. "Yes, indeed."

"You must think this a madhouse, Mr. Harlaw," Isabella said, blushing. "Allow me to present you. Mr. Waller Harlaw. Sir, my stepdaughter, Lady Wickenden, her husband, Lord Wickenden, and little David, their son."

Wickenden's bow was not cordial, but Gillie gave her hand in a friendly way, and Harlaw bowed over it.

"My lady. My lord. We have met in Town, of course, but it is a pleasure to see you in Blackhaven." He turned to Isabella, smiling. "You will excuse me, I know. I shall leave you to your family reunion. If you will just pass me my hat…"

"But no!" Isabella exclaimed. "You cannot go out in this weather!"

"Goodness, it's only a step to the hotel," Bernard said. "Harlaw is not such a milksop, are you, sir?"

Harlaw's smile was somewhat fixed. "I hope not indeed."

"Nonsense, Bernard," Isabella said firmly. "Mr. Harlaw must stay for dinner. By then the rain at least might have calmed down."

"No, no, dear lady, I shall not intrude upon you at such a time."

Bernard reached for the door handle, but it was too late. Isabella had Harlaw by the arm and was leading the way up to the drawing room.

Wickenden raised his eyebrows at Bernard, who shrugged philosophically.

"Well, he *might* melt," Aunt Margaret murmured vaguely, and Gillie giggled as she hugged her aunt's arm to her side and started after the others.

It was some consolation to Bernard that Harlaw must have felt distinctly left out as dinner progressed and the family caught up on the Wickendens' journey, their latest news, and the gossip in Blackhaven, all exchanged at high speed with many diversions into related events, and frequent repetition for the benefit of Aunt Margaret, who was occasionally quite deaf. No one cared that Harlaw was scandalized to find himself dining with small children—it was a special family treat.

Fortunately, he left after one glass of post-prandial port. Bernard saw him off the premises, collected the decanter, and joined his brother-in-law in the drawing room with the ladies. There was a good deal more talk, and putting the excited children to bed, and yet more talk before everyone gave in and retired, Gillie and Wickenden to her old chamber.

Bernard yawned, sat on the edge of his bed, and fantasized about Felicia joining him there. For high days and holidays only, for of course they would be in Paris or Rome or Munich or wherever for the rest of the time.

He twisted his lips into a crooked smile. Dreams were sweet, but they were only dreams.

He tugged off his cravat and stood to remove his coat. A scratch at the door told him exactly who was on the other side of it.

"Come in, Gillie."

She slipped inside and softly closed the door, smiling around the familiar walls with much the same pictures and furniture that had always been there. "Lord, it's so good to be home."

It was good to have her home. They had been very close growing up, comforting each other for their losses, and then pulling together in their determination to keep their home here. He missed her, and although he understood she would not change her life even if she could, he knew she missed him, too.

"Is Aunt Margaret well?" she asked, sitting down beside him on the bed.

"She seems so. Why?"

Gillie shrugged. "She seems a little...nervous. Is that the Harlaw creature's fault?"

"The Harlaw creature? Then you do know him?"

"I never met him before today. David calls him a commoner. He thinks he cheats at cards."

"He does."

"Then how on earth has he got his feet under the table here?"

Bernard wrinkled his nose. "Isabella. She likes him, and he appears to be courting her."

"But you don't approve."

"How could I? On the other hand, she can befriend whoever she likes. Neither of us has a say in that. And she is still a young and beautiful woman. There is no reason why she should not marry again. I can see why he is attracted to her. Only…"

"Only you don't trust him."

"No further than Aunt Margaret could throw him."

"I believe," Gillie said, "that he is largely pockets to let. Last I heard, he was hanging out for a rich wife." She held Bernard's gaze. "Could he have heard of Isabella's inheritance?"

"I don't see how. No one knows of it but us, and she was eager to keep it that way. There were no London solicitors involved, even."

"Perhaps Isabella told him," Gillie said doubtfully.

"She wouldn't. She would find that vulgar. I would suspect him of being in love, except…"

"Except he would never leg-shackle himself to a penniless female in a northern backwater," Gillie finished.

"You *do* know him," Bernard marveled.

"He was one of Nicholas Maitland's cronies. Selfish, hedonistic, self-serving."

Bernard's gaze snapped back to his sister. "You knew Nick Maitland?"

Gillie blinked. "I knew who he was. I think he and David had dealings in the past, but David shook him off."

"Did he cheat too?"

"No, but he was a vile husband."

"Felicia Maitland is in Blackhaven. She is one of Sir George Vale's daughters."

Gillie's eyes widened, either at the news or because, annoyingly perceptive sister that she was, she heard something in Bernard's voice.

"We have become friends," Bernard said as casually as he could. "She plays a mean game of cards, beats everyone to flinders."

Gillie smiled and stood to kiss him on the cheek. "Then no

wonder you admire her. Goodnight, Bernie."

"Goodnight, Gillie."

THE VALE SIBLINGS' first dinner party at Black Hill went very well. Lord Linfield and Miss Talbot were charming guests, and actually knew Sir George, so there were amusing tales aplenty to keep everyone's interest.

Felicia was delighted with the evening, not just for the fun of it but because she rather thought Julius was falling in love with Antonia Macy. Something had been lacking in him since he came home, as if he had retired from life, as the twins put it, but somehow he seemed *awake* again, and Felicia, Lucy, and the twins put it down to Antonia.

However, they knew better than to quiz Julius about it. Instead, the following day, Felicia followed the twins back to Lawrence's bedchamber.

"I am looking for old clothes," she stated. "Either to pass on to tenants or to make into rags. You must have lots of things you have outgrown recently."

Indeed, Lawrence had begun to sprout alarmingly in the last few months—which at least gave Felicia a reason to take away breeches and coats and pantaloons that no longer fitted. Inevitably, Leona passed on her own old dresses, too, which Felicia felt obliged to take away and sort.

There was no suspicion in their eyes when she left with a pile of clothing she could not see over, but she did catch them smiling.

In the privacy of her own bedchamber, she tried on Lawrence's old "Sunday" coat and pantaloons and made a cravat out of an old linen shirt. She had manly gloves, even boots, and a hat. Delighted with her appearance, she paraded up and down in front of the glass, laughing to herself and practicing male poses.

Of course, she could hardly hide her long hair under a hat while she played cards indoors. After a hunt in her chest of drawers, she found a length of narrow black ribbon and brushed her hair back severely from her face before confining it with the ribbon. The style was old-fashioned. Gentlemen in Tranmere's world would never wear their hair like that. But she could, at a pinch, be a very young gentleman bumpkin.

Over the next couple of days, she observed more closely the ways her brothers moved and sat and spoke. She practiced in front of the glass and addressed herself in a low voice until her throat hurt.

Quite aside from her own problems, Roderick had a particularly loud nightmare that scared the twins and obliged Felicia to intervene at last. He took it surprisingly well, even allowed the beginnings of a connection, and when she finally left him in order to reassure the twins, she had hopes of his mending whatever parts of him the war had damaged. And she was glad he was not alone.

Being alone with pain, however many people moved around you, was its own special hell.

There was a massive storm the following night, which could not have been good for Roderick's nerves, but at least it brought Antonia Macy back within their walls, this time with her small, engaging son. And the following morning, Antonia and Julius looked...happy.

Smiling to herself, Felicia took it all as good omens and made her own preparations for the evening.

Her worst dilemma was wondering how much of the money won from Harlaw she should take to Tranmere's card party. She stood by her belief that Bernard was owed half of it, but on the other hand, she wasn't sure there would be enough for the early part of the evening if Tranmere and his friends played for exorbitant stakes. Which Aubrey seemed to suspect.

In the end, she took it all, promising to pay back Bernard's half at the end of the evening. And she could not be too late, for the castle garden party was the following day, and the whole family had been invited. And oddly, the whole family seemed to want to go.

As the household retired, Felicia donned Lawrence's clothes, including his old traveling cloak, beneath which she hid her hat, and went around to the stables.

They had no regular grooms as such. The men who worked in the stables on and off were quite used to the family saddling and riding off at all sorts of odd times. So it was simple enough to saddle her favorite mare—with a man's saddle—and leave with a lantern to guide her way.

This, she thought with an overwhelming sense of freedom, *is an adventure. My adventure.*

IT WAS DARK by the time she arrived at the Black Stag. She had decided such a late arrival would be best, both to avoid the glare of daylight on her distinctly feminine features, and to make it less likely that her hosts would be sober enough to care that they hadn't invited her. With luck, they would each blame her presence on someone else. In fact, she also took the wrong fork in the road at one point and had to ask a grumpy farmer for directions.

However, she enjoyed the journey. Riding astride reminded her of childhood excursions with Cornelius and Aubrey. By the time she arrived at the inn, her heart was beating fast with excitement and sheer nerves. What if they threw her out? Worse, what if they discovered she was a woman? Dressed like this, she could expect no help from the inn staff. She would be considered fair game.

Well, she would just have to make sure she was *not* discovered.

She jumped spryly down from the saddle, tossed the reins to

the ostler, and, after a careless pat on the mare's nose, swaggered into the inn.

The noise was deafening. Tranmere and his friends seemed to have taken over both the coffee room and a private parlor that opened off it. A fiddler stood in the corner, sawing merrily away, though only snatches of his music were audible over the boisterous roars of the young men-and the occasional screeches of the blowsy women who flitted from lap to lap, table to table.

It was unquestionably a shock to Felicia. She had thought she was used to rakehell gatherings. Nick had frequently brought a gaggle of friends home in the small hours, and she had run into them more than once. Drunk and loud as they had been, they had never felt remotely threatening. She saw now that her position as Nick's wife, and his position as host, had kept some semblance of order. Here, there was none.

Not that they were accosting respectable women. The females here clearly chose to be for whatever reason, but it all fed the gentlemen's unfettered entitlement.

For one frozen moment, panic gripped her and she almost bolted. Then she looked beyond the badly behaved young men to the tables around which they sat, and the cards that many were playing more seriously than their drunken companions. She remembered that this was her opportunity to win, and gathered her chosen role about her like a cloak.

No one had noticed her arrival, but as she strode further in, searching the tables, she spotted Tranmere himself. Or at least someone very like him. She *had* met him once, shortly before Nick's death, though she hoped devoutly that no such recollections troubled Tranmere.

He was scowling over the faro table, deep in concentration while those around him either stared with him or yelled encouragement.

She changed pace, grinning directly at him and strolling toward him with her gloved hand held out. "Evening, Tranmere! Seems I'm late to the party."

Tranmere, a wild-looking young gentleman with glimmerings of intelligence behind his reckless eyes, and lines of dissipation already forming on his handsome face, looked up and blinked at her. Without rising, he reached up and grasped her hand.

"You might be, but I've no idea who the devil you are," he said.

"Nicholas," she replied. "Blackhaven? Tavern?" She pulled Aubrey's crumpled card from her pocket.

Tranmere laughed. "Lord, I don't need proof. Just don't recall you."

"Foxed," said the man next to him succinctly.

"Then and now," Tranmere agreed, "but I'll still trounce all of you. Take a seat, Mr. Nicholas, and bear in mind there's no special treatment for youth. Play and pay."

The stakes were eye-watering, and she lost steadily at first. She was dangerously near the end of her resources before she began to win it back. By the time she stood up, she was used to the noise and her own role in the company. She had won a certain amount of respect and gained all her money back and more. Her entire focus was on the plan.

As a result, when she rose, she had stopped worrying. Until she stepped backward onto someone's toes, turned to apologize, and gazed directly into the face of Bernard Muir.

This was one possibility she had, stupidly, never considered. Why not? Had she assumed the company would be too aristocratic or too wild for his respectability? Discovery rushed upon her, along with fear of his anger, his contempt. Her mouth was suddenly too dry to speak—which didn't really matter, since she could think of nothing to say.

The silence seemed to stretch tight like a rope. She could only tilt her chin with a mere hint of the old swagger. He did not seem to notice. His face gave away nothing except slight impatience.

Did he not know her? Why did that not delight her?

"Well met, Nicholas," he said casually. "I'll just take over your chair, since you're off." And he brushed past her without another glance and sat down.

Almost blindly, she moved away, passing various tables before she found herself in the private parlor that had been laid out with a buffet and copious bottles.

She had deliberately spilled more of her ale than she had drunk during the game. But now she felt the need for something stronger. Like Aubrey's brandy.

The inn's brandy tasted just as good, no doubt acquired from France via the same smugglers as supplied Blackhaven. The shock of it burning down her throat steadied her nerves. She recognized that Bernard had done her a favor by naming her aloud without introduction. Only, how had he known? How long had he been there?

It didn't matter. He was playing along, whatever his reasons, and in truth, it was much more comfortable to feel she had a friend present. She just hadn't expected him to be quite so casual about her appearing in this company, or in this guise.

With her brandy in her hand, she allowed herself to be inveigled into a game of vingt-et-un, where she lost a little and won a lot more. From where she sat, she could keep one eye on the faro table, though only the back of Bernard's head. A passing stranger clapped him on the shoulder and won a quick, very Bernard smile. It was more than she had done.

Why was she so surprised to see him among these wild young rakehells? He was surely younger than most of them and had probably played more games of cards. Because he was not rich? Because he troubled to look after his aunt and stepmother and was liked by everyone in Blackhaven?

Tranmere was exchanging some jest with him. Bernard gave a riposte, and the whole table shouted with laughter. She was probably glad she hadn't made out the words. She must remember to swear more.

On that thought, she realized she was about to signal for another card and could not afford it. She swore and shook her head emphatically. *Mind on the cards, Felicia!*

Next, before anyone could notice her run of luck, she made up a fourth in a game of loo that was really too easy, since her opponents were utterly foxed and had no interest in the game. They shoved a load of money at her, along with vowels she had no idea how she would redeem in this guise, and returned to the girls and the drink that were clearly their preferred pastimes.

While she gathered up her money, a girl sat down in her lap.

Chapter Six

COMPLETELY FLUMMOXED, FELICIA blinked at her. "Ain't you a handsome young gent?" the girl said, winding her arms around Felicia's neck. She smelled of alcohol and old sweat and something else Felicia did not care to contemplate.

But nor could she sit here, frozen, as if she did not appreciate the attention. She was supposed to be a lusty young man on a spree.

"Handsome?" she managed, reaching around the girl to gather the rest of her winnings and stuff them into her pocket. At the last moment, inspired, she dropped a coin down the girl's very obvious cleavage.

The girl shrieked with laughter. "Handsome is as handsome does!" she cried with delight, leaning in to kiss him.

Abruptly, she sprang off him, yanked by the waist.

"So am I," Bernard declared before giving her a smacking kiss on the lips. "But later! Nicholas, we have an appointment with piquet."

How weird to be addressed by her husband's name, and by *him*, of all people. She wished she had picked a different name altogether. There was nothing she could do except follow him to the one table set up for piquet. It was not a popular game among the wilder young bucks, requiring as it did more skill and concentration than blind luck.

Bernard sat down with his back to the room, leaving her to squash into the chair between the table and the wall.

"I'm glad of this chance to talk," she said low, as he began to shuffle the cards.

"Are you?" he said deliberately. Which was when she saw that he was not casual about her presence at all. On the contrary, he was furious. "Why? What can you possibly say?"

Stung, she raised her eyebrows haughtily. She had practiced before the mirror and knew it looked as effective as either male or female. "Why, that we should not waste our time playing piquet with each other. I have almost doubled our money already. I suggest we partner each other at whist for—"

"There will be no whist for us. You have spoiled my evening as well as your own."

Her face heated, more with anger than shame. "My evening is going splendidly. If you don't care for the company, go home."

"I fully intend to. Pick up your cards. One hand and then we leave."

Oh, no. No one ordered her around, not anymore. No one had the right, and she would not allow it ever again.

"One hand," she said, meeting his gaze. "No more until you recover your temper and your manners."

His eyes widened and swept over her. *"Manners?"*

His contempt chilled her, but at least it served to stoke her own anger. She laughed provokingly. "Confess. You are just jealous because that wench so clearly preferred me to you."

If she had meant to make him laugh, she failed dismally. If anything, his lips whitened. Unexpected rage, unexpected passion. How could something so damned *annoying* still thrill her?

"Dear God—"

"Don't rant, Muir," she interrupted. "Play."

His mouth snapped shut. They played in deafening silence. And as soon as the hand was over, with no money exchanged, she sprang up, deliberately rocking the table so that he had to spend time righting it before he could follow her.

By the time she felt the touch of his hand on his arm, she was sliding into the fourth chair at the whist table.

She glanced up at him. "I thought you were not in the mood for whist?" she said carelessly.

His face blank once more, he managed a smile. "I changed my mind."

"Lady's privilege," she said sweetly. "Not a gentleman's."

"Here, take my place, Muir," said her proposed partner. "Need some air."

There was curiously little satisfaction in forcing him to her will. Although his face betrayed nothing, he barely glanced at her, and there was an odd stiffness in his posture, slight but unmistakable, that told her she had ended their friendship.

Nevertheless, they played perfectly together, as if the game was separate from either of them. He was an intelligent and perceptive player and always seemed to know her aims as she guessed his.

They won a good deal, and could have won a lot more, but Felicia had spotted the frown of annoyance on one of her opponents' faces, not helped by Tranmere's remark that he was being fleeced by a stripling.

Ready to call it a night, she rose to her feet.

"How old are you, anyway?" Tranmere asked, peering at her more closely than was comfortable.

She scowled as aggressively as she could. "Old enough to win."

"And young enough to be missed by his mother," Bernard added, taking him by the ear.

The others roared with laughter as Felicia wriggled free and glared at him. By this time, they were halfway across the room, and she could see for herself that it really was time to go. A couple were lying together on a bench. One young man was pouring neat brandy into the open mouth of another while others stood around chanting. Two men were tugging a willing-enough girl toward the stairs. The cards were almost entirely forgotten.

Bernard threw his arm around Felicia's shoulders and raised a free hand by way of farewell and thanks. "Not a word," he murmured as he swept her out of the inn into the blessedly clear, cold drizzle.

The shock of fresh air made her stagger. Mocking male laughter came from close by. No doubt more of Tranmere's guests laughing at the youth who couldn't hold his drink.

"Lord, I'll have to tie you onto the damned horse at this rate," Bernard complained, to another chortle. "Stables, my lad."

It was actually quite clever. Causing everyone to laugh at her distracted them from realizing how much she had won. So she didn't fight him. They were almost free. The knowledge seemed to relax Bernard too, because when she let out a spectacular burp, his spontaneous breath of laughter stirred her hair.

"I know," she murmured. "I should be on the stage."

"You should be in Bedlam, you lunatic," he said frankly, pushing her over the stable door.

She peered around the unexpectedly dim light. "Where's the—"

The rest was cut off as she landed hard against his chest and his mouth covered hers. She gasped in shock. And in delight.

God, yes, sweet, welcome, heart-churning delight. There might have been no warning, let alone a granting of permission, but this was no violent, entitled assault, even though it probably sprang from frustration or anger with her, as though the force of his emotion had nowhere else to go but into this sudden, overwhelming kiss. And yet there was something delicate about his mouth, seducing, not forcing her into helpless response. This, *this* was what she wanted of him, had always wanted. Such passion, such intensity she had never dreamed…

A horse whinnied loudly in her ear, and she squeaked, jerking away.

Bernard released her at once. "You are quite right, my friend," he said, apparently to the horse. His voice sounded…strange. "Can you find your horse, or will I shout for the ostler?"

"No, let's saddle them ourselves and go."

The tack was easy enough to find opposite the mare's stall, but her fingers felt numb and clumsy, her mind not on the task at hand because her lips tingled so sweetly where they could still feel the pressure of his, the caress of his tongue...

"Let me," Bernard said quietly behind her, and he took over buckling the bridle. She let her hands fall to her sides, knowing she should move aside, but he smelled too good, *felt* too good... He pushed the reins into her hand and turned to his own mount.

Pulling herself together, she led the mare out of the stables.

A violent shove knocked her sideways. The mare objected, rearing and whinnying and dragging the reins out of Felicia's hand. Another buffet knocked her off her feet, and someone landed on her hard.

"Keep still or I'll cut your throat," came the growl of her attacker. "Where's the blunt?"

"Pocket," gasped Felicia, who had a very good reason not to be searched bodily. However, neither was she prepared to give up the hard-won money. While the man reached into her coat pocket, she opened her mouth to yell, and heaved at the same time. She only managed to dislodge him partially, and his hand closed around her throat. In the other, he held her purse.

And then, suddenly, he was ripped off her.

"Pick on someone your own size," Bernard said furiously, and ducked as the man lashed out at him.

He barreled headfirst into the thief's stomach, while Felicia scrambled to her feet and looked wildly around for a weapon.

Instead, she saw a second man several feet away, but approaching fast. Help? Or further threat?

"Oi!" he yelled out, and the thief, who now had one arm wrenched most of the way up his back by Bernard, raised his other hand and threw the purse to the newcomer.

Felicia did not hesitate. She leapt, almost flying to intercept the purse, and caught it in midair before tumbling to the ground.

She rolled and sprang up, swinging the heavy purse around her head like a medieval weapon.

But the second thief was closing on Bernard, and Felicia's heart flew into her mouth. He needed help, now. She sprinted after the second thief, and then had to swerve as Bernard punched him and he staggered back, all but losing his balance.

"Behind you!" Felicia called as the first thief crept up on Bernard. He whirled around, and as the second man closed in from behind, Felicia swung the purse hard against the side of his head.

He froze, half turned with an expression of surprise, as though he had forgotten about her, and then crumpled to the ground. Bernard struck the other, who fell almost on top of his comrade, and groaned.

By the light of the stable lantern, Felicia met Bernard's gaze. He was panting, scowling.

"Well," she said. "You are a man of unexpected parts."

Bernard began to laugh.

WHATEVER ELSE, BERNARD had to admire Felicia Maitland's cool.

As he boosted her into the saddle at last, she said disapprovingly, "Are we just going to leave them there?"

"I don't feel much tending their wounds," Bernard said. His knuckles had begun to sting.

"No, but they'll try to rob the others as they leave the inn!"

"They'll have to take their chances," Bernard said, swinging into his own saddle. "We can't really afford to have a magistrate poking around and asking us questions."

"You mean *I* can't afford it," she countered ruefully.

Fear for her had made him angry earlier, and he had gone the wrong way about making her understand. But in her quiet voice now, he heard all her vulnerability from the past as well as the present. She would not be bowed, but her self-belief hung by a thread.

"I mean *we*," he said clearly. "I thought we were partners?"

Her smile more than made up for the agony of the evening. It was almost as sweet as kissing her. *Oh God, why did I kiss her?*

Because he had always wanted to. She had obsessed him very quickly. Her beauty, her cool self-possession, masked the conflicting passions behind her eyes. Her inner glow. And yet there was something unfulfilled about her that spoke to him, binding them together.

He had not intended to kiss her. He just *had*. And now that he had tasted the merest hint of her passion, it had not cured him of his obsession at all. He wanted more, much, much more. All of her.

Partners…

They had a lantern each, enough to light the road if they paid attention. They set off at a fast pace that precluded conversation.

When they slowed enough to draw breath and give the horses a rest, he asked, "Will you be able to sleep in late this morning?"

"I never do. None of us seem to. And there is the garden party at the castle that will require much preparation."

"By you?"

"Not necessarily, but it is impossible to ignore a house full of Vales preparing for anything. Will you be there?"

"En masse. Gillie and Wickenden have arrived, so we will all go. Including my little brother and my even tinier nephew."

"It must be strange having a brother quite so much younger. Like Julius when he first met the twins. There are twenty years between them also."

A thought struck him. "Is your stepmother still alive?"

Her head turned toward him. "My stepmother? Oh, the countess, the twins' mother. She was never our stepmother. My father was not married to her when the twins were born. Apart from anything else, she was married to someone else. Her husband sent the twins to my father when she died. Like a bequest."

"Did he mind?"

"To give him his due, no. He kept them with him as much as he could, as he always did with the rest of us. I know what the Blackhaven gossips say. We are a ramshackle family. And they are quite right that Sir George was a shocking rake. But if he did anything right, it was the way he brought us all up together. He made no difference between the legitimate and illegitimate, so neither did we. And neither did his wives." Her teeth gleamed. "Only the twins themselves ever make use of it, to shock people or win their sympathy and their confidences."

"They sound formidable!"

"Oh, they are, but most people seem to find them charming."

Bernard smiled. "You love them."

"Did you expect me not to?"

"No, I just wanted to hear you admit it."

He could not see her frown in the darkness, yet somehow he knew it was there. "You are a loving person," he blurted. "I like that. Look, there is a shortcut through this meadow."

For a moment, he thought she would speed up over the dangerous ground, just because he had intruded. He was sorry, because his obsession had extended to breaking down her barriers, and it seemed he had pushed too hard, too fast.

But she rode beside him still. So he asked what he really wanted to know. "Did you love your husband?"

"Yes." It came out as a sigh and almost broke his heart, though he had known the answer before. She would not have married anyone without love. "I met him while my father was posted in London, and I had never encountered anyone like him. So handsome and charming and wild to a fault. The matchmaking mamas kept their daughters well away from him. He was like forbidden fruit." She let out a breath of laughter. "A bit like our friend Tranmere, I suppose."

"How did you even know about Tranmere's party?" Bernard asked, distracted. "Let alone be accepted there?"

"Aubrey. He had an invitation. And yes, before you say it,

even Aubrey had no intention of going. I took his card, and everyone tonight assumed Tranmere had been too foxed to remember he had invited me."

"It was clever," he allowed. "Even splendid, and definitely brave. But dear God, Felicia, do you have any idea of the dangers—"

"Rather more than I had when I arrived," she interrupted. "Young, entitled men, out of control. And with too much brandy to remove any lingering inhibitions. I should not have gone."

Bernard breathed more freely. "I apologize for my rudeness. I was just so afraid for you I thought I would explode."

"Bernard, I am not your responsibility."

It was the first time she had used his Christian name, and the sound on her lips enchanted him. "No," he said, smiling, "but one looks after friends. As you looked after me, delivering a very healthy wallop to the head of our thief. Thank you for that."

"It was nothing. You were managing fine without my interference. I didn't know you were a fighting man."

"I'm not," Bernard said firmly. "Though the science of it is quite interesting. Wickenden took me to Gentleman Jackson's boxing saloon a few times."

Again, she turned her head toward him. "There are many hidden parts to you, Bernard Muir."

"And to you, Felicia Vale," he retorted, forgetting momentarily about her marriage. "The flying catch to the purse, for example. I haven't seen anything like it off the cricket field."

She gave a strangely enchanting gurgle of laughter. "Well, considering what we went through to get it, I was determined not to lose it. We all but tripled our money, Bernard."

Had he somehow agreed to this after all? Yes, he had called her his partner and promised a card party at the inn. He was committed, and he could not let her down. He *would* not. "There are my own meager winnings to add to the haul."

"Then you are a little closer to your dream. And I can repay some of what I owe my siblings."

He thought of that dream he had harbored for so long, born during the card parties he and Gillie should never have hosted. The freedom to own a gaming club somewhere in Europe. Only the vision seemed to have altered. A shadowy lady shaped rather like Felicia strode through the gaming halls by his side.

He blinked the fantasy away. "We can canter over this part, down to the road to Black Hill."

They rode between the hills, until finally the house was in sight. Bernard, though suddenly aware of exhaustion, did not want to leave her.

"Will your family have noticed you were gone? Will they kick up a fuss?"

"I am beyond the age and stage in life of needing a chaperone," she said, just a little sharply. "They respect my independence." Then, in a different voice, she added, "Though somehow I am sure the twins will know!" She peered at him. "It is still a long ride to Blackhaven from here. Why don't you stay at Black Hill?"

He blinked rapidly in a futile effort to dispel the erotic visions dancing behind his eyes. "I would not disturb your household at this time of night," he managed. "Besides, your brothers would kill me."

"Not when you saved my life," she said lightly. "But I take your point. I don't want to answer questions either." Her breath caught. "Wait, though—there is the summer house. There are blankets there, and no one will disturb you."

Images of Felicia in the summer house with him threatened his sanity. Felicia, naked among all those cushions, warm and passionate as she reached for him with both silken arms...

She said, "You need a few hours' rest, and then you can ride home tomorrow in plenty of time to squire your ladies to the garden party. And your hand will need attention."

Oddly, it was the thought of his right-hand knuckles that did it. Dulcie, their old nurse, would be bound to hear about any blood in his washing water, and he would never hear the end of it.

Excuses, Muir. Excuses.

It was true. He would do anything for just another half-hour of her company.

Chapter Seven

FELICIA'S HEART DRUMMED as they quietly saw to the horses and left them both in the stable. Then she took him to the summer house, lit the lamp, and left him there while she fetched water and bandages from the kitchen in the main house. All the time, she tried to focus on practicalities, to keep her mind off his kiss and the way it had made her feel.

She found him sprawled among the cushions, with his gloves peeled off. She placed the bowl of water on the low table where they played cards the last time they had been here together. Without a word, he stuck his hand in the bowl. His knuckles were grazed and bloody, but not much worse than she had seen on the boys from time to time.

She sat beside him, a clean towel on her lap. When he took his hand out of the water, she placed it on the towel and dried it gently. There was an intimacy about the prosaic tasks that was curiously comforting. And she knew his gaze was on her face as she dried and salved his wounds, then bound a bandage around his hand.

"Just wear gloves in company for a day or two and no one should notice," she said optimistically. She rose and went to the other table, pouring ale into the cup she had brought. "Here."

He took it with thanks and drank.

She watched him in silence, then sank onto the cushions

opposite him. "Why did you kiss me?"

He met her gaze. "I wanted to. Why did you kiss me back?"

She flushed but did not think of lying. "I wanted to."

He smiled, that quick Bernard smile that always undid her.

She reached across and touched his cheek, a little rough with stubble. "You may kiss me again if you wish," she said huskily.

He caught his breath. "Don't," he said. "I do wish."

She let her thumb stray over his lips. "Then...?"

"If I kiss you now, I will not stop," he said. "And I owe you more than a weary tumble in the cushions. You are worthy of more respect."

God, he was *kind*. Her heart ached. Her body ached. "I would take that honest, weary tumble over a luxurious seduction."

"There is nothing wrong with luxurious seductions," he said, catching her hand and kissing it. "They can be honest, too." He held her hand to his cheek. "I cannot abuse your weariness or your trust. Or your hospitality. I would care for you. I would take you to bed and love you with all the time and luxury in the world."

Heat flooded her. He turned her hand and softly kissed the inside of her wrist. The tip of his tongue flickered over her galloping pulse.

"Is that an offer, Bernard Muir?" She meant it to be light and sophisticated, but it sounded too breathless, too excited.

"It is a promise," he said.

Without warning, he leaned over, his eyes dark with desire, and, despite what he had said earlier, took her mouth.

But there was little time to rejoice in provoking him thus far. He fell back almost at once, smiling and yet firm. "It must be goodnight."

And it seemed the right thing to do to smile back and leave him there. Yet she felt as though she walked on air across the garden and into the house. She did not remember climbing the stairs or undressing, but she found herself in bed, smiling into the pillows because Bernard Muir would be her lover. And because, at last, she had chosen well.

LADY BRAITHWAITE'S GARDEN party at the castle was not a formal affair. Children of all ages were welcome, and the twins were eager to meet young people of their own age. They cornered Felicia in the breakfast parlor, ostensibly to tell her so, although Lawrence followed it up immediately by saying, "Someone was in the summer house last night. They left early this morning."

Felicia knew that. She had gone there as soon as she wakened and found him already gone. He had taken his horse. She thought the new laborer, Farmer, who occasionally worked in the stables, might have seen him go, but he was a close-lipped man and appeared quite uninterested.

Felicia could not help being disappointed. She had wanted to speak to him again, see him again in the light of day just to be sure he had meant what she thought he had last night. Instead, she had to wait until the garden party, when they were likely to be surrounded by other people. The pleasurable knot of anticipation in her stomach grew.

But the twins were still looking at her, waiting for her response. "Oh, don't worry," she said carelessly over her shoulder as she made her way out of the room. "It was only a friend."

"Couldn't they stay in the house?" Lawrence asked.

"It was too late," she said vaguely. "Oh, do you both have something decent to wear this afternoon that is still clean?"

Having neatly turned the conversation, she swanned off to inspect their apparel.

Everyone was determined to attend the garden party, though, fortunately for everyone else, Roderick said he would make his own way there, thus leaving more room in the two carriages it would need to transport them all.

Roderick had been busy with some new business he was

trying out and looked a trifle grim. So did Julius, while Delilah and Cornelius both appeared merely troubled. This made Felicia a little uneasy, reining in her own happiness.

A new question was echoing around her head. *When?*

Oddly enough, after the Countess of Braithwaite welcomed them to the castle gardens and told them about the exhibitions, music, dancing, and poetry readings to be found both inside and out, the first person Felicia saw was Tranmere.

Glass in hand, he was talking to a couple she recognized as Lord and Lady Wickenden, Bernard's sister and brother-in-law. Well, Wickenden was the original "Wicked Baron," so no doubt Tranmere looked up to him.

They stood just outside the marquee on the lawn—a sensible defense against the almost inevitable rain, although it was dry at the moment. On impulse, Felicia walked toward them. She wanted to look Tranmere in the eye and spot any sign of puzzled recognition.

It was Lady Wickenden who saw her first and smiled in her friendly way. "Why, Mrs. Maitland! Why did I not know you were a Vale of Black Hill?"

They curtseyed and clasped hands, and her ladyship introduced her husband and Mr. Tranmere, whose slightly bloodshot eyes bore a gleam of admiration, but no recognition that she could see.

"I did not know of your Blackhaven connection either," Felicia replied.

In fact, she had once suspected that Lady Wickenden and she were bound in other ways entirely, namely being the wives of known rakes. Except that the Town gossips quickly began to say that "the nobody" had tamed the Wicked Baron, for he fought no further duels. No more ridiculous, dangerous, or expensive wagers were reported, and no other ladies' names were coupled with his. If he strayed, he did it so discreetly that his bride was at least never publicly humiliated.

This was a consideration that had never troubled Nick.

"Bernard tells me you play cards like a fiend," Lady Wickenden observed, walking with her toward the castle. Tranmere and Wickenden strolled on either side of them.

Felicia allowed herself one quick glance at Tranmere. She doubted he was even listening as his gaze roamed over her figure.

"I enjoy cards," she told Lady Wickenden. "Don't you?"

"Snap," Lord Wickenden said from his wife's side, and she laughed.

"It's true. I am not a great card player. People take it too seriously for me. Bernard, of course, will play anywhere, though I don't believe it's part of today's entertainment."

At that moment, she saw Bernard. Surprisingly at home in the ornate surroundings of a nobleman's castle, he strolled into the great hall from an inner doorway, with a small boy of about three on his shoulders. Though in immaculate morning dress, he looked gloriously casual—and so handsome that her heart tried to leap into her throat. The child held on to his head, chattering away and laughing. Bernard laughed, too, a carefree sound that made everyone else smile in response.

His gaze fell on Felicia, and their eyes locked—a tiny moment of joy and understanding. At least, that was how it seemed to her. He increased his pace toward them, much to the child's delight. Tranmere hastily made his excuses and sauntered off in search of more congenial company.

Felicia wanted to give Bernard her hand, but he was too occupied in holding the boy steady on his shoulders. She curtseyed instead, and he grinned in response, his eyes warm and unreservedly happy. To see her? Or just because he was enjoying himself?

"Our little brother, Arthur," Lady Wickenden said proudly. "Arthur, this is Mrs. Maitland."

The boy greeted her with a grin alarmingly like Bernard's. "How do you do, Mrs. Maitland?" he recited.

"I am very well. How do *you* do?" On impulse she reached up, and Arthur detached one of his hands from Bernard's hair to shake.

"My horse is taking me to find the other children," he told her. "And I'm to look after Davie. Giddy up, horse!" He raised one hand as though it held a whip.

"The horse will throw you," Bernard said, "if you hit it."

Arthur grinned and lowered his hand, though he wriggled impatiently instead. Bernard shrugged his burdened shoulders and ambled off out the door. It struck Felicia that he would make a wonderful father—attentive, fun, and yet firm. For an instant, she felt an unexpected ache that this would be with some other woman, and then she banished it. The present, the very near future, was hers.

⁂

FROM THE MEZZANINE gallery above the great hall, where an exhibition of paintings was on display, Waller Harlaw watched Felicia's entry with the Wickendens. He was irritated to see Tranmere in her company, presumably sniffing about her skirts—the boy was an inveterate rake—but she paid him no more attention than a wary glance.

"This one is particularly lovely," Isabella Muir enthused beside him, and he forced himself to turn back to her and the paintings. He was bored with both.

"I am surprised he has never painted *your* likeness, dear lady," he said, for she was referring to the work of Lord Tamar, the aristocratic if impoverished marquis turned painter who was considered a local celebrity after his marriage to one of the Earl of Braithwaite's sisters. "The gentle strength of your features, the character that shines forth—"

She interrupted him, blushing. "Actually, he has."

His eyebrows flew up in astonishment. He could not stop them, although it was hardly flattering to Isabella. But he recovered quickly. "But I have never seen such a painting! Is it such a poor likeness that you do not display it in your home?"

Her blush deepened. "It is in my bedchamber. He painted Arthur and me only a few weeks after the birth. I like to look at it in private. It—it connects me to my husband."

Harlaw was wise enough not to take a pet at that remark. If he had learned anything of Isabella, it was that she was supremely private in her feelings. That she had admitted as much to him, even blushed over it, was a major step forward in their oh-so-proper courtship.

It would not be like this with Felicia. Her cool, sophisticated manners were all for show. Beneath them, he knew she was all fire. But he must not think of her now. This was Isabella's moment.

He touched her hand, smiling gently. "I understand."

Her smile was warm, and she voluntarily took his arm as they progressed along the gallery.

It was not until the poetry reading—utter drivel—that he managed to escape, leaving her in the comfortable company of Lady Wickenden, the Countess of Torridon, and some other ladies he did not know. She was surprisingly well connected in the town. Cynically, he wondered if that was only since she had inherited her fortune. At least he would not have to be ashamed of her.

Back in the hall, he saw that the weather had driven most people indoors, although there seemed to be a racket outside, where some children were playing in the marquee. Really, what was Lady Braithwaite thinking about to permit children at such a party? He would have expected the haughty dowager countess to squash such foolishness.

Felicia. His pulse quickened, as it always had at the sight of her. She was with one of her sisters and Lord Linfield, moving toward the front of the room, where some fellow was preparing to play. The young countess was introducing him as Harlaw swept up a pair of wine glasses and made his way to Felicia's side.

She glanced up as though surprised to see him. He bowed

slightly, murmuring her name, and presented her with one of the glasses. From that, it must have been clear he meant to detach her from her current friends, and a shadow of irritation crossed her face. For an instant, he feared she would not accept the glass, but then she inclined her head and took it.

"Mr. Harlaw. My thanks."

"I always find listening to music thirsty work."

"Perhaps you should try the poetry instead."

He shuddered and won a laugh from her when he hadn't even been trying. "Do you care for music, Mrs. Maitland?"

"I do. And I am told this pianist has taken London by storm. He is already highly thought of in Scotland."

"Music or cards?" he asked her, smiling into her eyes.

"Music," she said at once. "There are no card games here, sir."

"Then when will you allow me my return match at piquet? Do I have to wait for the castle ball?"

"Possibly. Though I heard Mr. Muir was talking of arranging a charity card party. I am not sure exactly when. I imagine it will be at the King's Head or somewhere similar, though, for I believe Mrs. Muir does not care for cards in her home."

Well, she will have to get used to it. Harlaw smiled. "At the inn? What a charming idea. For farthing stakes?"

"Any stake you like, I imagine, if you can find someone to match it."

"I hope you will."

"You hope I will what?"

He smiled into her eyes. "Match with me."

She laughed and tapped his arm reprovingly with her gloved fingers. "The music, sir. Pay attention."

His smile broadened. For the first time he could recall, she was almost flirting. Unfortunately, when he raised his eyes, he saw Isabella staring straight at him. She looked stricken.

Damnation! Why can't the wretched woman stay in one place?

On the other hand, perhaps he was unwise to court two

women for two very different purposes under the same roof.

❧

FELICIA HAD GLIMPSED Isabella too and was appalled. Not so much that Harlaw's flirting might put Isabella off him—which had to be a good thing—but that Bernard's stepmother was hurt and might take her in understandable dislike. Even though it had been Harlaw doing the flirting.

What the devil was he up to, anyway?

It was the question she put to Bernard almost at once when she finally got the chance to walk with him during a gap in the rain.

"I think he was *flirting* with me, which he has never done before, and yet it looks as if he has some kind of understanding with your stepmother."

"God, I hope not," Bernard said, scowling. "He is always underfoot, though, and for some reason, she likes him. Gillie thinks she is just flattered by the attention."

"I am not. He is up to something, even if it's just to persuade me to lose to him at piquet. I told him about your card party at the inn. He definitely bit."

So far, they had been walking decorously along the path, well within sight of the great hall windows, her gloved hand resting lightly on his arm. But now he gazed down at her, his eyes warm and intimate.

"Last night, our partnership moved beyond cards."

Heat flooded into her face. "Beyond? Perhaps. But between you and I, are cards not always included?"

He guided her along a fork in the path that led past a walled orchard. "Curiously," he said, "I have this selfish desire to surpass the cards in your interest."

"Even more curiously, I have a notion to let you."

"Then I have not yet achieved my goal?" he said lightly.

"I'm not sure you have tried."

His eyes darkened. Without warning, he pushed a wooden door in the orchard wall and whisked her inside, spinning her in his arms. His head bent over hers. She inhaled his clean citrus and spice smell, grew fascinated with the texture of his lips so close to hers. His chest was broad, his growing arousal obvious against her stomach.

"And yet you would take me as your lover?" His breath whispered against her mouth.

She was so deliciously weak, she would have taken him there and then. But she had pride. "Perhaps. If you tried just a little harder."

His lips curved into a smile just before they sank on hers, slow and sensual and utterly devastating. In wonder, she reached up to cup his cheek, then, as his mouth began to move on hers, exploring and deepening the kiss, she had to clutch his shoulder with her other hand.

It seemed she was not so weak after all, for she pushed closer against him, caressing his cheek, the corner of his silken mouth, his hair, his nape.

He held her by the hips, pressing her against his hard body. His kisses spread out from her lips to her ear and her throat, whispering fire across her skin. One hand stroked upward, over her waist to her breast, and desire such as she had never known seemed to explode within her.

She flung both arms around his neck, desperately drawing his mouth back to hers. Sensation overwhelmed her with pleasure, with growing, urgent need. And when he began to move his body lazily against hers, she followed blindly, trying to reach the ache between her legs.

He released her mouth, but only to whisper in her ear, "What about now?"

She stared up at him, barely understanding. "You want to make love to me now? *Here?*"

"God, yes," he said fervently before returning for another long, deep kiss. "But I was asking if I had piqued your interest. Or shall we play cards?"

A breath of laughter shook her. "I did not bring any cards."

"What a shame. Neither did I." He trailed one fingertip over her lips and down her neck to the pulse that beat there. He lingered, then slid his finger lower, as far as the neckline of her gown would allow, so lightly that her skin clamored for more.

"You have seduced women before, Bernard Muir," she said, wondering if she was jealous. It seemed she could no longer think.

"I am no saint," he admitted. "But neither am I a rake. Shall we tryst, Felicia Vale?"

"You mean to climb up to my balcony under the moonlight?" she teased.

"Do you have one?"

"A balcony? No. But I can leave the window open."

She felt the breath of his laughter as he kissed her, and then kissed her again.

Reluctantly, it seemed, he drew back. "We should not linger here much longer. Most of the castle occupants use the orchard for assignations. Besides, beyond this tree, I believe it is raining again."

"Then we should wait until it stops."

"What an excellent plan."

It was another five rather beautiful minutes before she straightened his cravat, and he replaced the fallen pins in her hair. By then, it was barely raining at all, and a brisk walk brought them back to the castle dry enough not to cause comment.

But Felicia had taken her eye off the ball.

Lucy was behaving atrociously because the man she had been betrothed to since childhood had suddenly chosen to make his appearance at the garden party, and according to Roderick, she was in love with someone else. Antonia Macy seemed to have jilted Julius in favor of the slimy man who administered the charitable hospital. And when Felicia smiled at Isabella Muir, the other woman turned away as though she had not seen her.

And then Bernard danced with Genevra Winslow.

Chapter Eight

APART FROM THE fact he would rather have held Felicia in his arms, Bernard was quite happy to dance with Genevra. He had known her all her life, and her older sister, now Lady Sylvester Gaunt, was one of Gillie's closest friends.

She appeared in front of him just as the music struck up—the little orchestra having moved indoors from the marquee, where the children had been dancing with somewhat hilarious results. Bernard, who had been prowling straight for Felicia, was obliged to halt before Genevra or mow her down.

"Bernard!" she exclaimed. "It really *is* you."

Bernard regarded her with the tolerant irritation he normally reserved for his sister and small brother. "Do I detect a hint of sarcasm, Genevra?"

She pouted. "I just mean I have only seen you from a distance all day."

"Be grateful," Bernard said flippantly.

"I will be if you make up for your mistake by dancing with me now." She took his arm in a managing kind of way that was frankly annoying.

A quick glance showed him Felicia turning toward Wickenden and then Mrs. Winslow frowning in his direction. Mrs. Winslow had always had social ambitions for her daughters, and they most certainly did not include Bernard. He was well aware she only ever invited him to her parties in order to make up numbers or to please Gillie now that she was a baroness.

Prompted by a little devil of mischief, he let himself be drawn onto the dance floor, at which time he brushed her hand off his arm. "Don't drag a fellow about, Genevra. Most of us don't like it," he murmured, taking her hand instead and placing his hand lightly on her waist. The waltz began. "What did you ambush me for?"

Color flooded into her face. "Ambush you? That is hardly gentlemanly!"

"Not really ladylike to grab a fellow who has promised the dance to another lady, either."

She tilted her chin with somewhat childish defiance. "Then why did you come with me? Because I am so strong?"

"There's that sarcasm again," Bernard observed. "No, I came because other people were watching, your mother didn't like it, and I thought there might be something wrong."

She blinked. "Wrong? Why should there be something wrong because I choose to dance with an old friend?"

He said nothing, letting her work out for herself that she had done *all* the choosing. Of course, it wasn't really fair. A lady—unless she was not dancing at all—was really obliged to dance with whoever asked her, so he was only having the favor returned and being somewhat ungracious about it.

"*Is* there something wrong?" he asked more gently, searching her face.

"What makes you think I would come to you if there were?" she snapped.

"I hope you would, since we are indeed old friends."

She met his gaze with suspicion, and then began to look slightly mollified. But she said nothing, as though he had somewhat taken the wind out of her sails. They danced in silence for several minutes while Bernard wondered more seriously what it was all about.

"I suppose it was Mrs. Maitland," she blurted at last.

Bernard blinked. "You suppose what was Mrs. Maitland?"

"Whom you were going to dance with."

"Actually, it was."

"Well, you needn't worry, for she is dancing with Lord Wickenden."

Bernard glanced around and saw Felicia waltz by in his brother-in-law's capable arms. Despite knowing that David was devoted to Gillie, he felt a sharp twinge of jealousy. He and Felicia made a very handsome couple, they had moved in the same world, and that world had not called him the Wicked Baron for nothing. He was a very charming fellow, damn him.

"I expect she'll have her claws into *him* next," Genevra said with contempt.

Bernard jerked his attention back to her, realizing many things. That he had been blind to Genevra's growing affection and, perhaps, her expectations. Perhaps willfully blind because he had not wanted to deal with it. But this kind of spite he could not allow, not against Felicia.

"That is neither kind nor worthy. Not toward Gillie or Lord Wickenden, and most certainly not to Mrs. Maitland, whose reputation is of the highest."

Genevra's cheeks burned. She turned stiff in his arms, even made a half-pull as though to be free of him.

"Do you want to sit down?" he asked.

She swallowed hard. "No. Unless you wish to be rid of me. You will hate me now."

"Of course I don't. We've all said things, done things, we regret."

She was not a stupid girl. She understood the importance of regret—and of not repeating her mistake.

"Are we still friends, Genevra?"

Her gaze fell and then came back to his, miserable but proud. "Of course we are still friends."

He had to make a bit of effort after that, to steer the conversation and make her laugh, to walk with her to her sister Catherine and linger a little before he could go in search of Felicia once more.

At last, he swung away with relief—a small scandal and a lot of damage averted—only to find himself face to face with a very young lady and gentleman who were like mirror images of each other.

He had noted them before, now that the older children like Rosa Benedict and the visiting Michael Gaunt, who were not quite regarded as adults, were allowed to join in the dancing that would close the garden party.

He glanced from one to the other, wondering whether to be amused or annoyed by the second ambush of the afternoon preventing him from seeking Felicia.

The girl smiled and held out her hand. "You are Mr. Bernard Muir."

"I know," Bernard said gravely. "And you are the youngest Miss Vale."

"I am. Leona. This is my brother, Lawrence."

"How do you do?" Lawrence said, also shaking hands.

"I'm very glad to meet you."

"We wanted to meet you too," Lawrence said. "Since you are Felicia's friend."

Bernard could not easily grasp the boy's tone. It was not quite disapproval or warning, or even idle curiosity. "I hope I am," he said. "I don't suppose she gave you a message for me?"

"No," Leona said, looking uncertain for the first time. "I don't think she would do that."

She glanced at her brother, who said, "Felicia is very open and honest by nature."

Somehow, they were strolling through the quieter part of the hall, a twin on either side of Bernard.

"I know," Bernard said. "I imagine she shares those traits with the rest of you."

Leona smiled. "Well, Lawrence and I are always honest. I suppose we are not always as *open* as some people imagine. Our brothers are, though. They have expectations."

"Of their sisters' friends," Lawrence added.

Bernard regarded him, not quite amused now. "Is this where you point out to me how large they are, how honed in battle and—"

The twins laughed. "We know you are not blind!" Leona said. "And we like that Felicia is making new friends and having fun at last. She deserves some happiness."

"I agree," Bernard said. "Cut line, Vale twins. Is there something you want me to do?" *Or not do…*

Lawrence frowned, looking unexpectedly stern. "Look after her."

Leona smiled. "Make her happy," she said, and they vanished out of the French doors, speeding off to who knew where.

❧

WALLER HARLAW, DANCING with Isabella, watched the little drama between Bernard and Genevra Winslow with some amusement. He could easily recognize the signs of jealous womanhood, and was more than happy for her fury to be turned on Bernard. On the other hand, he did not like the way it was turned on Felicia Maitland.

Anyone could see that Bernard was at Felicia's feet. However, the thought that there could conceivably be reason behind Genevra's jealousy—such as Felicia's favoring of Bernard—did not please Harlaw at all. Bernard was a boy, a young man of no account who had been nowhere and done nothing. He would not even be invited to castle parties were his sister not Lady Wickenden. Their father might have been a gentleman—just—but in the grand scheme of things, he was a nobody.

And yet, where Isabella was concerned, he always seemed to be in Harlaw's way. Well, the boy would not block his path to Felicia. That, he would never allow.

Having some slight acquaintance with Genevra's sister, Lady Sylvester Gaunt, Harlaw strolled over, engaged the pair in conversation, and eventually contrived to edge Genevra away from her family.

"Forgive me if I overstep the mark," he said, "but young Mr. Muir appeared to upset you."

"Oh, no," Genevra said brightly. "We have quarreled and made up since we were children."

"Ah, I see. Then all is well. I just wondered if your upset was caused by anxiety over an old friend of my own."

She frowned, clearly uncomprehending.

He leaned forward and murmured, "Mrs. Maitland. He is merely dazzled, you know. She is too old for him in both years and...experience. Marriage between them will never happen."

Genevra flushed a dull red. "Mr. Muir's marriage—or lack of it—is no concern of mine."

He held her gaze until her breath caught.

"She is not old," Genevra blurted. "And she is beautiful and clever, everything I am not."

"Well, they would be miserable together," Harlaw pronounced, "so you and I should put our heads together to prevent our old friends making any such terrible mistake."

Genevra stared at him until he snatched a glass of lemonade from a passing footman and pressed it into her hand. "How do we do that?" she asked.

Harlaw smiled.

OF COURSE, THERE was no reason in the world why Bernard should not dance with Genevra Winslow. Felicia assumed they were old friends, which might be allowed to take precedence over his vague plan to waltz first with her. She would have felt no more than mild disappointment had it not been for Genevra's triumphant glance, cast directly over Bernard's shoulder to Felicia.

There was no reason for that look. Felicia was already dancing with Lord Wickenden. And Bernard was not a bone to be fought over by animals!

Then, for the first time, it came to her that Bernard's life was not quite as simple as she had assumed. Although she knew he was not married, he might well have entanglements, expectations that she knew nothing about. She had never asked.

He might not have been engaged to marry Genevra—he would surely have told her that, and even if he hadn't, she would have heard of it elsewhere. But it looked to Felicia very much as if the girl was in love with him and had some cause to hope.

Quite suddenly, she saw her own behavior in a whole new light. Not as a young widow looking for the consolation of a love affair, but as a siren who could affect someone else's life, as all those women of Nick's had torn her in pieces.

And Bernard... Bernard was undoubtedly attracted, but did he see her merely as a mature woman of experience, a source of the physical pleasure he could not take from the innocent Genevra before marriage?

She felt suddenly sick. She knew, had always known, that selfish pleasures had their price, usually paid by others. She had paid for Nick's. Should someone else now pay for hers?

Beyond that was a fierce, aching disappointment in Bernard. Was he no better than Nick? Were all men brothers under the skin?

She was confusing herself. Had she not gone to the assembly room ball with the idea of seeking a little pleasure of her own, firm in the belief that all men *were* basically the same? She would never look at a married man, but the unmarried were surely fair game. When had she begun to expect more of Bernard? *Why* should she?

"Are you quite well, ma'am?" Lord Wickenden asked. "Would you like to sit down?"

"Actually, I believe I would like a breath of fresh air, if you don't mind…"

Lord Wickenden gave her his arm, and they walked outside. The rain had gone off again, and everything smelled fresh and clean. By chance, they found Delilah sitting on a bench alone in the marquee. Wickenden left her with her sister and departed.

For a while they said nothing to each other, but the comfort of her older sister's presence washed over her. Delilah had always been there, long before Nick, through every family loss and every joy. Tears pricked her throat, tears of gratitude for Delilah, for all her siblings. She was so lucky, because they made each other strong.

"It will pass," Delilah said quietly at last.

Felicia had no idea whether she was referring to Felicia's troubles or her own. And she could not ask, because Delilah immediately began to tell her about the mistakes she had made concerning Antonia and Julius, and how she meant to help put things right. And then, together, they went back to the hall to help Antonia in any way they could.

❧

OVER THE NEXT couple of days, Felicia regained perspective on her trivial troubles. Lucy was still furious and miserable and would not confide in her. Julius got involved in the capture of horse thieves and gun smugglers, and the slimy bookkeeper from the hospital abducted Antonia. Naturally, this involved the entire family, duly warned of some of it by the twins, going immediately to Blackhaven Harbor to help, and ended in a celebration at the hotel of Julius and Antonia's betrothal.

Felicia, despite her views on marriage, could not help being delighted for Julius. After all, not all marriages were like hers. Julius was a genuinely honorable man, and Antonia clearly adored him. They were *matched*, and Felicia was very glad to welcome a new sister to the family.

For the hours they took over the hotel's tearoom, it was like a release of tension, and she simply let the joy enfold her. There was one potentially awkward moment when Lucy came face to face with her betrothed, Lord Eddleston, but even that passed quickly, and to her credit, Lucy did not let it interfere with her genuine pleasure in Julius's happiness.

The tea party was reaching its natural end when Felicia happened to glance over to the foyer. Through the glass windows, Miss Muir, Bernard's aunt, stopped dead, like a startled deer, then turned and fled toward the back of the hotel.

A young man Felicia did not know turned and followed her.

"Excuse me," Felicia murmured to the table in general, and went after them.

She had no reason to suppose the young man a threat to Miss Muir. There just seemed something wrong, both in her flight and the apparent pursuit by a stranger. Not that he was necessarily a stranger to Miss Muir, of course. But instinct propelled Felicia through the passage past the kitchen stairs to the door leading out to the stables and other outbuildings.

Only then did she realize she should have brought one of her large and fit brothers with her. But surely there were ostlers and other servants in the yard? She stepped outside, and to her right, approaching the arched exit to the alley beyond, she glimpsed Miss Muir and the same stranger.

The lady seemed nervous, about to glance over her shoulder, and Felicia started toward her, her mouth already open to inform her—and the man with her—that she had a friend nearby.

But abruptly, her arm was seized and she fell back against the wall. Or at least she would have fallen against it had not her attacker's arm been in the way. As it was, she flung up both hands to pummel him, and would have cried out, except his mouth seized hers.

She got in one desperate thump to the side of his head before she registered the appearance, the smell, the feel, of the man who held her.

Bernard let out a grunt that seemed to be half pain and half laughter. "Hush," he whispered against her lips. "Forgive me and humor me."

Was he watching out for his aunt? *Spying* on her?

He shifted position subtly. His hat had fallen forward over his forehead, or perhaps he had pushed it there, presumably so that the two people under the arch would not recognize him so easily. They certainly wouldn't, seeing him engaged in this activity. Her face and body burning with shame as well as unwanted desire, she was just grateful they wouldn't see her face.

But she glimpsed them, somewhere between the wall behind her and the brim of Bernard's hat. The young man held Miss Muir's hand. He bent and kissed her cheek. Not her enemy, then.

Miss Muir smiled and hurried off up the lane toward the high street. Her companion turned and walked in the other direction.

Bernard's gaze came back to Felicia. His lips—those sensitive, devastating lips—quirked into a half-smile.

"One more. Since I'm here." He kissed her again, this time with his full attention, turning her knees to water.

So much for her resolution to maintain a more proper distance between them. At least she made herself pull away first, and he released her at once.

"Are you spying on your aunt?" she demanded.

"Yes, but only because she was being furtive," he said ruefully. "I was here in the yard talking to a friend of mine who works in the stables when she appeared with that fellow I've never before seen in my life." Bernard scowled. "Mighty friendly he is, too."

"At least he is no threat to her, which is what I feared when I followed her out here. You startled me out of my wits, Bernard Muir!"

"Sorry." He grinned, not looking sorry in the slightest. "I could see you were about to attract her attention, and then she would have seen both of us."

"So you don't want her to know you are spying on her?"

"Well, no," he said. "But I do want to know who the devil that fellow is and what he wants with her."

A memory stirred. "When I had tea with her, she talked of a friend coming to Blackhaven, and of not having room for them to stay in the house because Lord and Lady Wickenden would be with you."

Bernard frowned. "What friend?"

"Someone she usually stays with in Scotland. Or, at least, that is what I understood."

"He doesn't look like a little old lady to me," Bernard said with rather touching grimness.

"Perhaps he is the son of the little old lady," Felicia said, trying not to laugh.

Still, he must have seen the gleam of amusement in her eyes, for he smiled reluctantly. "Am I being an ass? I'll speak to Gillie before I do anything else. But if you find out who that fellow is, let me know?"

"Of course. I should go back to my family. Julius is engaged to marry Antonia Macy."

"I know. The whole town knows. I saw you all at the harbor."

"Oh."

He glanced around to be sure the yard was still empty, then touched her cheek. "Will you tryst with me, Felicia? Tell me when."

Something seemed to land in the pit of her stomach, jolting her, reminding her of dangers and pitfalls and sound, good sense.

"I'll think about it," she said, rather more calmly than she felt. "If you tell me something."

"What?"

"Do you mean to marry Genevra Winslow?"

His jaw dropped. "Marry Genevra? Good God, no. It would be like marrying a little sister."

Relief seeped through her veins, almost painfully. "I'm not

sure she knows that," she managed.

Bernard grimaced. "I'm not sure either. She was dashed odd at the garden party—seemed jealous of you, which should have been a clue. Either way, I think I disabused her."

Felicia nodded. "Good."

"And our tryst?" he insisted.

"I shall see you at church tomorrow."

"We cannot tryst at church."

She smiled and walked away. "Neither we can. Good day, Mr. Muir."

Chapter Nine

W ALKING HOME, BERNARD rather thought he had let his feelings get in the way of good sense. He'd thought she was teasing, but there had been an edge to it, an edge to *her* that was unfamiliar. And no wonder, he thought ruefully. He had more or less assaulted her in a backyard and then demanded a tryst.

What had those wretched Vale twins said to him? *Look after her. Make her happy.*

He thought back to his earlier conversation with Kate Grant. *She needs respect.*

Did Felicia imagine his only aim was to take her to bed?

It was certainly at the forefront of his mind and body, had been since he first saw her at the ball. And it was true that part of him hoped that bedding her would ease his obsession to manageable proportions. But God help him, there was so much more to his feelings than that. Her smile, her courage and determination, her outrageous sense of fun that had led her to Tranmere's card party... He actually laughed aloud at that memory, and a passing lady swerved to give him a wide berth.

Part of him could not believe she would even consider him. Had he not told Kate that Felicia was above his touch? Which was nothing to do with rank, or even experience. It was just some-thing he *felt*.

She had loved her husband and endured his betrayals, his neglect, and the tangle of debt he had left her in when he died. Yet there was no self-pity in her. She cared for her family and sought her own independent future, and he admired that beyond words.

He knew all those things about her, and yet still he had seized her in a back alley and said only, *"Will you tryst with me, Felicia? Tell me when."*

She deserved so much more than his schoolboy eagerness! He would give Felicia her heart's desire if he could... If he ever found out what that was. He was certainly not coxcomb enough to imagine it was *him*. Although the very thought startled him into a sudden, desperate longing.

Felicia was all passion, all emotion and feeling. To have all that focused on him...

Keep dreaming, Muir, keep dreaming.

Surprised to discover he was entering his own front door, he glanced from habit at the hall stand and was relieved to see no sign of Harlaw's fashionably tall beaver hat and cane.

He found his sister in the drawing room, playing with the children, who interrupted their game to charge at him in an excess of affection.

"Where is everyone else?" he asked Gillie, walking forward with a small boy attached to each leg.

"Isabella has gone to help at some charity of Kate's. David went up to the castle to see Braithwaite, who is in a tizzy about Helen."

"Helen?" Bernard repeated in surprise. "Sweet-natured girl."

"She is. I daresay Braithwaite has the wrong end of the stick. Serena seems to think he has. What else is new in Blackhaven?"

"Sir Julius Vale is engaged to be married." He frowned and sat down, bumping his legs up and down like a bucking horse, to the delighted squeals of the small boys. "Gillie, who are Aunt Margaret's friends in Scotland?"

"The ones she visits every year? I don't think I've ever met them. Mrs. Bryson? No, Bryant. Edith Bryant."

"Is there a Mr. Bryant?"

"I believe so... Wait, though, did he not die? I think she is a widow now, but there are children."

"How old?"

Gillie widened her eyes. "I really have no idea. What on earth has prompted this unprecedented interest in Aunt Margaret's cronies?"

"I saw her at the hotel with a strange man. Being furtive."

"Furtive," Gillie repeated. "Are you sure it was Aunt Margaret?"

Bernard did not trouble to answer that. Instead, he asked, "How long has she known them?"

"Forever. Certainly, she's talked about them for as long as I can remember. She goes to stay with them at least once every year."

"And they have never come here..."

"Lots of people never come here," Gillie said flippantly. "Did this strange man appear to threaten her in some way?"

"No," Bernard admitted. "But what if—" He broke off, not quite sure where his mind was going with this.

"You think he is some flim-flam man making up to her to get at her money?"

"It crossed my mind, except that she has no money." He sighed. "This business of Isabella with Harlaw has me seeing fortune hunters and scoundrels everywhere."

"I thought we were agreed Harlaw could not be a fortune hunter, since he cannot possibly be aware of Isabella's fortune?"

"I still don't like the man."

"Isabella does."

Gillie was right, of course, and his own misgivings gave him no right to interfere in the respectable relationships of his adult family. He turned his mind instead to pleasing Felicia. To making her happy.

And funnily enough, the plan to do so made him happy too.

Accordingly, he accompanied Wickenden and their women-folk to church on Sunday morning. He saw Felicia at once, among her own large family. Disconcertingly, the twins turned their heads toward him at the same time and waved.

The banns were read for Sir Julius's marriage, and there was a lot of Vale grinning and nods of approval and interest from the rest of the congregation.

Bernard liked Grant, the vicar, very much, but he had never been so eager for a church service to end. Released at last into the damp, fresh air, he stood in the churchyard a little apart from his family and waited for the opportunity to speak to Felicia.

Inevitably, Harlaw glued himself to Isabella like a limpet. Bernard tried not to scowl. In a few moments, he saw Felicia a little apart from her own family, as though they had moved nearer to the gate and she had been too preoccupied to notice. With new concern, Bernard started toward her but was stayed by Gillie.

"Bernard, are you free for dinner at the castle tomorrow?" she called to him.

"No," Bernard said at the same time as his brother-in-law.

"Gaming club night," Wickenden explained. "It's a tradition. I doubt Braithwaite is free either."

Bernard left them to it and approached Felicia. "What is bothering you?" he asked at once.

She looked up quickly. "Oh, I am not *bothered*, precisely. It's only... Just as Julius engages himself, Lucy has *un*engaged herself, and I don't know why."

"I thought none of you wanted her to marry a man she had never met."

Felicia nodded in the direction of Lucy, who stood with the twins, a smile on her lips that didn't fool even Bernard, a stranger. "Then why is she not happy?"

"Did you ask her?"

"She brushes me off."

"It does bother you," Bernard said.

"I failed to look after her once," Felicia said. "I won't do it again."

"Felicia. You can't look after all of them all the time." Even as he said the words, he realized he could as well be advising himself with regard to both Isabella and Aunt Margaret. He gave a lopsided smile. "Shall we run away together? Just for an hour?"

Something leapt in her eyes. A smile hovered on her lips. Her beauty took his breath away all over again.

He smiled back. "Go toward the beach. I'll tell your twins to let your family know."

The twins smiled upon him, which he took to be a blessing of sorts. Wickenden, when told Bernard would not be joining the family until later in the afternoon, looked even more amused, and Bernard strode off after Felicia.

He caught up with her as though by accident and offered his arm. And after that, he concentrated only on her.

It was easy and fun and curiously peaceful. They walked on the beach quite openly among the other Sunday strollers, until they reached the quieter end. Bernard went and took the rock from his favorite hiding place and removed a blanket and a basket.

Felicia laughed with delight. "What a wonderful idea!"

"Well, church makes most people hungry," Bernard said irreverently. He glanced at the sky. "We might have to wolf it down before the rain arrives."

"No, today is a dry day." Felicia spread the blanket on the sand, while Bernard unloaded the sandwiches, cake, and cheese he had purloined from the kitchen, along with a bottle of wine and two glasses.

It was the sweetest afternoon he could remember, and their hour of escape quickly turned into two. They spoke of many things—childhood fun, family tragedies, plays and books and poetry, and then about the difficulties of ever knowing another person completely.

"I like the surprise," Bernard said. "And people will always surprise you, in good ways and bad."

She thought about that as they wandered along the sand to the water. Since this part of the beach was empty, he took her hand, and she let him. In fact, he wondered if she noticed until he brushed his fingers over her wrist and felt her galloping pulse.

He knew a moment of gladness, even triumph, but he would not rush her. He would court her as the wonderful, beautiful lady she was.

In fact, he did not touch more than her hand for the entire afternoon, not even when they packed up the basket and Bernard carried it back into town to find a carriage for hire. He traveled to Black Hill with her, on the opposite bench, content just to look at her and to talk when the notion hit them.

"It's been a lovely afternoon, Bernard," she said warmly. "Thank you. I believe it is just what I needed."

"Me too." He leaned forward and took her hand as they turned in the Black Hill gates. Softly he kissed her fingers, glad she had removed her gloves and he could feel her soft, warm skin beneath his lips. He imagined her fingers clung to his mouth, just for an instant, before he laid her hand back in her lap. "Until next time."

On this occasion, he said nothing of trysts or secret assignations, but somehow their intimacy was greater and his desire more intense. He was glad to have given her the happiness he read in her eyes... Or perhaps, he thought, as he handed her down from the carriage, it was just a reflection of his own.

THE FOLLOWING EVENING, Bernard and Wickenden strolled together down to the hotel. The staff took a great deal of trouble to keep separate their respectable guests and the somewhat mixed company who attended the gaming club. Bernard, however, was well known in the establishment, and even Wickenden, only an occasional visitor, was easily recognized. They strolled through the foyer to the double doors at the back, which opened to a large hall used for various events like musical recitals, private parties, even banquets. Every few weeks, it was set up as a gaming club, and anyone who could pay was admitted.

"Good evening, gentlemen." The old soldier guarding the doors opened them, letting out the wall of noise, and Bernard felt his excitement rise as it always did.

It had never been the gambling that drew him. It was the cards, the play, the pitting of wits and riding his luck, knowing when to quit and when to persevere. He understood that in the end one always lost more than one would ever win. So he never played for high stakes. When he won, he saved at least half. And at the end of the night, if he was ahead, he put that money away too, leaving only his original stake for the next game.

The system worked for him. He often lost, but not too much. He used his winnings for extra things—gifts, clothes, outings with friends. And some of it remained in the ever-growing "dream" fund that might, eventually, buy him a club of his own abroad.

And yet, in a moment of outrage, he had committed to high-stakes games to bring down Waller Harlaw. He wondered if Isabella would ever forgive him.

But all that was in the future. Tonight was to be enjoyed. Among the habitual gamblers and the Captain Sharps, the women of the *demimonde* and lower who haunted the lucky winners, he found a scattering of familiar faces. Lord Sylvester Gaunt waved from across the room. Braithwaite and a few of his guests, including Lord Daxton, beckoned to Bernard and Wickenden to join them at faro. Mr. Winslow, the squire and magistrate, was present at the hazard table.

Just as Bernard sat down to play faro, he caught sight of another face he recognized—the man who had been in the hotel yard with Aunt Margaret. *How interesting...*

Faro was too unpredictable for Bernard, so before long he moved to play macao, at which he excelled. His table attracted something of a crowd, including a sultry, underdressed lady with whom he had had dealings in the past. As he acknowledged her with a quick smile, he saw the man nearest her was Aunt Margaret's man.

The end of the game—from which he emerged the winner—earned a spontaneous bout of back clapping and laughter, even from his opponents, so he was grinning and sweeping up his coins and vouchers when the major stir of the evening occurred.

A beautiful lady strolled alone into the room. She walked with incomparable grace, her head held high, and she was dressed in black lace with only a brightly painted fan by way of contrast. The gown was exquisitely cut. Bernard had no idea whether it was this year's fashion, but it did not seem to matter. Despite her surroundings and her lack of escort, she looked every inch a lady.

Braithwaite swore under his breath. "Is that not one of the Vale sisters?"

"It is," Bernard said. He felt torn in pieces by conflicting emotion—anger, pride, even admiration, for she was undeniably magnificent, but whether brave or foolhardy was another matter.

"What the devil are her brothers thinking of? None of them are here..."

"Be reasonable, Braithwaite," Wickenden drawled. "Have you ever been able to make your sisters do or not do anything?"

"No," Braithwaite said with unexpected bitterness.

Felicia gazed around her but did not appear to be looking for anyone in particular. Bernard stood up, and her gaze found him. He did not quite know what he intended. More importantly, neither did she. In the instant their eyes met, he understood that she would not be escorted out, that she would bear his and the world's contempt rather than back down. And he knew how much such contempt would hurt her.

"As a family friend," he murmured, "I escort her."

"Which of them is your friend?" Braithwaite demanded, staring at him.

"Aubrey," said Bernard, who had run into him at the tavern

once.

"Good fellow, Aubrey," Sylvester Gaunt murmured, apparently unaware that his endorsement carried little weight with the respectable.

Bernard waited no more and strolled toward Felicia like a host welcoming a late guest. By then, she had a swarm of men around her—a mixture of card sharps, chancers, and the disreputable. One or two glanced up at Bernard's approach and warily hung back. He caught sight of Waller Harlaw, his mouth open, his hand frozen on a card halfway to the table. But his eyes gleamed as though he saw his chance.

Before Bernard could clear his throat and scatter the insolent flies buzzing about Felicia, she sailed through them, shedding them like discarded layers of unwanted clothing. With no more than a freezing demeanor and a haughty glance or two, she was already rid of them. For now.

Only Bernard remained blocking her way. He bowed and offered her his arm. "Mrs. Maitland, welcome. May I escort you to a table?" He raised his free hand peremptorily at the same time, and a footman hurried toward them with a tray of brimming wine glasses.

Felicia's eyes softened as she realized he had not come with the intention to eject her from the room. "Indeed you may. Thank you," she added, accepting a glass. "Perhaps some piquet, if you are free?"

"Perfect," he said. As they made their way to the side, Braithwaite and Wickenden bowed, and she inclined her head in acknowledgement. Aunt Margaret's man—who looked much younger up close—watched them both with curiosity and, for some reason, approval.

"Thank you," Felicia murmured as Bernard held a chair for her. "But you did not need to put yourself out. I learned long ago how to protect myself from most insults."

"The matter is simpler if they know you are protected."

She met his gaze as he picked up the cards. "I understood you had refused me your protection to this place."

"And yet somehow I knew you would come anyway. I was looking for a very unconvincing boy."

"I was *not* unconvincing," she said dangerously, and he just grinned and dealt the cards.

"Then why come as yourself tonight and risk the tabbies tearing you to shreds?"

She shrugged. "Another thing I learned long ago is that to have your eccentricities accepted by Society, one should never, ever apologize for them. I shall play in the public eye and retire alone in public, before the night gets too late."

"It is a good plan." He picked up his cards. "And there are many possibilities for the night's end."

FELICIA'S GAZE FLEW to his face. What did he mean by that?

"There are many possibilities for the night's end." Something warm and beguiling stirred deep inside her, but his face was unreadable. His attention appeared to be on the cards, so she turned hers in a similar direction, glad of the distraction.

"Harlaw is here," he said casually. "What is your plan?"

"I thought I might give him his chance of revenge at piquet. I might even let him win, if I can."

His lips quirked. "Lulling him into a false sense of superiority?"

"If he refuses to play us, we are undone."

"I have arranged our charity card party at the King's Head," Bernard said. "Or, at least, I've left it to the Grants to arrange. Entry fee and a percentage of winnings to the hospital—it needs funds since Dunnett cleaned it out."

From both Julius and Antonia, Felicia knew all about the fraud perpetrated on the hospital.

She nodded. "Good idea. They have hopes of getting most of

the money back, but that doesn't really help with the present. So we shall be killing two birds, as it were, with one stone. And with luck... Bernard!"

He glanced up, one card between his fingers. "Yes?"

"That man is here," she whispered excitedly. "The one with your aunt."

"I know. He's been watching me. What the devil does he want with my family?"

"Have you asked him?"

"No, but I will as soon as I can do so discreetly. I certainly don't want a public fight." He frowned. "He looks too dashed unthreatening to be true. I'd swear he is younger than I am."

"Then I'm surprised he is allowed out late to play cards," she said flippantly, and then regretted it as a shadow passed over his face.

He held her gaze. "Is that it, Felicia? You think me too much of a boy to be taken seriously?"

In fact, it seemed a long time since she had considered his age at all. And she rather thought she had always taken him seriously. A man who played macao with such *savoir faire* was not to be trifled with. But it seemed he could be hurt.

She raised her eyebrows. "Are you calling me old, Bernard Muir?"

He blinked and then laughed. Only the faint color seeping along the line of his cheekbone betrayed him. "How could I? What are you? Four or five and twenty?"

"Five and twenty."

"I am four and twenty. Not so different."

"And you are much older in sin," she mocked him.

He smiled, unoffended. "You don't know that."

"I am not the first woman you have trysted with, am I?" she asked boldly.

"You have not trysted with me at all, yet," he pointed out. He played and then raised his gaze to hers once more. "We can change that if you like. Tonight."

Her whole being fell into turmoil.

Tonight...! She had not even *considered* tonight.

"Think about it," he said softly. His gaze moved beyond her. "Harlaw approaches. Shall I give up my seat to him?"

"Why not? We've lost track of the game anyway." Or, at least, she had.

He gathered up the cards, and Harlaw appeared beside them. "Good evening, ma'am. Sir. Dare I hope I am in good time?"

"Please," Bernard said generously, rising to his feet, though before he could move very far, someone else accosted him.

The mysterious young man they had seen with Miss Muir.

"Do I address Mr. Muir?" he asked pleasantly.

"You do."

The young man offered his hand. "Alan Bryant. Care to play?"

Felicia had to force herself not to gaze after them as they wandered off. Instead, she turned her attention to Harlaw and wondered how difficult it would be to lose to him.

Chapter Ten

As though impressed by Bernard's round of piquet with Felicia—unfinished as it was—Bryant dealt the cards.

"Is the lady a particular friend of yours?" Bryant asked. There was a pleasant hint of Scottish in his accent. His face was youthful, his eyes unexpectedly shrewd.

"I count Mrs. Maitland a friend," Bernard said steadily.

"But not the gentleman?"

"Not the gentleman," Bernard agreed. "But perhaps he is a friend of *yours*?"

"Indeed not."

Bernard didn't expect him to admit it, though a conspiracy between the two had begun to make a ghastly kind of sense in his mind. He just could not yet see the purpose.

Bryant picked up his cards and met Bernard's gaze. "Were Mrs. Maitland a friend of mine, I don't believe I would abandon her to Mr. Harlaw's company."

Bernard was an old hand at making conversation while playing complicated games, and he was well aware his opponent might have set out to distract him. "And why is that, Mr. Bryant?"

Bryant made his play before he answered, and then he appeared to choose his words carefully. "I have observed his manners to be…disingenuous."

Bernard's lips quirked. "And where have you observed this,

sir?"

"Here in the hotel, where I am lodging for a few days." His gaze flickered beyond Bernard's shoulder to where Harlaw and Felicia were playing. "He would appear to be courting two different ladies."

Interesting that Bryant had picked up the nuance that even Bernard could not have sworn to. It was just a feeling, hovering below his skin that he had dismissed as jealousy, because he was so obsessed he did not want any man near Felicia, even one she loathed. *Especially* one she loathed.

"And which of them concerns you, Mr. Bryant?" Bernard asked pleasantly.

"Both." Bryant gave a quick, self-deprecating smile. "And neither. Which is why I confide my concerns to you."

"Because you believe I have a connection to both?" Bernard challenged.

"Don't you?"

"Perhaps. It is certainly my intention to spike our friend's guns if I can."

For a while, they concentrated on the game. Bryant was a thoughtful player but not, Bernard suspected, a habitual one.

"What is it you do, Mr. Bryant?" he asked. "Are you a gentleman of leisure? A landowner?"

"No. I am among the despised who works for his living."

"I would not despise a man for such a reason. I have a notion to do the same."

"Why don't you?"

"My skills are limited, but I'm working on them. What is it you do?"

"I clerk for a shipping company." Bryant's voice remained modest, even deprecating.

And yet no clerk's salary had bought Bryant's excellent evening coat, let alone paid his shot at the Blackhaven Hotel.

Bernard held his gaze. "I suspect you do rather more than clerk."

"It does not always seem so, but you are correct that I am in a privileged position. My father owns the company."

"Does he, by God?"

"He does. Are you playing, Mr. Muir?"

Bernard liked him, though he was not quite sure why. Which didn't mean he trusted him, especially as, despite many opportunities, Bryant never once mentioned Aunt Margaret. Still, as the game ended, Bernard decided he owed him for the warning about Harlaw, even if it was unnecessary.

As they shook hands and parted, Bernard murmured, "I would not play cards with our friend."

Bryant stared at him. "And yet you permit Mrs. Maitland to do so?"

Bernard laughed. "One does not *permit* Mrs. Maitland. When it comes to cards, she is entirely up to snuff. A pleasure making your acquaintance, Bryant."

He knew exactly where Felicia was. Her game had finished earlier, and her perfume had wafted behind him as she moved around the tables, mostly watching. Now, she was playing vingt-et-un. Many men ogled her, but she appeared blissfully unaware, and her manner was such that no one dared address her except with respect and on matters of the game.

She rose, a minor winner, as Bernard passed her table.

"Did he win?" he breathed.

She nodded delicately in Harlaw's direction. He was playing faro again and looked decidedly pleased with himself. "Of course he did."

"Well done. Would you care to play loo?"

"Why not? What did you discover about our other friend?"

"That he is the son of a shipping man and seems surprisingly decent. Close-mouthed as the devil, though. Gave nothing away that I actually wanted to know."

"Then he did not mention his connection to your aunt?"

Bernard nodded to a passing acquaintance. "No. But he has the same surname as her friends in Scotland."

They found a game of loo about to come to its conclusion and hovered nearby.

"Bernard?" she said low. "Did you mean it? About tonight?"

He hadn't truly expected her to mention it again. That she did caused his heart to leap. And other parts of him.

"Of course I meant it," he said intensely. He turned his face to her so no one would hear or read his lips. "Will you come?"

"When?"

"After this game?"

"Where?"

"Here."

Her eyes widened. Then she looked away toward Lord Braithwaite and smiled in acknowledgment. He could have yelled with frustration, because the moment, so close, had clearly passed. But he must not push her. He would wait.

The game before them was breaking up. Bernard stepped forward and held a vacant chair for Felicia.

She smiled her thanks. "Yes," she said, so casually that he almost did not realize she was answering his question.

He could not breathe. He could not think of anything except Felicia and the night to come. And yet he had to play loo and win, and treat her with distant respect so that no one would know...

It became part of the game, a pounding heart behind an impassive face, a mind kept ruthlessly on the cards and the bets, while every inch of his body was as aware of her as if she physically touched him. Her every tiny movement, every slightest change of expression, moved him. He watched subtle color ebb and flow as she won and lost, the soft dart of her tongue over her lips as she thought, the intensity of her eyes, every alteration of her breathing. And he knew she was anticipating the night to come, just as he was. Perhaps it added an extra excitement to the game, as though every moment was both pain and pleasure.

For Bernard, the game became purely secondary. He played almost mechanically, and though he never saw her calculating, he knew she was doing so all the time.

Inevitably, she won. They agreed an increase in stake, and Bernard won. And then Felicia rose and announced that she must go home, and Bernard offered to escort her to a hired carriage. A line of them would be waiting by the front door.

She laid her gloved hand lightly on his arm. He thought her fingers trembled.

"My door is right opposite the staircase on the second floor," he murmured.

She said nervously, "Does Lord Wickenden not expect you to return with him?"

"Wickenden left an hour ago." He opened the double doors and bowed her through. "I stay here occasionally to avoid disturbing the household. If…"

But abruptly, he had lost her attention. She dropped his arm and strode forward to the staircase. *"Lucy?"*

Bernard almost groaned aloud. His sweet, desperate dreams of the night began to crumble around him.

⚬⚬⚬

FELICIA'S SHOCK AT discovering Lucy in the hotel at this time of night might have been a shade hypocritical, but Lucy was unmarried and not yet nineteen years old!

Then, with some relief, she saw Julius's distinctive figure striding across the foyer after her, and he did not appear to be angry. Bizarrely, young Lord Eddleston was there too, along with a friend of Lucy's and an old lady.

Only when she realized Lucy was in no danger did Felicia pause to consider that Julius might not be terribly happy to see her here on gaming club night. At least she had left Bernard a little behind her, out of Julius's line of fire, as it were. Although she was aware of him hovering close by, as though to step in if he could make things better.

In fact, the little drama unfolding had nothing to do with Felicia or Bernard, although the people swarming after them out of the gaming club were treated to an attempted arrest as Lucy accused someone Felicia did not even know of murder.

Felicia, it seemed, had lost track of events in her own family life. Again. Perhaps that was why she found herself leaving the hotel with her brother and sister, without even a word to Bernard.

"Have I spoiled your evening, Fliss?" Lucy asked ruefully.

"Of course not!"

"We have the carriage," Julius said. "Are you coming with us?"

A breath of cool night air brushed her cheeks. It came to her that Julius had no intention of interfering. That he trusted her to make her own decisions. It did not matter what they were or whether he approved. They were hers to make.

He was right.

She searched Lucy's face for signs of trauma and saw only excitement and exhaustion. She did not need Felicia.

Felicia hugged her. "I'll come home later, and we shall talk tomorrow. Goodnight."

What am I doing? she wondered as she walked back into the hotel.

Bernard had not waited for her. The small crowd that had stayed to watch Lucy's little drama had dispersed or gone back into the club. Without looking left or right, she swept across the foyer to the staircase. Only when she was halfway up did she realize the hotel staff probably thought she was going to visit Lucy's friends.

She did not. She went straight to the top of the staircase and, without much hope, turned the handle of the door facing her. It gave easily, and she walked in.

The room was lit, and she closed the door quickly behind her, leaning against it for support. Bernard sat on the edge of the large bed in his shirt sleeves, without his cravat. He rose at once, taking a step toward her and then halting.

"Felicia," he said hoarsely. "I did not think you would come."

"Neither did I." Laughter trembled in her throat. "I didn't know if it was right. But this is my life, and Lucy does not need me."

He moved toward her again, slowly, stretching out his hand. "And you, Felicia, what do *you* need?"

She spoke haltingly, trying to arrange her thoughts while her heart galloped and her whole body trembled. "I think... For a long time, I think I have needed you. Before I even knew you. Before I met you."

He closed his fingers around hers, light but firm, and searched her face, not accusing or offended, merely trying to understand. "You wanted a lover."

She could not help smiling. "I went to the assembly room ball to play cards, to prove to myself I could still win. And yes, I hoped to meet a man there who might become my lover. He had no face, no character in my mind, only that he would want me. That he would *see* me and want me still."

"And then what?" he asked, his fingertips gliding over her cheek. "You wished to recapture the physical pleasures of marriage?"

"I miss the warmth," she whispered. "The intimate attention of another human being, to see the worship just for a moment, without pretense or pain. I suppose I wanted that power, without it mattering."

"I would never knowingly cause you pain," Bernard said, cupping her cheek. She leaned into his hand, closing her eyes. "And I would certainly never pretend. Can you not see that I worship you already?"

She opened her eyes, startled all over again. There was such warmth, such feeling in his eyes that her heart melted.

"I expect that is blasphemous," he said. "Let me rephrase. I adore you. I love you."

She gasped, sliding both arms around his neck and hiding her face in his shoulder. "Don't say these things. You don't have to say these things. I am not a child."

"Neither am I. You obsess me, Felicia. I want to be with you, look after you, laugh with you, and talk long into the night about everything and nothing. I want to play cards with you, run on the beach and paddle in the sea with you. Right now, I want to make love to you so badly I can barely speak."

Laughter shook her. "You are doing pretty well so far. With the speaking."

"Yes, but I'm not really sure what I'm saying."

She raised her head and looked into his eyes. Honest, caring, lust-filled eyes. He bent his head slowly and kissed her. Emotion tightened her throat, but the sensation was too wonderful to weep. She kissed him back, stroking his hair, his nape, and reveled in his arms folding around her, holding her so close to his lean, hard body.

"Will you marry me, Felicia Vale?" he whispered against her lips.

She drew back, startled. "*Marry* you?"

"Marry me," he confirmed.

She shook her head dumbly, and now the tears prickled again. "I do not want a husband. You do not need a wife."

"But you will let me try to convince you otherwise?"

"You may take me to bed. But I will never change my mind."

He smiled as he kissed her with devastating sensuality. Deftly, he unhooked the fastening of her gown. "Never is a very, very long time."

Nick was the only lover she had ever known. She always imagined that if she ever got so close to a man again, she would not be able to help comparing him to Nick. But curiously, her late husband barely entered her head now. There was only Bernard, his warm, tender mouth and clever hands on her skin, caressing, arousing her even as he undressed her.

He was her lover. She ran her hands boldly over his wide shoulders, loving the play of muscles beneath warm, smooth skin.

She drew off his shirt, stretching high over his head, and as soon as he was free of it, he lowered his lips to her breast, and she let out a muted cry of delight.

They were both naked now, half lying in each other's arms across the bed. She waited for him to climb on her and take her. She wanted it with an intensity she never had before. It wasn't about the power or even that tiny moment of worship she would read in his eyes. It was about her, about *feeling*.

But Bernard was in no rush. Every inch of her seemed to delight him. With exquisite delicacy, he caressed and kissed each part of her, discovering what made her gasp and clamor and then repeating it until the pleasure and the hunger were one. She ravished him in return, her caresses increasingly bold and passionate.

She drew him inside her with slow bliss. He did not push or pound. He stroked, soft and sensual, seducing her, building the excitement until it was truly unbearable. And then, his gaze locked to hers, he stroked harder and faster as she clung to him, moving with him as though in some wild, heady dance. The heavy sweetness she barely recognized soared far beyond the familiar, like a rolling tide, and exploded into something so wonderful she cried out, reaching with blind, gasping gratitude for his mouth.

But he only held her, avidly watching her joy before he gave her his kiss at last, deep and worshiping. Only then did he push harder and withdraw, shuddering and groaning into her mouth as he spent outside her body.

Somewhere, even then, she acknowledged his care, his consideration. Most of her was too lost in wonder and bliss.

❧

MAKING LOVE TO Felicia was a revelation in many ways. He had never wanted any woman as much as he wanted her. And no woman had ever driven him to such heights of pleasure. The way she kissed, the way she moved beneath him, above him, and then beneath again, alternately submissive and demanding, enchanted him. In fact, she almost undid him. He almost forgot to withdraw before he left his seed in her, and he had never in his life found anything so difficult to achieve.

Even so, the pleasure was uniquely profound, paralyzing, soul deep.

He rolled, gathering her close against him in a tangle of satisfied, lethargic limbs. He already loved her. Was that why she was the sweetest, most exciting lover he had ever known?

"Which of us seduced the other?" he murmured against her sweat-dampened skin, when his heart had calmed enough to speak.

She smiled. "Does it matter?"

"Not if it gave you pleasure."

"You know it did."

This was another revelation. Her passion was moving, delicious, and entirely instinctive. And the climax of loving had astonished her. What kind of selfish or incompetent ass had her husband been? Everyone told him Maitland had been a hedonist, but what pleasure was greater than holding Felicia in his arms and bringing her to bliss?

It all increased his tenderness, though he knew better than to mention her husband's name at this point. This was *their* night, Felicia and Bernard's.

He kissed her hair, her forehead. "You see what delights we could have if we were married?"

Her eyes gleamed in the lamplight. "I know what delights we had *un*married."

"I would love you every night," he said in her ear. "And during the day too. Whenever the notion takes us. Not just when we can find a secret moment that does not ruin your reputation."

"I found the secrecy quite fun, though I nearly let Lucy and Julius spoil it."

He propped his head up on his hand. "Will you tell them the truth? That you spent the rest of the night with me?"

"They will not ask. Well, Lucy might. But there is something between her and Eddleston..."

"Are you changing the subject?" he asked.

To his surprise, she pushed him over and rolled on top of him. "Yes. I am changing the subject. You give me joy, Bernard Muir, but I will not marry you."

And before he could stop himself, he blurted out, "Because I can never measure up to Maitland?"

Her eyes widened. To his horror, he saw tears there, and would have given anything to take back his crass words. He threw his arms around her, holding her as though to prevent her leaving him.

"Don't, Bernard," she said shakily. "Never even imagine that. Yes, I married Nick for love, and he is the reason I will never marry again. Because I will never, ever give anyone that kind of control over me again. I will not risk my happiness, my livelihood, my family's safety..."

Startled, Bernard dragged himself into more of a sitting position, still cradling her in his arms. "Your *family?*"

"I loved him when I married him—not blindly, but stupidly, childishly, imagining he would give up all the women and the vices for *me*. But of course he did not. And I—I did not even see that half his attraction was the danger of those vices. If he had given it all up for me, I wonder if I would still have loved him..."

"But he didn't," Bernard said gently, sadly. "And you did."

She clung to him harder, in an anguish he could not yet understand. "No," she whispered. "No. Bernard, I did not love him when he died. I could not. Because of Lucy."

"Lucy?" he repeated, startled.

With no further warning, words began to spill out of her, words he suspected she had never said before, and probably never meant to at all.

"It wears you down after a while, the hurt and the humiliation and the pretense of not noticing or caring. But I forgave him. I even tried to adjust, mitigating what damage I could—which was hardly any—until I realized he truly had no self-control, no decency. He even told me himself, as though I would forgive him as I'd forgiven everything else. He told me he'd kissed Lucy but that it would not go any further."

Her fingers dug painfully into his shoulders. "Bernard, she was fifteen years old, my innocent, curious, maddening, lovely little sister. She was in my care, and she was not safe from my husband. The very fact that he said it would go no further told me he had already considered it. It was inevitable. Even if Lucy would not allow it—and no one knew better than me how he could seduce—he would take her when he wanted. He was that entitled. To him, she was only a girl."

He was almost afraid to ask. "What happened?"

"I sent her to my great-aunt in Bath and packed the twins off to our father. I did not even trust him with Leona. The twins didn't question my decision, but Lucy knew the reason. I read the pity in her eyes. For the first time I was truly ashamed of my husband, and that sort of shame cannot live with love. I'd probably been pretending for years. But from the moment he told me about Lucy, I knew. I broke my vow. I did not love him until death did us part."

He hugged her closer, his heart breaking for her pain. "Oh, my poor sweet. No wonder you trust no one. But Felicia…" He found her chin, gently tipping it so that she had to look at him. "Felicia, none of this was your fault. You are kind and beautiful and wonderful."

He did not know how to make her believe except with words that seemed so inadequate to the task, but she clung to him fiercely, suddenly urgent once more, and he saw his way clear.

With my body, I thee worship. He did, and she so clearly adored it that he had hope for her healing and her love.

Chapter Eleven

ELICIA WOKE WITH the dawn, as she usually did. What was strange was the sense of wellbeing, of happiness, that came too. And the large, warm body curled around her back. There was even an arm flung across her waist, too heavy for comfort, perhaps, but curiously protective and welcome.

Memory flooded back. *Bernard.* Bernard's astounding love-making. The overwhelming physical joys she had never tasted before. His tenderness. His strength. His body. She began to tingle with awareness, with the stirrings of desire.

Only very occasionally had she ever wakened with Nick still in her bed—usually only when he had passed out drunk.

Bernard had not been drunk.

Bernard...

Very slowly, careful not to wake him, she turned, easing out from under his arm. He shifted, mostly onto his back. Daylight seeped through the curtains onto his face, his naked arms, and his shoulders.

God, he was beautiful. She had never appreciated male beauty before. Nick had always been in too much of a rush, and, she realized now, he had begun to go a little to seed with too much brandy and self-indulgence. But she would not think of Nick. She could not when her eyes feasted on this very different man.

A wave of tenderness took her by surprise. Asleep, he looked so young, so boyish. And yet he had all a man's strength and understanding and knowledge. A tear prickled.

I could love you, Bernard Muir...

The thought frightened her, and she slid out of bed. She dressed hastily and quietly, with no time to fasten the hooks of her gown. Last night's evening cloak lay on the back of the chair. She picked it up doubtfully, for though it would cover the gaps of her gown, no one would wear such a thing in the morning. Anyone would saw her would know she had not been home. And that was too blatant a flouting of the conventions. In Society, discretion, not truth, was king, and she had already taken a chance attending the gaming club.

Beneath her evening cloak was another. Too short to be Bernard's, she realized it might once have been his sister's, that he had brought it for Felicia, so that she could leave incognita.

A lump came to her throat. If she had met him before Nick...

But then, perhaps she would have been too young and silly to appreciate Bernard at that time. In any case, when she was seventeen, Bernard could only have been sixteen years old! No, *this* was the time for her and Bernard, for however long it lasted.

With a quick, fugitive smile toward the sleeping figure on the bed, she swung the dull traveling cloak about her, found enough pins to cram her hair out of the way, and drew up the hood of the cloak.

On the bed, Bernard stirred. She froze, taken aback by her sudden longing to stay.

Which meant that it was definitely time to go.

She opened the door a crack to see that all was quiet and slipped out, closing the door softly behind her. Instead of going directly down the staircase, she hurried along the long passage to the staff stairs. She passed one or two maids, but kept to the shadows, her face covered, and no one spoke to her. She doubted she was the first woman to sneak out of the hotel at dawn. Should that make her ashamed?

Perhaps, though it did not. For last night, everything was

worth it. Even though she had told him too much, more than she should ever have told anyone. But Bernard had understood, and he would never betray her. She knew that from instinct as well as her knowledge of him.

She emerged into the yard where they had seen Miss Muir with Mr. Bryant and kept walking. The ostlers ignored her as though she were a gray ghost in the gray light.

She walked all the way home, only partly because she did not want to be seen going home to Black Hill at this hour. Mostly, she just wanted to, because she was happy, and full of vitality, and because she wanted peace to think of Bernard and remember and smile whenever she wished.

By the time she had slipped into the house and up to her bedchamber, where she washed and changed, and re-emerged to join her family, ready to hear the tale of Lucy's adventures, the family was celebrating Lucy's re-engagement to Lord Eddleston.

BERNARD COULD NOT deny to himself that he was hurt by Felicia's rejection of his offer of marriage. Except in Blackhaven, where everyone knew him, he was no one. But Felicia had always made him feel more than that, even before she gave herself to him. The sight of her in the gaming club, beautiful, alluring, and sailing coolly through a crowd of predators without a moment's rudeness, had spoken to him.

His dream of his own club had another facet Felicia by his side.

Which was mad. Felicia was a gentlewoman, and he would never want her running a men's gambling den. He would hate her to be within a mile of it. Yet the dream lingered through all the next day, along with the simmering desire.

Gillie and Wickenden dined with the Grants that night, so there was only himself, Margaret, and Isabella in the house.

Rejoicing that Harlaw did not join them, Bernard left the house after dinner, strode along to the livery stable, and hired his favorite horse, which he rode out to Black Hill.

Only as he tied the horse to a tree branch on the edge of the wood and approached the house on foot did he realize his problem. He had no idea which window was Felicia's.

There was a light on the ground floor, presumably the drawing room. And in one of the upstairs windows. After a few minutes watching, the upper light went out. Bernard guessed this was Cornelius, who looked after the land and retired early in order to rise early in the morning.

One eliminated, eight to go.

This was impossible. Should he simply knock on the front door and ask to see her? Or would she hate him to involve her family? Perhaps servants in the stables or the kitchen could be bribed.

The kitchen seemed to be in darkness, as though the servants had been given leave to retire. He walked around the edge of the woods to discover the stables, and another light began to glow in an upstairs window.

He held his breath, for the shutters were not closed, nor the curtains drawn, and the figure in the room was definitely female. As she approached the window and opened the sash, he could not believe his luck. It was Felicia.

Grinning, he loped out of the wood and toward the house, until a lantern shone in his face.

"Well, that's a surprise," said an unexpected female voice close to him. "We thought you were Eddleston."

Bernard spun around to face the twins. It would have been funny if it wasn't quite so annoying to be foiled this close to his goal.

He glowered at them. "Aren't you two supposed to be in bed at this hour?"

"It's as well we are not," Lawrence said tartly. "With strangers running loose about the garden."

"We have been introduced," Bernard reminded them.

"But not invited to each other's homes."

"An oversight," Bernard said. "You are welcome in mine."

Leona looked skeptical. "Even in the middle of the night?"

"Yes," Bernard said recklessly. "Will you take a message to your sister for me?" It was the best he could hope for now.

"No need," Lawrence said, jerking his head toward the window where Bernard had already seen her.

"Bernard?" Felicia's voice drifted down. He couldn't be sure, but he thought she was laughing. "What are you doing out there with the twins?"

"Waking the dead," Bernard replied, "to say nothing of the living."

A breath of definite laughter made him smile and ache.

"Then be silent. I'm coming down." Felicia vanished from sight, and Bernard regarded the twins.

"What's in the bundle?" Leona asked.

"Cards," said Bernard.

"That is a lot of cards," Lawrence said.

"It is," Bernard said.

A gray figure flitted gracefully out of a side door to the house, and Bernard's heart turned over just because she was there.

"Mr. Muir brought cards," Lawrence said.

"Of course he did." Felicia, wrapped from head to toe in Gillie's old cloak that he had taken to the hotel for her, sounded perfectly serene.

"Can we play?" Leona asked.

"No," Felicia said. "You have to go to your own rooms. Just because the last lot of thieves, smugglers, and highwaymen has been dealt with, that does not mean you are allowed to run about the grounds at night. Bed, if you please."

The twins hesitated a moment. "Have you met Lucy?" Leona asked Bernard unexpectedly.

"Yes, once or twice. And your brother Aubrey. Why?"

"Lucy likes him," Felicia said with finality. "Go."

This time, the twins trotted off with the briefest of good-nights, leaving Bernard to follow Felicia to the summer house where had slept once, dreaming of her so close and yet so far away.

"Why do they ask about Lucy?" he murmured.

"She is like a touchstone. She is never wrong."

She opened the summer house door, and when he had followed her inside, she closed and bolted it and then walked into his arms as though she belonged there.

⸎

"Did you really bring cards?" she asked some time later, glancing at the bundle he had dropped on the floor.

Bernard unwrapped the bundle to reveal her evening cloak and a pack of cards. She smiled, reaching over him for the cards. Since she was totally naked after a passionate loving, he hauled her onto his lap, and it was some time before they got around to the cards.

Even that was fun, as was the wine they shared from his flask, and the banter exchanged.

It became the pattern of the next few days. Felicia passed most of the daylight hours in a haze of memory and anticipation, living for the night and their clandestine meetings in the summer house. There, they made heady love that was increasingly intimate, the pleasure growing only more intense. But they also talked and played cards.

Sweet as it was, Bernard never stayed all night. He rode home in the dark, and for some reason she missed the sensation of that first morning in the hotel, waking in his arms.

Those days were also important for finally closing the distance that had existed between her and Lucy since Felicia had sent her to Bath out of Nick's reach. Lucy had not wanted to go, whether because of Nick or because she imagined Felicia had wanted rid of the responsibility of her little sister. Either way, neither of them had ever broached the subject. It had got lost in Nick's death and their father's, and the mess of worry and debt.

And then, out of the blue, Lucy brought it up while discussing the ridiculous costume she wished to wear to the Braithwaite masquerade ball. Almost in tears, and clearly unaware that Felicia already knew, Lucy confessed to kissing Nick and apologized for hurting Felicia.

Felicia, although perhaps she should have guessed, was stunned by the guilt Lucy had been carrying for years. Somehow they ended in each other's arms, crying, while Felicia assured her sister the blame was Nick's and that Lucy had been sent away only for her own safety.

"I sent the twins to Papa at the same time," Felicia reminded her.

And then Lucy's tongue loosened and she began to talk about Tyler—her name for Eddleston—and love, and how much Felicia had loved Nick. And Felicia's pain grew, because in the end she had not loved Nick anymore.

She did love Bernard. That knowledge was sweet and secret, and she had no intention of ever telling anyone, least of all Bernard himself. She knew there would be heartache, but at least she could prevent the pain of disillusion. She wished only that he would be happy, and she wanted to help him make that so.

Once, sprawled among the cushions in the summer house, she asked him about Bryant. "Has he never visited the house?"

"Never. And I haven't mentioned him to Aunt Margaret. Gillie asked her about the family, though, and apparently she has known Mrs. Bryant since they were girls. She was born in Blackhaven, married a Scottish shipbuilder or an importer—Aunt Margaret is a trifle vague on details. She has been going to stay with the Bryants every twelve months or so for more than twenty years. Usually just for a couple of weeks, but once, early on, for several months. Neither Gillie nor I remember that, so it must have been when we were very small."

"How odd that she does not mention their son being in Blackhaven. If he *is* their son?"

"It's a bit of a coincidence if he is not," Bernard said. "But if he wants anything of my aunt, she is showing no signs of distress. I should go."

"Whatever you wish."

He met her gaze, and it struck her that while she waited for him to suggest staying until morning, he was waiting for her to suggest the same thing. It surprised her so much that her tongue stuck to the roof of her mouth, and by the time she had unstuck it, he was already dressed and ready to go.

She went to him and kissed him, trying to make him understand what she did not—her feelings for him.

❧

THE FOLLOWING DAY, it came to Felicia that about twenty-one years ago, when Margaret Muir had probably first gone to stay with the Bryants, her own family had been here at Black Hill. Julius might have just gone to sea, but Roderick and Delilah must have been here, for it was just before that their father had married Lucy's mother, Emma.

Encountering Delilah at breakfast, Felicia asked her, "Do you remember Miss Muir from when you stayed here before? Lady Wickenden's aunt," she added, deliberately avoiding all mention of Bernard.

Delilah, who had been gazing at her and frowning, raised her eyebrows in surprise. "Yes, I do. She was here a good deal."

"In Blackhaven?"

"Well, yes, but I meant here in the house, too. She was kind to us and had twinkly eyes when she slipped us treats. Actually, she still has twinkly eyes."

"Was that after Papa married Emma?" Felicia asked.

"It might have been." Delilah looked doubtful. "I don't remember them being friends, or ever seeing them together, though. But then, Emma never cared much for me—not that I blame her. Bad enough having your new husband's legitimate children foisted upon you without the bastard daughter."

Felicia frowned and wondered aloud, "When did she go away, then?"

"Emma?"

"Miss Muir! She went to stay in Scotland for a while."

"Good for her," Delilah said, regarding Felicia over her tea-cup with a mixture of amusement and bewilderment. Then she set down her cup. "Actually, now you mention it, I do remember her being here a good deal, and then suddenly she was not. When Emma came, I remember thinking I liked Miss Muir better than her. Why are you so interested?"

"I'm not sure," Felicia admitted. "There's a mysterious Scotsman in Blackhaven who may be connected to the Muirs."

"Never listen to Blackhaven gossip. Everyone will advise you so, even while they spread it. You're looking tired, Fliss. Is everything well?"

"Oh, yes," Felicia replied, trying very hard not to blush. "I suppose I have been working too much on this costume of Lucy's."

"Is it very mad?"

"Oh yes. Quite insane. And its sole purpose seems to be to amuse Eddleston."

"Bless them," Delilah said indulgently. She rose and went toward the door.

"Do you still have Papa's letters?" Felicia asked her.

"Of course." Delilah glanced back over her shoulder. "Do you want them?"

"Yes, please."

"Then I'll leave them in your room."

"Thanks, Delly."

What with the housekeeping duties she had taken on, and preparations for Julius and Lucy's weddings to consider—to say nothing of readying herself and Lucy for the ball—Felicia had little time to study the packet of letters Delilah left on her bed.

Finally, having declared an hour's rest before dressing, she unwrapped them and spread them out. It felt odd to be touching things that were so close to Papa—not letters he had written to her but that others had sent to him. She had not expected to feel the connection to him through them, but she did.

And she missed him.

She had been close to her father growing up. He had been proud of her mathematical skills, abilities that her mother, aunt, and stepmother had all called useless. And he had been so intrigued and delighted when she began beating everyone at cards. They had spent a lot of time together...

And, quite suddenly, she did not wish to pry into his private life. He had been a charming rake, and she did not want to read that kind of devotion. She saw at once they were personal letters, nothing remotely diplomatic. Yet of all the huge amount of correspondence he had received over the years, these were the only epistles he had chosen to keep, to carry with him from place to place. There was a letter from a childhood friend, several from Julius and Roderick, one from Cornelius at school. Even one from Felicia written after her marriage when she had been pretending happiness.

She thrust that away and glanced through the others. Interestingly, there were none from any of his three wives, nor from Delilah's mother, nor the twins'. Three letters were tied together with a plain black ribbon. She did not recognize the handwriting. She untied the ribbon and unfolded the first paper. It was signed only M. So were the other two.

Reluctant still to read them—though why else had she asked Delilah for them?—she put them in order of date. Two had been written in 1795, one back in 1787.

The earliest had been directed to him in Paris, even before the revolution, and was an amusing letter about goings-on in Blackhaven. Written with fun and humor, it made Felicia smile, because it was the letter of a friend, not a lover.

The other two were different and caused her a serious dilemma.

Chapter Twelve

WALLER HARLAW DID not find masquerade balls sophisticated entertainment, but at least a large part of the company was tonish, thanks to the noble Braithwaites and their guests. One could be assured of decent wine and conversation while one danced and played cards. He hoped the food would be just as good, for he had declined dinner at the hotel in favor of the anticipated free meal at the castle.

The dowager Countess of Braithwaite was terrifying, of course, and Harlaw had always found the earl too serious and stuffy, but the man had a lovely wife and several beautiful sisters who were not stuffy at all. Two of those sisters were unmarried, but he knew Braithwaite would sniff out a fortune hunter at a hundred yards. No, his best bet was still Isabella Muir—rich, foreign, ageing, and grateful. Plus, while her blood was Spanish, it was definitely noble.

Tonight was the night he meant to propose to Isabella.

And, with luck, ensure a tryst with Felicia Maitland. He had waited for her long enough.

His initial opportunity came after the first waltz of the evening—a dance enlivened by one costumed lady in a large, hooped gown and a ridiculous headdress, from which leapt an excited puppy.

With great aplomb, Isabella ignored the fuss and hilarity.

Harlaw, who found it rather amusing, kept his face straight and continued to dance. Wearing a mask had never suited him, so he had let his slip down around his neck and adorn his cravat. Isabella's was a pretty confection of lace and glittering jewels that might just have been real. For some reason, it lent her an air of pride and consequence that was almost…daunting.

Almost. Waller Harlaw, son and brother to viscounts, was rarely daunted for long. And Isabella was clearly his for the plucking.

"Perhaps a turn on the terrace?" he suggested with aplomb as the waltz came to a close. "A little air would be welcome, and I have something particular to say to you."

Her bosom heaved in a gratifying manner. The color in her cheeks heightened as though she knew what he would ask, and she laid her hand on his arm to accompany him.

The terrace beyond the French windows, whence the head-dress lady and her partner had fled, pursued by a curious, laughing crowd, was quiet once more. The smell of cigarillo smoke drifted over from the far side, where a couple of army officers stood in idle conversation. Harlaw led his lady in the opposite direction.

"The evening is delightful, is it not?" Isabella said with enthusiasm. "This is the first castle ball I have attended."

"An oversight on Lady Braithwaite's part, I am sure."

"Oh, no, I was invited. Bernard and Gillie always went, but I never liked to leave my little Arthur."

Harlaw took her hand. "Then dare I hope I might have had something to do with changing your mind this time?"

Her blush deepened beneath the line of her mask. "Perhaps."

"Mrs. Muir—Isabella—you must know how I feel about you. My respect, my esteem for you, is incomparable." He kissed her fingers ardently. "As is my love."

"Oh, sir," she whispered. "You must not say such things."

He gazed down at her, knowing he had won. The emotion in her eyes, in her voice, was clear. "But I must. I know I cannot compare to the heroic Captain Muir, but please, please allow me at least to hope."

"For what?" she asked hoarsely.

"For your hand and your heart, Isabella. I would give you my name, my protection, my eternal devotion. Please, say you will be my wife."

"Oh, Mr. Harlaw..."

"Waller," he insisted, smiling down at her.

She began to smile back. "Then you truly mean it?"

"Oh, my dear, how could I not? Put me out of my misery and answer. Will you marry me, my sweet love, my Isabella?"

"Yes," she whispered, smiling up at him. "Yes, Waller, I will."

He kissed her chastely on the lips. In truth, he had little desire to do more, and certainly not with that oddly chilling mask in place. Beneath it, his bride was certainly beautiful, but it was Felicia Maitland who set his blood on fire. "You have made me the happiest of men."

Really, it was ridiculously easy. He barely even needed to think to say the right things, paint the right expression on his face, touch her with just the required amount of respectful ardor.

Then she said, "Come, we must tell Bernard and Gillie and Margaret our good news."

At this, he did have to hide a smile. Bernard had made no secret of his dislike, and Harlaw was delighted to rub his face in the engagement. Even masked, the boy's expression would be a picture to treasure.

Bernard, however, dressed as Julius Caesar, gave little away, and rather belatedly, Harlaw remembered his skill at macao where one always kept one's opponents guessing. The boy's mouth curved into a smile, eyes amiable behind the mask.

He merely bowed and said to Isabella, "You know how important your happiness is to us."

It was the old lady who fluttered, looking alternately appalled and frightened and hopeful as she twittered, "Oh goodness, what a... How charming... We wish you every happiness, and... When will you be married, do you think?"

"Oh, not for a month at least," Harlaw said smoothly. "So you must not feel you need to find a new home before then."

That got Bernard's attention! Something definitely flared in his eyes before he could conceal it. Harlaw smiled, bowed, and excused himself, well pleased with his evening's work. "One must do one's duty," he told them, strolling away to find more congenial company.

Felicia was easily discovered. Even masked and dominoed, her hair, with its beautiful silver highlights, gave her away, as did the unique grace of her movements and the alluring shape of her smiling mouth. Besides which, he had seen her gown before, at some ball she had attended years ago with poor Nick. Harlaw rather liked that she was brazen enough to wear something so old, even semi-concealed by her domino cloak.

She was dancing with Lord Wickenden, which caused him a moment of genuine jealousy, for the wicked baron had been too much the dangerous rake in his day. Since his marriage, he appeared to have learned discretion—which poor Maitland never had, the fool.

It was another dance and a game of cards later before Harlaw saw his opportunity. Felicia spoke to one of her sisters in passing and darted out of the ballroom—not via the French windows or even toward the ladies' cloakroom, but further into the castle, to apartments that were not open to guests that evening.

Curiously, he followed her. He had learned long ago that one could go anywhere one liked if one did it with enough confidence.

He found her entering a small, semi-lit sitting room and followed discreetly. She went immediately to the sofa, where, with a smile, she lifted up a familiar if bizarre headdress and wrapped it in a voluminous gown and petticoats that had been abandoned on the sofa's arm.

"Good Lord," he drawled. "That ridiculous costume was never yours, was it?"

She spun around, clearly startled behind her mask. "No. Just a friend's. I promised to remove it for her."

"I always thought you had a mischievous soul." He did not pretend not to recognize her, and she appeared happy enough to follow his lead.

"Not I, Mr. Harlaw," she said coolly. "I am quite dull. I keep house for my family and I play cards, and that is my very pleasant life."

"Sounds confoundedly dull."

"Well, that must remain one of the many issues on which we differ. You will excuse me?"

"In a moment. Stay a while, Felicia. Keep me company."

"I thank you, but no. And I must point out that I did not give you leave to use my name."

"Felicia! We are old friends."

"No, you and my husband were old friends. That is not the same thing." She walked toward the door, which he continued to block. She was quite splendid, aloof, graceful, unafraid. And yet he had glimpsed fire in her eyes before now. That was what had first fascinated him, even before he had realized what a dog-in-the-manger Maitland was.

"I shall give you a fair chance of revenge at cards," he offered.

"Thank you, but not this evening. Excuse me."

Curiously, his body almost obeyed without his brain's permission. He really was about to stand aside for her, whether from the remains of the gentlemanly manners once instilled in him, or from Felicia's clear assumption of his obedience to her wishes. But he halted the impulse in time.

Instead, he leaned toward her, touching the soft skin of her cheek, just below the line of her mask.

"You have not yet heard my proposal. Only listen, and then, if you still wish, I shall let you go."

"Say your piece, sir," she snapped. "I am expected elsewhere."

It was hardly the warmest of invitations, but, determinedly, he did not drop his hand. "So busy, so urgent about everyone's business but your own. Deep down, I know you are lonely."

"I cannot imagine what makes you think so."

"You are a widow, and poor Nick has been dead, what, two years? Near enough. Felicia, you are a beautiful, red-blooded woman, and I have wanted you for years."

"Stop. I will never marry again."

He laughed, which at least had the benefit of surprising her. "Oh, my dear. I would not be so crass as to try to step into Nick's shoes. No, I do not offer marriage but something more to both our tastes. Carte blanche."

She stared at him so blankly that he wondered, just for a moment, if she had any idea what he meant.

"Pleasure," he clarified. "A contract between us, promising mutual pleasure without the inconvenience of marriage."

She searched his eyes, and his loins threatened to burst out of his satin breeches.

"I cannot work out," she said slowly, "whether you are being insulting or merely silly. Assuming the latter, I shall answer in kind. I thank you, sir, for the *honor* of your offer, but we should not suit. Good evening."

With that, she turned on her heel so fast he had no time even to seize her, let alone kiss her, and marched out of the other door that must lead further into the bowels of the castle.

Harlaw swore and was already striding after her before another movement in the room caught his eye. He halted and spun around to see Margaret Muir arise from the high-backed armchair facing the fireplace. Her mask dangled from one ear.

How very farcical... But at least she is deaf.

"Miss Muir," he said loudly, bowing elaborately.

She stared at him, two spots of angry color on her cheeks. Her normally soft, vague eyes were hard, her body rigid, so perhaps she was not quite as deaf as she pretended.

"Despicable," she pronounced. "Unconscionable. Insulting two beautiful and kind women to whom you are not worthy even to raise your eyes."

"I have no idea what you are talking about."

"I shall not bandy words with you, sir. You will leave Blackhaven on the morrow, and you will never see Isabella again. You will not speak to her; you will never write nor send messages through anyone else."

"Far be it from me to contradict a lady," Harlaw said, smiling, "but in this case, you really are quite mistaken."

"No," Margaret said. Was she actually shaking with anger? Or with fear? "I am not. You will leave Blackhaven, or I will tell not only Isabella but Lady Braithwaite, and everyone else I know—which is, you must be aware, everyone—what I overheard in here today."

"What, and ruin both ladies?"

"It will be neither lady who is ruined."

Harlaw strolled toward her, amusing himself. "You are quite right in that, of course. It will be you."

She blinked. "I?"

"Indeed. Should you be foolish enough to mention any of what you overheard to Isabella or anyone else, I will be forced to reveal *your* secrets, and then only think of the damage."

"I have no secrets."

"Dear lady, you are the mother of an illegitimate child and very, very far from being the respectable old spinster you pretend."

The flush had vanished from her cheeks, leaving them ghostly white. She gripped the arm of the chair so hard her knuckles shone palely in the candle light.

Harlaw winked. "I spent a very convivial evening in London with some Scotch tradesman who could not hold his drink—or his tongue. Name of Bryant." He smiled at her. "So you see, my dear lady, discretion is most definitely the better part of valor. Good evening."

As he strolled out of the room, he wondered if he could get her pin money out of her too. Before he married Isabella and stopped her allowance.

❧

FELICIA WAS STILL furious by the time she had hidden Lucy's costume with their other things in the cloakroom and found her way back to the ballroom.

How dare Waller Harlaw accost her and issue such an insulting proposition? Did he imagine she was some lightskirt, some female version of the "loose screw" Nick had been?

And then she flushed all over with shame.

Was that not what she had become? She was Bernard Muir's mistress. Was that really any better than sharing her favors as Nick did?

But I love Bernard!

The world did not know that. Bernard did not know that.

Now she felt chilled. Had Harlaw somehow found out about her *affaire* with Bernard? Perhaps she had not been as discreet as she imagined. After all, they had left the gaming club together, and she had walked home from the hotel early in the morning. She had imagined she was unrecognizable, but was that the case?

She pulled herself together sharply. Rumors did not matter. She was a widow, playing as so many did, at being just a little fast. It was past time for some fun. She had promised herself that before the assembly ball. Now, she had two choices. She could carry on with Bernard as her discreet lover until he tired of her, or she could end it now.

Ending it now was too painful to contemplate. But she was getting herself in an emotional tangle again. After Nick, she did not want to love Bernard or anyone else. And there was going to be pain whenever Bernard tired of her. That much was already inevitable.

She straightened her shoulders. *He will never know. I will see it is ending and walk away first. And it will be worth it, for however long it lasts…*

At that moment, she saw him in the ballroom. Masked and

dressed as Julius Caesar, he was part of a group of laughing, beautiful people. For a moment the scene held a sickening sense of familiarity. The man she loved at the center of fashionable attention.

It took her by surprise, not least because she had got used to regarding Bernard as *ordinary*—not in his person but in his rank and social position. To see him hobnobbing with Braithwaite's fashionable guests, to say nothing of Braithwaite's beautiful sisters, brought its own shock. Of course, he was Lady Wickenden's brother, and he had known the Braithwaites all his life, but she had never truly seen before how comfortable, how at home he was among them.

At that moment, he looked up and saw her. He was already smiling at something, and his expression did not change. He did not acknowledge her. She only had a moment to feel the exquisite hurt of that before she realized he was easing away from them, that he was walking indirectly yet inexorably to intercept her. This was Bernard's discretion, his consideration, not the waning of his interest. Even the relief felt like pain.

"What is it?" he asked at once, though he bowed as if to a mere friendly acquaintance.

That toad, Harlaw, just made me an offensive proposition. Similar to the one she had already accepted from Bernard. But she could not say such things. Apart from anything else, he would probably pick a fight with Harlaw, and she would not have that.

"Oh, nothing," she said mildly. "Just feeling slightly harassed. In case you did not recognize her, that was Lucy with the canine headdress, but she never clears up after herself. It is a minor inconvenience."

"Then come and dance with me and be at peace again."

"You are not a peaceful person, Bernard," she teased.

"I can be," he assured her, and offered her his arm for the waltz.

And curiously, he *was* peaceful. Ugly thoughts and doubts disintegrated in his presence, leaving only happiness to be with him, waltzing in his arms. She wanted to lay her head on his chest, though fortunately, she resisted.

After the dance, they walked on the terrace.

Bernard said, "Harlaw is engaged to Isabella."

"Oh no!" She had to bite her tongue to prevent the story of Harlaw's other proposal pouring out, but inside, she was incensed. To propose marriage to one woman and a carte blanche to another on the same night, under the same roof! He really was a scoundrel. But it was worse than that. Isabella had accepted him. "She is going to be hurt by this. Whatever we do, or don't do, she will be hurt."

"It is unavoidable," he agreed. "I think I will have to talk to her tomorrow, explain about his cheating Maitland and how you were left."

"Perhaps I should speak to her, too." In private, probably, and tell her everything...

"Thank you," Bernard said, clasping her hand on his arm. "I think that might help. Will you marry me, Felicia?"

"You know I will not."

"I wish you would change your mind."

There was such sadness in his voice that a lump formed in her throat. She swallowed it down. "I won't. You should not even ask when the examples before us are so awful."

He frowned. "Meaning?"

"Meaning Nick and me. Meaning Harlaw and Isabella."

"And Gillie and Wickenden, the Braithwaites, the Grants, Benedicts, Lamptons, Dovertons, Gaunts. There are examples all around us of good marriages as well as bad, you know. Many more of the good, in fact. And you seem happy enough to welcome the institution for your siblings. I think what you are actually doing is comparing me to Harlaw."

She withdrew her hand from his arm, flushing because there was an element of truth in what he said. "The problem is not in character. It is in the nature of marriage, the control it confers on a husband. I will never cede that control again, not even for you."

He gazed down at her, his expression stricken. "You don't trust me."

She shrugged, as though the matter were of no account, when she knew that it was. "Where marriage is concerned, I suppose I don't really trust anyone."

"Then I *am* another Maitland in your eyes. I play and I gamble. I could easily be another Harlaw. A cheat, a deceiver, a thief, a rake of no morals."

"I did not say that." She did not need to. Her lack of trust implied it, and she could not now go back on her words without giving in on marriage. Or so it seemed to her.

Was it her imagination that his face looked paler?

"Oh, Felicia," he said, so softly, so sadly, that she barely heard him.

But she knew. The pain was coming so much earlier than she had imagined. "I told you from the beginning. I will not marry anyone. Not even you."

"You did," he replied. "But I hoped. I still hope."

"Don't," she uttered.

He did not even touch her. If he did, she could make things right again. She could. Just for a little…

"I love you," he said. "I will always want to marry you. But it seems…"

"Bernard," she warned, panic rising.

"It seems what I cannot do, without your trust, is be your lover. It is…wrong."

"*Now* you will preach morals?" she said in disbelief.

He shook his head. "It is nothing to do with morality. Just *feeling*."

His words stuck in his throat. She seemed to be too numb, too helpless to stop this tragedy that had galloped out of nowhere at such devastating speed. He stepped back from her, bent his head in a bow, and walked away.

I have lost him. Felicia's knees began to give way. She gripped the balustrade at the edge of the terrace and tried to pull herself together.

So, she had taken a risk, and she had been burned because she cared for him—loved him, even. But she had known happiness. She had known *him*. And at least she was not married.

On that note, she turned and walked slowly back into the ballroom. Vaguely, she was aware of Lucy's Eddleston lurking in the shadows near the doors. And inside, Lucy was making her way toward the doors, no doubt for her own romantic assignation.

Felicia could not choose for her siblings, only for herself.

She wanted very badly to go home, to cry, to hide. But she had felt like that so often before, and she knew how to deal with it. She pinned a bright, social smile to her face and strolled around the ballroom, nodding to acquaintances, pausing occasionally to exchange a few words about nothing.

And then a crack like a gunshot sounded from outside, and people looked at each other as though wondering whether to be alarmed. And Lucy's voice cried out.

Lucy! With a gasp, she bolted for the French door, true horror filling her mind. But there were too many people blocking her path to her distressed little sister, who might have been *shot*, who might already be dead. Dementedly, she pushed past them, until someone caught her around the waist and dragged her back.

"It's not Lucy," Bernard told her. "It's Eddleston. They have the man who shot him. Your brother is there, and Braithwaite, and Lucy is fine."

She stared at him. "She can't be fine. Not if Eddleston—"

"He is alive," Bernard said. His voice and his eyes were caring. How could he be so tender and still leave her? A puzzle for another day. He handed her a handkerchief. "Wipe your tears."

None of it was remotely funny, and yet she had an insane urge to laugh. Hysteria... Lucy, with Dr. Lampton and Braithwaite's sister, Lady Maria, were walking swiftly from the ballroom. Young Lady Braithwaite announced there had been an accident but that there was no danger and the dance should continue.

And so the terrible evening went on. Felicia and Bernard came upon a white-faced Delilah, and Bernard left them together. Then Roderick came back with the news that Eddleston's wound was not too serious and that he was expected to live.

By then it was the supper dance, after which came the unmasking—during which a complete stranger to Felicia, a rather beautiful woman dressed as Cleopatra, claimed to be engaged to Roderick, of all people. Unamused, Roderick stated in clear, precise tones that he could not possibly be engaged to Cleopatra because he was already betrothed to Lady Helen Conway, their host's youngest sister.

It was like a bad play, or a bad dream that made no sense.

Lady Helen smiled vaguely, as though her mind was somewhere else entirely, but agreed she and Roderick were indeed betrothed.

The whole world seemed to have gone mad. Or just her whole family.

Funnily enough, it was Bernard who saved the supreme awkwardness of the moment by declaring the unknown Cleopatra's pronouncement a jest and laughing with her as they walked away together as though he was leading her into supper. So everyone could be comfortable again, congratulating Roderick and wishing Lady Helen happiness.

Looking from her brother to Helen, Felicia did not believe they were happy at all. No wonder. Why was everyone rushing into marriage?

A new thought struck her. Was this all, somehow, the twins' doing?

Chapter Thirteen

B ERNARD ACTED TO be rid of Meg Maven, alias Cleopatra, largely because of his old friendship with Lady Helen. He was not sure he believed in Helen's engagement to Roderick Vale any more than he believed in Meg's, but he had sensed she was about to break somehow. And so he swept Meg out of the room, laughing as though it was all hilarious.

Meg did not laugh. She looked flabbergasted. Probably, she had been outmaneuvered, but Bernard did not want to know the details. There seemed to be something about the Vales that made people behave badly.

No, that was not fair. No one had compelled him to seduce Felicia or to love her. His tragedy was that she did not love him, that her past seemed to have rendered her incapable of love.

"So you're the earl's lackey now, Bernie?" Meg said spitefully. "You throw out the drunks and the unwanted guests?"

"You don't look drunk to me," Bernard said, and had to duck to avoid her swinging hand. He caught and threaded it forcibly through his arm. "In fact, I am as sure as I can be that you were not invited either."

"I could buy this castle and the estate twice over."

"Everything is not about money, Meg."

"Isn't it?" Her shoulders suddenly drooped, and he found he felt sorry for her. He was even fond of her with the casual affection he felt for all his past lovers. Except Felicia. There had never been anything casual about that. It had been a soaring, singing joy from the first. And now...

But he would not think of that.

"Mrs. Maven's carriage, Jem," he said to the stable lad.

"Since when do you give orders for me?" Meg demanded.

"Don't worry, I won't do it again. Whatever you were about, Meg, it's over. Let's just make this as dignified as possible."

She didn't say another word. They waited in tense silence, but Bernard didn't mind. He didn't want to be in the castle anyhow. Perhaps he could just walk home after this and leave the carriage for the others.

Someone, a lady in a ball gown, still masked, flitted out of the shadows beside the stables and hurried to one of the castle's side doors. Someone who knew the place well, then. In fact, she resembled Genevra Winslow. He hoped her assignation had been with someone trustworthy.

Bernard handed the now-regal Meg into her carriage and closed the door. He waited until the horses trotted off down the drive before he turned and walked reluctantly back to the castle.

It was just a matter of getting through the next couple of hours. Surely there could be no more drama left in the evening.

※

AFTER SUPPER, BERNARD went to play cards. Felicia came in just a little later and sat with a group of ladies. She did not look at him. Harlaw entered half an hour after that, and strolled over to the ladies' table to watch. Without looking at him either, Felicia rose and left the card room.

Which was odd. They had agreed to lull Harlaw into a false sense of security so he would walk into the King's Head charity card party suspecting nothing of their plan. Perhaps she had given up on punishing him with exposure and ruin.

It would be no bad thing for her. Revenge was unhealthy. On the other hand, Bernard had not given up. If it was the last thing he did, he would see she was compensated fully for Harlaw's cheating.

Geoffrey Winslow, Genevra and Catherine's brother, marched up to Bernard's table.

"A word with you, Muir," he said with unusual abruptness.

"Let me just finish this game, then I am all yours."

Geoffrey scowled and waited in impatient silence. Then, as Bernard glanced up at him at last, he turned on his heel and stalked out of the room.

Not quite amused, Bernard followed him along the edge of the ballroom to the staircase, mounting the first few steps to obtain privacy.

Bernard stood a step below him. "Say on, my man."

"Your flippancy is unwelcome," Geoffrey said stiffly.

"Then stop being an ass and tell me what the devil's the matter with you."

"Not with me," Geoffrey said between his teeth. "With Genevra. You have slighted her."

Bernard blinked. "I most certainly have not."

Geoffrey peered at him with the first sign of uncertainty, and more than a little relief. "Then you are honoring your betrothal?"

"What betrothal?" Bernard asked bitterly. "I am not betrothed to anyone." *Felicia, Felicia…*

Geoffrey raked his fingers through his hair. "Damn you, Bernard, that's not what Genevra says!"

"Then she's playing some trick on you. Who does she say I am engaged to?"

Geoffrey glared at him, growing fury in his eyes. "Genevra herself! What has got into you, Muir?"

Bernard had had enough. "Nonsense. Tell her to grow up and pick on someone her own size."

As soon as the words were out, he knew they were wrong. Geoffrey was trying desperately to protect his sister's honor and was in no mood to recall childhood games.

"Oh for the love of... Look, Geoffrey, if I offered for Genevra, would I do it behind your back, your father's back?"

"Apparently so! You must know my mother is looking higher for her. She would oppose the engagement."

"So do I," Bernard said. "So we are all in agreement."

"Except Genevra," Geoffrey said.

"Then I advise you to have a word with her."

"Are you calling my sister a liar?"

The whole conversation was ridiculous. "Yes," Bernard said. "If she says I offered for her or gave her any reason to expect me to, then she is quite clearly either misunderstanding or downright lying." He searched the room for Genevra and found her with her mother, glancing in her brother's direction. Her posture betrayed nervous excitement. "Why don't we go and speak to her and clear the matter up?"

"No!" Geoffrey burst out so loudly that several people glanced at them. "You will not go near my sister again! Ever."

Bernard stared at him. "Right now, Geoffrey, that suits me perfectly." He swung away from his old friend, who seized his arm to detain him.

"Oh, no, I have not finished with you yet. You have deceived and insulted my sister, and I am calling you out."

"Oh, take a powder," Bernard said in disgust.

"You are refusing to meet me?"

"Yes!"

"Then you leave me no choice." Geoffrey raised his hand with the clear intention of slapping him.

Bernard seized his wrist and bore it downward while he laughed for the benefit of any watchers. "Have you lost your mind?" he hissed. "You accuse me of trifling with your sister—on the basis of no evidence, because there can't be any—and then challenge me publicly in front of everyone? Do you want her name dragged into this?"

"Oh, I think people are more likely to bandy Felicia Maitland's name, don't you?"

Bernard dropped his old friend's wrist and stared. "Have you annoyed her?"

Geoffrey curled his lip with contempt. "Is that the word you use? Then half of Blackhaven has annoyed her!" He recoiled from whatever fury spat from Bernard's eyes. Or it might have been from the half-raised, fully clenched fist.

With an effort, Bernard forced both hands to his sides and spoke between his teeth. "Wickenden. Send your second to Wickenden." With that, he leapt down the steps and strode away before he struck his old friend full in his vicious, lying mouth.

It took him some time to track down his brother-in-law and then to extract him from his conversation with Lord Linfield and Colonel Doverton.

"Well, Bernard?" Wickenden said tolerantly when Bernard had dragged him outside under the vaguely spitting rain. "What can possibly be so urgent?"

"I need you to act for me."

Wickenden halted, staring down at him. "*Act* for you? As in a duel?"

"Geoffrey Winslow challenged me, accusing me of insulting his sister, which I never did."

"I would be surprised," Wickenden said. "But what the devil gave him the idea that you had?"

"Haven't a clue."

"I thought you would have had the sense to find the truth of it without resorting to duels. It's a fool's road, and as you know, I speak from experience. And you've known these people all your life."

"I know, and I tried. I refused to fight him, and then he insulted…someone else, and that, I could not allow."

Wickenden gazed at him, his eyes unusually piercing.

"Thing is," Bernard added quickly, "I named you as my second, so I wanted to warn you someone will approach you on Geoffrey's behalf. It will have to be hushed up, David—"

"Not least from Gillie."

"Exactly. But the whole thing is ridiculous."

Wickenden considered, strolling on a little further. "Where did young Winslow get the idea you insulted his sister?"

"From Genevra herself, apparently. She claims I offered her marriage and then reneged, neither of which is remotely true. All I can think of is that she's having a tantrum. But surely a brother should see that!"

"She must have gone to a good deal of trouble to convince him," Wickenden said thoughtfully. "Why would she do that? Has she shown any signs of wishing to marry you before?"

"None," Bernard said in disgust. A memory nudged him, and he frowned. "Except at the garden party, she was a bit odd, seemed jealous of...another lady."

"The same lady her brother insulted to get you to fight him? No, don't name names. I can work it out. So you think this is Genevra's revenge for the garden party slight, real or imagined?"

"It's all I can think of, but I've never known her to be so damned vindictive. And in any case, I thought we had sorted it out and were friends again."

"Could someone have put her up to it? Egged her on?"

"I suppose so, but why? I'm no catch. Mrs. Winslow would hardly welcome me to the family with open arms, even if I wanted to be there." Another thought struck him, and he swore. "Unless she needs to be married for other reasons entirely."

"Well, don't repeat that, or Geoffrey *will* have reason to fight you."

"You know I wouldn't," Bernard said impatiently.

"Perhaps we should send Gillie to have a word with her. Or Catherine."

"I'd rather leave Gillie out of it," Bernard said uneasily. "She doesn't like duels."

"Credit me with a little discretion," Wickenden advised, clapping him on the back. "I'll tell you what, though, London parties are pretty dull compared with Blackhaven..."

❧

"AUNT MARGARET HAS gone."

Bernard, who had finally fallen asleep with his head full of duels and Genevra's lies and anxiety over Felicia, awoke to a much more urgent problem, as hurled at him by his sister from his bedchamber door.

He sat up in bed, confused and still disoriented by sleep. "Gone where?" he asked, rubbing his eyes and trying not to be irritated.

"If I knew that, I would go after her," Gillie said, stalking across the room. She threw a folded letter onto the bed, inscribed with his name in Aunt Margaret's hand. "We all got one—you, me, and Isabella. Isabella's just made her furious. Mine makes no sense. So we are depending on you."

"I don't see why," Bernard muttered. "I didn't write the da— *wretched* thing."

He unfolded the letter.

My dear Bernard,

You have brought such joy to my life and grown into such a wonderful young man that I know I may rely on you utterly to care for Isabella and little Arthur and even Gillie, although she also has David, who has proven such a boon to the family.

I am going away for a little—or perhaps for good—because I will not bring scandal upon the rest of you. When opprobrium is heaped upon me, and you are bewildered by the sudden judgments and accusations, do not fight in my defense, but know in your heart that I am ashamed of nothing, that I live for you and Gillie and now Arthur, too. Help Isabella, and do not attempt to find me. I am well and have the means to live as pleasantly as I may.

Ever yours,
M.

Frowning over the bizarre words he could not quite grasp, he raised his gaze to Gillie's. "What...?"

She took the letter from his fingers and scanned it before dropping it back onto the bedclothes. "More or less the same as mine. What has got into her, Bernard? Where would she go? And why? Who could possibly *heap opprobrium* on Aunt Margaret?"

"I have absolutely no idea. What does Isabella's say?"

"She won't let me read it. She is too furious."

"With Margaret?"

"I can only suppose so. Get up, Bernard. We have to decide what to do."

Bernard did not waste time arguing with her but clambered out of bed to stick his head in the washing bowl.

Ten minutes later he was in the breakfast parlor with Gillie, Wickenden, and Isabella. His stepmother was tight-lipped and pale, her eyes spitting fury he had not seen since she first walked into the house in the midst of a card party three years ago.

"She cannot do this to us!" Isabella fumed. "Release her vitriol and then flee so that we have no—"

"*Vitriol?*" Bernard interrupted. "Aunt Margaret? What the devil did she write to you?"

Isabella waved that away, just as the door opened and Danny said, "Mrs. Maitland to see Mrs. Muir. I just brought her straight here."

Bernard leapt to his feet, joy soaring because she had come before he even registered Danny's statement that she wished to see Isabella.

Gillie began, "Danny, this is not a convenient time. We are in the middle..." But Danny had already made way for Felicia to hurry into the room.

She paused to curtsey. "Forgive the intrusion." Her gaze slid over Bernard to Isabella. "Mrs. Muir, might—"

"You!" Isabella uttered with loathing. "You have the nerve, the insolence, to come to my home after what you have done?"

"*Isabella,*" Bernard said sharply.

But Felicia did not look angry. "I? What have I done?"

"Always flirting and leading him on, trying to entice him from me, filling my family's ears with lies!"

"What lies?" Gillie asked with apparent interest.

"None," Felicia said, but without looking at Gillie. Her entire attention was on Isabella. "What do you imagine I said, and to whom?"

"To Miss Muir, my poor, trusting, sister-in-law who has been driven from her home by your lies!"

Felicia blinked, then glanced around the other occupants of the room. "Now I am confused. Miss Muir has nothing to do with my visit, and I am surprised that you bring her up."

"She has left us!" Isabella exclaimed. "Because of you."

Before Bernard could speak, Gillie did. "If you're going to make such accusations, Izzy, you'll have to explain them. Please, sit down, Mrs. Maitland."

Bernard held out his hand to his stepmother, and after the slightest pause, Isabella took a folded letter from under her plate and gave it to him. As he read, his lips fell apart and his breath caught. He raised his eyes to Felicia's face.

"Harlaw accosted you at the ball. Why did you not say?"

"Because you would have picked a fight with him. What *is* this about your aunt?" she asked.

"She appears to have left Blackhaven," Wickenden said.

"And warned Isabella against Harlaw," Bernard added. "She overheard his proposition to you."

Felicia flushed, but she looked directly at Isabella. "I came to warn you, too, because I could not in conscience remain silent. That is the kind of man he is, and believe me, I know there is no happiness to be won from such a man."

"Because your husband was one?" Isabella snapped.

The pain twisted Felicia's mouth before she smoothed it. "Yes."

"Actually, that is a little unfair," Wickenden said. "Maitland was a shocking rake, but I never knew him to lie. Harlaw lies as a

way of life, cheats at cards, and hunts fortunes. And if Margaret is
gone—"

"It is because he frightened her," Bernard said grimly, "forced
her to be silent. But she could not be silent, for Isabella's sake.
Whatever he holds over her head, she knows it will fall now and
is trying to protect us. Damn it, where would she go?"

"Bryant," Felicia said suddenly, staring at him. "He might
even have gone with her, though to what end..."

"Who is Bryant?" Gillie demanded.

"An acquaintance of Margaret's whom she has signally failed
to introduce to any of us." Bernard strode to the door. "I'm going
to see him now."

"I'll come with you." Felicia sprang up, seemed about to say
something to Isabella, then merely curtseyed and passed out of
the door in front of him.

"IT DOESN'T MAKE sense," Bernard said as they walked rapidly
along Cliff Crescent. "What on earth could frighten Margaret? He
must have threatened Gillie or me or Arthur in some way."

"Something in her past, perhaps, that she is afraid will reflect
badly on all of you?"

"Aunt Margaret?" he said in disbelief. "If you..." He trailed
off, frowning as the words of her letter came back to him. "She
has done nothing she is ashamed of...and yet she runs. Do you
suppose she has gone to her friends in Scotland?"

"Perhaps. Mr. Bryant might even have taken her."

"And we could be wrong. What Margaret witnessed might
have nothing to do with the reasons for her departure. She might
simply have needed to tell Isabella what Harlaw is like before she
left. Either way, it leaves Bryant with much to explain!" He cast
her a sideways glance. "Did Harlaw hurt you last night?"

"No. He angered me, but that is not the same thing."

"It will be added to his account," Bernard said savagely.

She said nothing more until he seized her arm and barged across the high street, to the annoyance of several vehicles forced to swerve or halt to avoid them.

"Sorry," he muttered.

"Yes, well, don't charge the hotel with similar aggression or you will be repelled. Besides drawing the sort of attention that I believe Miss Muir is keen to avoid."

She was right, of course. Crashing so dementedly after Bryant and Harlaw would achieve nothing.

"Do you suppose they are in together?" he asked.

"In what together?"

"I wish I knew." He drew a deep breath, summoned an amiable smile for the doorman, whom he knew well, and conducted her inside the hotel. "Which room is Mr. Bryant's, if you please?" he asked Tom, the clerk at the foyer desk.

"He told you," Felicia said in amazement, a few moments later as they began to climb the stairs.

"He shouldn't really," Bernard agreed. "But I have known him since we were children. We played soldiers together."

"I have a feeling this happens a great deal," she murmured. "People do things for you, tell you things, whether or not they should, just because you are Bernard Muir."

"It's hardly a position of much note. This way."

Arriving at the correct door, Bernard swung up his arm to knock loudly and found it caught by Felicia's hands. He stared at her in surprise.

"Don't begin with anger," she said. "You don't know that he has done anything or is in any way involved. Either way, his enmity will not help you."

He wanted to deny that he was so stupid, but, in fact, the reminder was timely. Margaret had been like a second mother to him, a constant background to his life, and his anxiety for her was too raw to be sensible.

He nodded curtly and knocked more moderately on the door.

"Enter," called the male voice within.

Bryant was packing. Clothes and personal items were strewn across the bed around an open bag and a small trunk. He glanced around as they came in. His jaw dropped and the shirts in his arms fell on to the bed.

"Mrs. Maitland!" he said. "Mr. Muir."

"Forgive the intrusion," Bernard said, mindful of Felicia's advice. "I see you are busy. Are you leaving us, Mr. Bryant?"

"Yes, it seems I must. Er... I'm sorry, I do not have the means to entertain guests. Perhaps... What is it I might do for you?"

He glanced from one to the other, mystified but also wary.

"We are looking for my aunt, Miss Margaret Muir. The matter is urgent."

"Well, she is not here, sir," Bryant said tartly.

Bernard held his gaze. "Do you know where she is?"

"No."

"You hesitated, sir," Felicia said. "Please, if you know anything, you must tell us. Mr. Muir and his sister are afraid for her."

You could tell a great deal, Bernard thought, from a man's reaction to such an announcement. A villain would dismiss it, or even make fun of it. Bryant did neither. In fact, he looked exceedingly uncomfortable.

"I don't believe there is any need for anxiety," he said. "She has merely left Blackhaven."

"How do you know?"

"She left a letter for me."

Bernard blinked. "You got one too?"

Bryant hesitated more obviously this time, then took a folded letter from inside the open bag and passed it over to Bernard.

My dear Alan,

Bad things are afoot, and I do not know how they will fall. It is best for everyone that I go away for a time, and I advise you to flee as soon as you may, to avoid unpleasantness. The man staying at the hotel, Waller Harlaw, is to blame, so above all, do not trust him. Go home or go to London, but do not stay here in Blackhaven. I will write again when I arrive.

All my love,
M.

"All my love," Bernard repeated, raising his gaze from the letter to Bryant's face. "Exactly how well do you know my aunt? What is she to you?"

Bryant stared at him as though measuring his seriousness, the depth of concern. His lips twisted. "She is my mother."

Chapter Fourteen

FELICIA HAD NO idea how Bernard would respond to that blunt statement, how he might adjust to the enforced change in his view of his aunt, from slightly dotty but essentially pure spinster, to the mother of this large, young son. Disbelief, anger at the perceived insult…

But after the first instant of shock, he showed neither. Instead, he clung to the matter of first importance.

"Where is she?" he asked steadily.

Bryant turned once more to the fallen pile of shirts, picked them up, and crammed them into the trunk anyhow. "I don't know for sure. She has the keys to my cottage in Cheshire. It's my bolt-hole, if you like. No one else knows of it, not my parents or my brother—"

"Your parents?" Felicia interrupted.

"The Bryants. They brought me up as their son."

"Then you did not always know that Miss Muir…"

"They told me when I was old enough to understand the importance of the secret." He closed and fastened the trunk, then swept everything else into the bag. "I'm going to the cottage now. I might catch up with her on the road."

"And if she is not there?" Bernard demanded.

"I'll write to you. She will have left some sign on the road, or she will write. But if she felt it necessary to leave, we should respect her decision."

"You'll forgive me if I don't accept that," Bernard snapped. "I don't know you from Adam."

"No," Felicia agreed. "But this does make sense, Bernard. This—Mr. Bryant—is clearly what Harlaw held over her head. She overheard how Harlaw spoke to me at the ball, threatened to tell Isabella, and he threatened her in turn with this exposure."

"Yes, but how did he *know* about Margaret? No one knew!" Bernard swung back on Bryant. "Unless you or your family blabbed?"

Bryant's smile was twisted. "In case you have not noticed, my family does not move in fashionable circles. I believe you call us *cits*. My older brother goes to London occasionally, on business. He might kick up the odd lark with noble young gentlemen, but he is not admitted to the best clubs or invited to *ton* parties. How would he blab to this Harlaw?"

Felicia met Bernard's gaze.

"Odd larks with noble young gentlemen," he repeated.

"I'm not sure it matters right now," Felicia said. "We should let Mr. Bryant get off after your aunt."

Bryant went suddenly to the desk and scribbled something on a piece of paper, which he shook to dry the ink before holding it out to Bernard. "The address of my cottage," he said. "I know you don't trust me. Truth to tell, I don't really trust you. She tried to keep us apart because she was afraid of what you and your sister would think of her if you discovered my existence."

"And we never asked," Bernard said slowly. "All these years, she had her little holidays in Scotland. Those frequent letters from Mrs. Bryson, and we never questioned any of it. We labeled her without understanding."

He snatched the paper from Bryant. "Thank you," he said curtly, then he drew in a breath. "Who is your father?"

Again, Bryant's crooked smile dawned. "That, I do not know. She will not tell me. She never even told my mother."

It was none of Felicia's business. It was not her secret to tell.

But Margaret's letter to her son lay open on the bed where Bernard had dropped it. And she thought, perhaps, that it was time to end the dangerous secrecy, at least between Bernard and Alan Bryant.

"Perhaps I can help you there," she blurted. "If you really want to know."

They both turned to her with astonishment, and then she saw understanding begin to dawn in Bernard's eyes.

"Oh no," he said.

"Tell me," Bryant said hoarsely.

"Sir George Vale," she said. "I think you are my half-brother."

Bernard sank down on the edge of the bed.

Bryant kept staring at her. "What reason do you have for imagining such a thing?"

"My father was something of a rake," Felicia said. "Not a bad man, or a deceiver, but a charming gentleman who liked women. My sister Delilah is the daughter of an actress he was excessively fond of. He loved his wives. Well, the first two... Margaret and George, my father, knew each other all their lives. They were friends, in a close but entirely platonic way. However, when he came home twenty or so years ago, around the time my eldest brother Julius went to sea, I think something changed between George and Margaret, and they fell in love. The time must have been right. My mother was dead, he was unmarried... I think the relationship went too far, and *you* are the result. She probably did not know about you when she sent him away."

"Why would she send him away if she loved him?" Bryant demanded. "Would he not marry her?"

"From her final letter, I gather he did propose. But she did not trust him to mend his ways. She could not believe he would be faithful to her, and she could not live with that. And so she sent him away without her. He went to London and in time married Emma, whom I don't think he ever loved, and Lucy was born. By then, so were you, but I don't believe he ever knew."

"How can you possibly know all this?" Bernard said. "You

must be guessing, imagining…"

"There are three letters," she said. "From *M* to George. *M* must be Margaret—if you read them, you would agree. They *sound* like her. My father kept them with his most precious correspondence. The first is the letter of a friend—I gather they had kept in touch since he first left Blackhaven. And then, there are two letters she wrote to him while he was at Black Hill. These are very different. Love letters. The second is also a letter of parting. He kept them both. I think he loved Margaret. Perhaps she would have been the one great love of his life. We will never know."

Bernard appeared speechless.

"Sir George Vale," Bryant said, as though trying the name on his tongue. He gave a short, bitter laugh. "Well."

Felicia caught his gaze. "I'm afraid you have rather a lot of half-brothers and sisters. Nine, to be precise."

He stared at her. "Nine that you know of!"

"He cared for all his children," she said defensively. "Delilah has always lived with us. So have the twins since their mother died. You are different. You have your own family, your own life. But you are still welcome in ours. I wish you would come and meet us. Soon."

Bryant reached for his coat. "I need to go."

❦

TWENTY MINUTES LATER, Felicia found herself on the beach, walking beside Bernard.

"How long have you known?" he asked.

"I only read the letters the other day and began to wonder if *M* could be Margaret. She, of all people in Blackhaven, seemed to be the most interested in his life, in us. She appeared very…*intense*. Julius and Delilah both remember her being around Black Hill a good deal when they were children. Roderick too. And then she wasn't."

"I wish you had told me last night."

"I'm not sure I should have told you now. It is not my secret. But I don't feel you and Alan Bryant should be enemies through mere misunderstanding."

"He is your brother," Bernard said slowly. "My cousin." A breath of laughter shook him. "I wonder what Isabella will make of it all? She is so...proper."

"I suspect she is more concerned with Mr. Harlaw."

Bernard nodded. "How do you think Harlaw found out about her?"

"I think the Bryant brother blabbed in his cups, or was induced to. Harlaw is exactly the kind of weasel who will store up information in case he ever finds a use for it. I think he used up all his credit in London, and no one will let him near an heiress there—he is too well known. So he came here for Margaret."

Bernard looked at her, his eyes widening. "That must be it! He did not come to Blackhaven with friends. The Braithwaites did not invite him until they ran into him at the assembly ball. I'll bet he *did* come to squeeze money out of Margaret in return for his silence. Only then he discovered she was not wealthy enough for it to be worth his while, and..."

He shook his head as though at his own stupidity. "I didn't really think about it before, but I'm sure he *did* ask first for Margaret. He claimed Gillie was the reason for his call, that when he had told her he was coming to Blackhaven, she asked him to visit us and give Margaret her love. That doesn't sound like Gillie to me. She doesn't even like Harlaw."

"No, she wouldn't—"

"Because we did not know him," Bernard went on, "Isabella made me accompany her and Margaret to the drawing room to greet him. He had been left alone there to wait. And Isabella had left an open letter on the table by her chair. I saw it and tidied it away because it was private." His eyes gleamed. "It was from the bank, about her inheritance and the investment of the funds. *That* is why he courted Isabella. Margaret turned out to be of no use to him. But a rich young widow? No wonder he is always underfoot. Why did I not remember this before?" He bumped his fist against his forehead.

Felicia shrugged. "It never entered your mind that a stranger purporting to be a gentleman would lower himself to read private correspondence."

"I thought worse of him than that," Bernard said with a hint of savagery. "I still do. It's why I didn't go with Bryant in the end. I think we need to deal with Harlaw *now*."

✥

CLUTCHING THE FLOWERS he had made one of the hotel servants buy for him, Harlaw left the hotel and walked around to call on Isabella.

"No one is at home, sir." The large former soldier the Muirs employed as a servant looked far too satisfied with this news.

"Stuff and nonsense," Harlaw said pleasantly.

"No one is at home."

"Then I shall wait." As Harlaw stepped forward, so did the family guardian, and for several tense moments they glared at each other over the threshold, neither willing to give way. With growing anger, Harlaw realized he could not win this battle, though when he won the war, this grizzled old brute would be dismissed without a character.

Then Isabella's heavily accented voice spoke from within. "It is fine, Danny. I will see him."

Harlaw smiled. Danny scowled and very reluctantly stood back to admit him. Without wasting another glance on the old soldier, Harlaw passed him his hat and strolled forward to present his flowers to Isabella.

His betrothed, however, had already turned away, leading him not up to the drawing room, but into the ground-floor salon where less favored callers were received. For the first time, Harlaw grew uneasy.

"My dear, what is it?" he asked with genuine concern, taking her hand as soon as he was inside the room.

She made a halfhearted attempt to withdraw her hand, but he hung on.

"It is Margaret," she said tragically. "Margaret has gone."

"Miss Muir?" he said in surprise. "Gone where?"

"We do not know. Gillie and David have gone to the livery stables to see if they can find out which way she left town at least, and Bernard is asking questions of a stranger at the hotel."

"My dear, you are all behaving like mother hens with a chick! Miss Muir is a sensible lady! She has probably gone to visit friends. Why should you assume she is *gone?*"

Isabella's face twisted with pain, and this time she did tug her hand free. "Because she left us all letters to say so. And it is my belief that *you* have something to with it!"

"*I?*" He stared at her in astonished disbelief. "Why would I tell her to go away? I assure you, I never did."

"Do you deny you spoke to her at the ball last night?"

"Of course not."

"About me?" she challenged, tilting her chin. "About Mrs. Maitland?"

Damn. Margaret had blabbed. That, he had not expected...

How *much* had she blabbed?

"Both your names were mentioned," he said innocently. "Miss Muir seemed angry, though I could not quite understand why. She appeared to misunderstand something about Mrs. Maitland. Perhaps someone had said something unkind or jealous. I do not know. My thoughts were all of you."

She looked uncertain. Which was an improvement. But if Margaret had really fled where he could not reach her, and Isabella's entire family was aware of her accusations against him... He could not risk them coming home and bolstering Isabella's hostility. Matters were urgent, and she really was his last throw of the dice.

"Miss Muir said something to make you doubt me," he said softly. "That breaks my heart. Come, walk with me in the fresh air, where we can talk uninterrupted. You will tell me your doubts and fears, and I will do my best to allay them before we return."

Still she hesitated, though at least he could see she was tempted.

"Isabella," he urged. "Last night, you promised to be my wife. Feelings do not alter so quickly. We must talk. We owe it to each other, to ourselves, and little Arthur, to straighten things between us, make them right if we can. And I have to believe we can."

She stared at him. Her eyes were reddened and a little puffy from weeping.

Come, he willed her. *Come.*

"Very well," she said, walking past him to the door. "I will fetch my bonnet."

He breathed again. But when Danny gave him his hat on the way out the door, the old soldier kept hold of it an instant too long, forcing Harlaw to look at him. There was warning in the man's eyes, an unmistakable threat. This really would be his last chance.

So he would have to make the most of it.

"SHE WENT SOUTH," Wickenden said, striding into the drawing room behind Gillie.

"We know," Bernard said. "And we know—we think we know—where she has gone. I believe she is safe."

Gillie sat down rather suddenly. "Thank God."

"There is more," Bernard said reluctantly. "About Margaret's past."

Some time later, after a prolonged silence, Gillie's gaze refocused on Felicia's face. "Your father and our aunt," she said vaguely.

"I'm so sorry," Felicia said. "It must seem to you he behaved quite without honor. But I believe he genuinely loved her and would have married her if she would have allowed it."

"Aunt Margaret can be unbelievably stubborn for someone so good-natured," Gillie allowed. She blinked several times. "And she *must* have loved him... She looked after his son from a distance all these years in the best way she could. It must have broken her heart to leave him. We always imagined she gave us all her love because she had no children of her own, but it was worse than that."

"Not worse," Lord Wickenden said. "She has a son. And if he is the decent man Bernard believes him to be, then he is part of the family. We can keep her secret." He looked questioningly at Felicia.

"Another half-brother is a drop in the ocean to the Vales," she said. "I'll talk to the others. In confidence, of course."

It seemed to be expected that Felicia stay for tea, and she was happy to do so. Gillie sat beside her while Bernard and Wickenden were distracted by an argument over some prize fight or other.

"So, is history repeating itself?" Gillie asked quietly.

"In what way?" Felicia asked.

"You and Bernard," Gillie said, causing Felicia's gaze to fly to hers.

"What makes you say so?" Felicia asked evasively.

"The fact that you do not answer. The fact that Bernard has never looked at anyone as he looks at you."

Felicia could think of nothing to say. She stirred her tea forcefully.

Gillie said, "When he was a boy, a stripling, if you like, he had a penchant for unattainable women. Like Kate Grant or heiresses whose family would never consider him."

"I think he also had a liking for perfectly attainable women, too," Felicia said wryly.

Gillie waved that aside. "Which are you?" she asked.

Felicia twisted her lips. "Neither. You may be easy, Lady Wickenden. I shall never marry again."

Gillie's eyes narrowed. "That does not make me easy. It makes me sad. But then, I was not married to Nicholas Maitland."

Felicia blinked. That was straight shooting, and she had no answer.

"Where is Isabella?" Bernard said from the other side of the table. He reached over and rang the bell.

A few minutes later, the old soldier, Danny, came in. "She went out with that Harlaw. I thought she'd be safe in the town, but she still isn't home."

Bernard groaned. "What is it about the women in this family? Why will they suddenly not sit still?"

Felicia's blood ran cold. "Because Harlaw is pulling the strings."

HARLAW WAS, IN fact, pulling tight the knots at Isabelle's wrists and ankles while she screamed at him in incomprehensible Spanish.

When he grasped her nape and took the handkerchief from his pocket, she must have finally realized the little time she had left to make him understand her point of view. "Wait, you fool," she uttered. "You cannot imagine such treatment will make me marry you!"

"Indirectly, yes," Harlaw said. "You will be too afraid—for your son's sake, if not your own—to defy me. For your soul's sake, too. A betrothal is a promise before God, you know, as binding as marriage. And you betrothed yourself to me not four and twenty hours ago."

"God would not hold me to such a promise in the face of

such treachery, such cruelty! My family will scour the country for me, make so much noise they will be bound to find me...!"

Harlaw smiled delightedly. "You are right. They will! And it will be so much worse for you. They won't find you until morning, and by then you and your son will be ruined. You will have no option but to marry me to salvage what is left of your reputation. The damage will still, of course, be considerable."

"The damage of being found like *this*?" she said incredulously, jerking her arms and legs. "*Who* will be ruined?"

"You, my dear. You will not be found bound and gagged..." He shoved his handkerchief into her outraged mouth and began to remove his cravat. Her eyes widened with gratifying terror and then closed. He tied the cravat around her mouth to keep the gag in place. "This is just to make sure you stay here and silent all night. I will come and rescue you in the morning, and then we will have Mr. Grant marry us. Unless you want to marry me now?"

She tried to speak, then shook her head violently.

He laughed. "No, but you will. It is the only option. Especially after all the noise your family will make to find you. The world will know you spent the night with me." He patted her shoulder mockingly. "Now do not fret, my love. I shan't really spend the night anywhere so disgusting. But you will, since you won't agree to marry me. By tomorrow, without food or warmth or company, you will have changed your mind."

He rose to his feet, and her eyes followed him, spitting hatred. She really was quite magnificent when angered. Perhaps the marriage would not be all bad after all. Even without Felicia to leaven the experience.

"I will leave you now to contemplate the folly—nay, the *sin*—of defying your husband. Goodnight, my sweet."

Chapter Fifteen

L EAVING THE MUIRS making discreet inquiries in the town—for Harlaw could have fled with Isabella to Scotland—Felicia went home to Black Hill. She tried desperately to think herself into Harlaw's head. He was not above forcing an elopement, but would he exert himself to that extent, knowing Bernard and Wickenden would pursue them?

If they had not eloped, what the devil had he done with her?

Felicia was sure he would not harm Isabella before he got his hands on her money, so he must have hidden her somewhere to make her agree to the marriage.

Now that Margaret had told her about his indecent proposal to Felicia, Isabella would surely have rejected him, or at least postponed the wedding. And Harlaw did not have the luxury of waiting. He would not have come so far in pursuit of a minor extortion if he were not desperate.

So where would he have hidden Isabella, at presumably short notice? Outside of town, surely, in case she was seen or heard. Some isolated cave along the shore, or a disused farm building? How many of those were there? How long would it take?

She found her family worried about Roderick.

"He has gone to Carlisle," Delilah said. "To obtain a special license—well, a common license—so that he can be married on Friday."

"Friday?" Felicia repeated, startled. "That's less than a week! Why does he not just call the banns like Julius? And Lucy?"

"There is something going on there we don't understand. You know Lady Helen, do you not?"

"Sweet-natured girl, I always thought. And Rod would never take advantage of someone so young and innocent!"

"But would she take advantage of *him*?" Delilah asked. "He has not been himself, Felicia."

"No," Felicia agreed. "We should keep an eye on him, but who are we to interfere with his marriage plans?"

For some reason, perhaps recalling her earlier interference in Julius's romance, Delilah flushed. But since Roderick was away, there was nothing they could do or say, either for or against his marriage. She left Delilah and went in search of Cornelius, whom she found unsaddling his horse in the stables.

"Don't," he growled, as soon as he saw her. "Leave Roderick to his own marriage. She's probably the best thing for him."

"Why do you think so?" Felicia said at once. "Do you know her well?"

"I know Roderick," Cornelius snapped. "And I have it on good authority that Lady Helen is devoted to him. Is that all?"

"No, grumpiest of brothers," Felicia said. "It is not. In fact, it's not at all what I came to ask you. You know the land around here and all around Blackhaven. Can you tell me where there are disused buildings? There would have to be lockable doors, probably boarded or shuttered windows, and they would be a long way from other dwellings, roads, and pathways."

Cornelius, saddle in hands, turned to stare at her. "Why the devil do you want to know that?"

"I'm trying to help a friend who is in trouble."

Cornelius strode past her and deposited the saddle. "Is it the sort of trouble that needs us all to help?"

Felicia's heart warmed. Even after a long day's work, he was willing to drop everything and help someone in need. She was lucky in brothers.

"Thanks, Cornel," she said. "It's just information, really, to pass on."

Cornelius rattled off several names and locations that she had never heard of. She remembered them all—her memory had always been faultless—and found each on a map while changing into her riding habit.

Half an hour after she had arrived home, she set off again, this time on horseback.

BERNARD HAD LOOKED in all the caves between Braithwaite Cove and the town when it came to him he could do worse than ask around the ne'er-do-wells in the tavern. And he could be more honest in his questions there, since the denizens were generally too close-mouthed to say anything unnecessary to their business. But Bernard knew these people, and many of them knew him.

The first person he saw was Smuggler Jack, leaning against the counter amidst the fug of tobacco smoke.

"Evening, young Bernie," said Jack, grinning.

"Evening, young Jack." It was an old joke between them since childhood, when Jack had taken Bernard and Gillie out in his boat and taught them to row and sail, and where to avoid the most treacherous rocks around this part of the coast. In return, they had saved his life and looked after his family when he had been shot during one of his more nefarious trips. "Buy you a pint?"

"Go on, then."

The ale was pretty grim, though the brandy, being smuggled, was excellent. Bernard had no actual intention of drinking it. But he ordered them amiably and, leaning against the sticky counter, peered into the fug for possible sources of information.

"Evening, Bernie," said a voice emerging from the darkness.

"Porgie. How's life?" He and Porgie had played together as boys, got up to all sorts of mischief before their lives had diverged into crime on Porgie's part and education and gaming on Bernard's. Even so, the bonds formed in childhood were hard to break.

"Rough," Porgie replied, grinning. "Don't know what the world's coming to. Tell you what, though, Bernie, very glad to see you. Lost anyone recently?"

For an instant, Porgie's eyes looked deadly serious.

"Tell me," Bernard said.

"Bloke comes in here—stranger, thinks he's a gent—offering work. Don't mind relieving the rich of a little wealth myself, but I didn't like his offer. Fredly and Bosk took it."

"Was the job abduction?" Bernard asked, his heart beating coldly against his ribs.

"Nope. Just guarding someone overnight. Easy enough, money for old rope. Only Fredly came back 'cause he didn't like it. They were guarding a lady, goes against the grain with him. So, soon as our gent's gone, Fredly peers through a crack to see if she's hurt. Turns out she's one of yours. Foreigner what married the captain."

"Where is she?" Bernard said steadily.

❧

IT WAS GROWING dark, and Felicia knew she should go home. This was the fourth of Cornelius's disused buildings, and it should probably be her last of the evening. She would ride home via Blackhaven, though, and tell Bernard or the Wickendens where she had been looking.

Of all Cornelius's suggestions, this one was the place closest to Blackhaven, a small barn next to a cottage with no roof, abandoned more than a decade ago—swallowed up, no doubt, by Braithwaite or another tenancy. Whatever paths had once led here, they were now overgrown, and with the woods so close, it had an air of doom and darkness. Part of her hoped Isabella was not here, because anyone would be frightened alone in such a place. And the more sensible part knew that anything was better than to be left here or anywhere else all night, a captive of Waller Harlaw...

Her gaze darted all around her, behind as well as all around the ruined cottage and the barn. There were no windows in the latter, but it did have a door, bolted on the outside, with a padlock holding it in place.

Her heart began to beat faster. Why would anyone padlock a disused barn?

Because something was kept in there that shouldn't be. Like smuggled brandy. Or Isabella Muir...

She urged her horse closer to the barn, and someone moved from the shadows on the far side of the building.

Her stomach lurched.

It was not Harlaw but a roughly dressed stranger who did not bother taking off his greasy-looking cap.

"Help you, missus?" he asked in a hoarse voice, his manner repelling.

"Possibly," Felicia said. "I am wondering why a barn with parts of its roof missing has such a carefully locked door."

"Doesn't do to wonder about things like that around here, missus."

"You think not? I believe I'll just have a glance through these little holes in the wood. Unless you're prepared to tell me...?"

"No reason to tell you anything."

Something moved inside the barn. She was sure of it. It could have been a mouse, or Isabella...or several large, angry smugglers protecting their goods.

Now she was so suspicious, should she not gallop posthaste to Blackhaven and tell Bernard? He could come with soldiers, or the watch at the very least... And by then, Isabella—if this was Isabella—could be gone, taken somewhere even worse.

She sighed and made to dismount, knowing she was taking a chance, and indeed, the scruffy individual grabbed at the bridle, causing her horse to snort with alarm and back up.

"Nothing for you here, missus," he growled. "Best go home."

Her ears had picked up another sound, someone else approaching from the woods. Her blood ran cold. Now she was in trouble. What to do? Bolt to Blackhaven or brazen it out?

"Don't be silly," she said with sudden inspiration. "Mr. Harlaw sent me."

"Don't care if the devil himself sent you. You've no business here. Ain't your land."

"How do you know?" she retorted. "It most certainly isn't yours."

The tiny hairs on her arms stood up as the footsteps came nearer. Her one consolation was that the man holding her bridle seemed uneasy too, shuffling his feet to try to peer between the barn and the ruined cottage.

She drew a quick breath. "Look, I'm clearly alone. What harm can I do you? All I want to know—to tell Mr. Harlaw, of course—is what you have hidden in there. And then we shall follow his instructions."

"*Shall* we?" he mocked, grinning fiercely to show a gap in his front teeth.

"Generally best to do what a lady says," said an entirely unexpected voice as Bernard strolled out from between the barn and the cottage.

Her captor spun around, reaching for a wicked-looking knife at his belt, and in alarm, Felicia kicked the horse forward. He snorted, nudging the stranger into a stumble.

"I'm sure she's in there, Bernard," Felicia blurted.

"Is she, Bosk?" Bernard asked the man who now stood still again, his hands loose by his sides.

"Course she is. Fredly tell you?"

"Porgie. Got the key?"

"Nah. His nibs didn't want anyone going in there. You could kick the wood in, though. Rotting to bits."

"Well, don't just stand there," Bernard said, striding up to the nearest rotted plank and kicking it hard. "All's well, Izzy! We're coming in."

Felicia quickly came to terms with the new state of affairs. Bernard clearly knew the villainous guard, who seemed happy enough to change sides for him. So she dismounted, and as soon as the men had kicked a hole large enough, she crouched in front of it. Bernard yanked Bosk back by the shoulder, and she wriggled through before they returned to kicking and wrenching the wood to make it larger.

"Mrs. Muir?" Felicia peered into the darkness.

A muffled noise reached her, a desperate shuffling along the floor. Terrified now as to poor Isabella's condition, Felicia stumbled blindly toward the noise and almost fell over the obstacle.

She dropped to her knees, feeling breath and trembling flesh. From sheer instinct, she wrapped her arms around the shivering creature. "You're safe now, you're safe. Bernard is here, and we'll take you home. There, there…"

A sudden blaze of lantern light swung over them, and she saw that Isabella was helplessly bound and gagged. While Bosk held the lantern, Bernard threw himself on the ground beside Felicia and Isabella. Muttering something beneath his breath, he pulled the gag from Isabella's mouth, took the proffered vicious knife from Bosk, and cut her bonds. All the time, Isabella lay shivering and weeping uncontrollably in Felicia's arms.

Bernard laid his cloak over her and sent Bosk to find Danny and the carriage and bring the blanket from inside.

By the time he returned, Isabella was speaking and weeping together, telling them how she had taken a walk with Harlaw to discuss the previous evening, and how they had left the town and he had all but dragged her in here and abandoned her bound and gagged.

"He said he would ruin me, oblige me to marry him because I would have spent the whole night away from home. Oh, Bernard, I hate him too much to marry him, even to live in the

THE GAMBLER'S LAST CHANCE

same house..."

"You never will," he said grimly.

"But my reputation, Arthur—"

"My dear, you are a widow," Felicia said. "Everyone would have turned a blind eye to a night spent away from home with your intended husband. Your reputation is secure enough— though since you won't be marrying him now, I propose we make it doubly safe by calling in on the Braithwaite ladies on the way home, thus proving to the world you are with us."

"Oh, I could not face them in such a state!"

"They'll just exchange a few words through the carriage window," Bernard said comfortably. "They will be happy to oblige us."

Everyone, it seemed to Felicia, from the dowager countess to the villainous Bosk, seemed happy to oblige him.

"Sorry, Bernie," Bosk said as Felicia wrapped the blanket around the still-trembling victim. "Needed the money and didn't know who she was. Wouldn't have let anyone hurt her."

Felicia glared at him, and he looked unexpectedly alarmed.

"Bosk's idea of hurt and yours are a little different," Bernard said. "Experience..." He put his pocket flask into Isabella's hands, and she took a sizable gulp without choking. "Good girl. Can you walk as far as the carriage? It's just a hundred yards or so away, on the forest path."

"You brought a carriage?" Felicia stared at him, registering the fact fully for the first time. "You knew you would find her here?"

"I did. So long as he hadn't moved her. How did *you* find this place?"

"Cornelius. He rode every inch of the country as soon as he arrived in Blackhaven. He prefers to understand all the land round about, and he is very thorough. This is the fourth place I looked."

"Thank you," he said quietly, rising and drawing Isabella slowly to her feet. "Can you walk, Izzy?"

She took a couple of uncertain steps between Felicia and Bernard, and nodded.

"Then let us go and make a few plans. Bosk, can you take Mrs. Maitland's horse to the livery stable? I'll bring it over to Black Hill tomorrow."

Bosk sighed. "Aye, of course. I'm not going to get paid for this either, am I?"

"Only by me," Bernard said, delving into his pocket. "I've only a guinea with me, but—"

"But I think we should get Harlaw to pay," Felicia interrupted. "And in more than coin. Bosk, how would you feel about putting up your hire price?"

Both men frowned at her. Isabella looked confused.

Then Bosk grinned. "What, say I've moved her and doubled my price and will release her when he pays?"

"Multiply it by ten," Bernard advised, catching on. "He'll try to avoid paying until he wins it in the card party."

"Only he won't," Felicia said happily.

"No, he won't," Bernard agreed. "And then we'll pay you what he owes out of the winnings."

Bosk grinned, looking thoroughly menacing in the lantern light. "Give us the guinea, then. I'm in."

THE RETURN TO Blackhaven went pretty much as they had planned. The Muirs' man, Danny, was driving the carriage. Bernard sat opposite the two women, and Isabella clung to Felicia's hand for the whole journey. In fact, when they clattered into the courtyard of Braithwaite Castle, her fingers gripped convulsively, especially when Bernard got out, saying curtly he wouldn't be long.

"What is it you fear?" Felicia asked urgently. "If there was even a chance of insult, Bernard would never have brought you here."

"I know," she whispered. "I am being foolish. Again. How could I have believed in such a man? Am I so desperate to have another husband?"

"He is very plausible. I know."

Isabella gazed at her. "He courted you, too?"

"No, he was too busy cheating my husband to risk stepping on his toes, but for months—years, even—I believed he was my friend, looking out for my husband and keeping him as safe as he could manage. He wasn't. He was encouraging Nick's worst excesses and robbing us blind."

"Then you hate him as much as I do," Isabella said.

Felicia shook her head. "No. It was a different kind of betrayal. And I never had your shock. But we will make him sorry for all of it."

"I am sorry," Isabella whispered, wiping her face again. "I was rude to you."

Felicia squeezed her hand. "No, you were not." And then Bernard emerged from the front door, surrounded by a bevy of beautiful noblewomen. Lord Braithwaite was there with his wife and his sisters Lady Torridon, Lady Tamar, and Mrs. Hanson. And then, behind them, Lord Tamar escorted old Lady Braithwaite herself.

Isabella shrank back against the squabs, but she needn't have.

"Bernard says you cannot stop," young Lady Braithwaite said gaily, "so we have come to wave you off instead! I'm glad you've had such a pleasant evening, Mrs. Muir, Mrs. Maitland. Come for tea on Tuesday."

"We're *at home* again then," Lady Tamar said. "But ices on Monday sounds much more fun."

"Bring Gillie," said Lady Torridon.

"How pleasant to see you both," the dowager said grandly. "Don't keep the ladies waiting, Bernard."

Lord Tamar opened the door, and Bernard climbed in. As those outside stood back, waving, Felicia raised her and Isabella's joined hands, and Isabella roused herself to wave.

"Now there will be no speculation, let alone scandal," Bernard said firmly.

Ten minutes later, Bernard let down the steps, and the front door of his house opened to reveal Gillie and Wickenden.

"Wait for me," Bernard threw at Felicia. "I'll only be a moment."

"There is no need," she began, but he was already down and handing his stepmother out of the carriage. He swept her inside the house, where she collapsed in Gillie's arms. Bernard spoke urgently to Wickenden while the women vanished from view, and then Bernard leapt back into the street and sprang into the carriage.

The horses moved forward as soon as he closed the door.

"I'm grateful for the loan of the carriage," Felicia said, "but there is really no need to accompany me."

"I want to," Bernard said. "I have hardly spoken to you, and yet you have spent all day about my family's business."

Felicia smiled. "So has everyone else. I have the impression the Muirs are as central to Blackhaven in their way as the Braithwaites are."

"And the Vales will be."

"Perhaps, since we are to be connected to the Braithwaites by marriage."

His lips twisted. The carriage lights played over the delicate angles and planes of his face as the horses turned onto the coast road. "But not to the Muirs."

"Or to anyone else through me," she said steadily.

"And yet you went for mere friendship's sake to find and save Isabella, someone you barely know and cannot have liked much after her behavior this morning."

"I know you. My friend and ally."

"And lover."

Heat simmered beneath her skin. "No longer, apparently."

"Does that mean you miss me?"

She gave an unhappy smile. "Bernard, I even missed Nick when he died. I might not understand love and marriage, but I know you can't turn feelings on and off like a tap. Something remains of the love, whether you want it to or not. In his own way, Nick loved me. It doesn't mean I could ever have been happy married to him."

"No, but you might be happy married to me."

"I might not be," she countered. "*You* might not be. You barely know me, Bernard."

"I know enough."

"That's what I told myself about Nick."

He sat back. "So it all comes back again to the dead husband. When I first met you, I imagined I would be competing against him, but I never suspected it would be against his faults."

"Mock me as much as you wish. It changes nothing."

He moved abruptly, landing beside her on the bench, threading his fingers through hers on her lap. "I am not mocking you. I am trying desperately to understand why you will not let us be happy."

She did not mean to respond, but her fingers clung to his. "We were happy, were we not? In the summer house."

"I was deliriously happy in the summer house. And at the hotel. I would like to be similarly happy everywhere, in my own bed, in yours. I want to be beside you at family parties and Sunday luncheon, to walk with you as we did on the beach, to be alone with you, whenever we choose. I want to give you children—"

"I am barren."

He blinked. "According to whom?"

"According to evidence. I was married for almost five years, and I never once conceived."

He shrugged it off. "What will be, will be. Even if it ever came to choosing between you or children, I would still choose you."

"You will change your mind when you are four and thirty

179

rather than four and twenty."

"You are very certain on my behalf. Do you think me a child who doesn't know my own mind?"

"I never thought of you as a child at all," she said impatiently. "You must know that much. There are a bare twelve months between us. It does not change what I think, what I feel." She dragged his hand suddenly to her cheek. "I care for you, Bernard. But I will never marry you."

They sat unspeaking for some time, the carriage bumping over pits in the road and sloshing through mud, while his fingertips stroked her cheek, her lips, and she still cradled his hand.

Eventually the horses turned off into the Black Hill drive.

She met his gaze. "There is still the summer house."

She counted her heartbeats through the silence until the carriage came to a halt at the front door.

Bernard carried her hand to his lips. "But not for us," he said sadly.

And then he released her, opened the door, and jumped down to hand her out. She knew he watched her walking up to the front door, but she did not glance back.

Chapter Sixteen

Harlaw was almost afraid to go to church the following day. He did not know who, or what accusations, he would face. His recent interview with the tavern villain at the empty barn still rang over and over in his mind.

"Don't worry, the woman is perfectly safe. But my price has gone up, now I know who she is."

"Then you'll have to wait for your money. And I don't want my goods damaged."

And now he had to pretend nothing was wrong, in case the bastard had freed the girl and she had told everyone exactly who abducted her.

His flesh crawled as he walked into the church alone. He smiled and bowed to acquaintances, trying not to search too avidly for the Muirs. He found Bernard at first, beside his sister and Wickenden. No Margaret. And, thank God, no Isabella.

No one was glaring at him or summoning the magistrate.

The situation was still salvageable, though the Muirs and Wickenden were not helping. They did not look remotely like a family who had lost two members in as many days, one of them quite without warning. Why were they not distraught?

Bernard glanced around and met his gaze. His eyes narrowed. His nostrils flared. But he nodded curtly, as though not quite sure he looked at an enemy.

Oh, you do, you do? Harlaw thought savagely. *And come Saturday night, I will fleece you of everything else you own. Including Felicia. And Isabella's money.*

Less what he would have to give the tavern villain, damn him.

Emboldened, he approached Lady Wickenden in the churchyard, where she was gossiping with the Earl of Braithwaite's sisters, the Countess of Torridon and the Marchioness of Tamar. It was interesting that the Braithwaite ladies seemed to regard her as an old friend rather than an upstart who had married above herself—which she undoubtedly had. However, Harlaw had no horse in that particular race.

"Ladies," he said, bowing. "You looked almost lonely in church, Lady Wickenden. Has Mrs. Muir perhaps gone to join your aunt?"

"Oh no," Lady Wickenden said in apparent surprise. "She is resting today. The ball and then yesterday's festivities have quite worn her out."

"Yesterday's festivities," Harlaw repeated, trying not to look as flummoxed as he felt. "She did not mention any such party when I saw her yesterday afternoon. But then, I daresay you have seen her since."

"We certainly have," said Lady Tamar. "Though I did think she looked a trifle fatigued. Did you not, Frances?"

Lady Torridon shrugged elegantly. "A little, perhaps. No more than the rest of us, I am sure."

"Well, perhaps I shall call upon Mrs. Muir this afternoon," Harlaw said, almost afraid of the response.

"Oh no," Lady Wickenden objected at once, calming his anxieties. "We will none of us be receiving until Isabella is returned…to good health."

Harlaw pushed back, partly to keep to his role, but mostly to see how far he could. "I know such a prohibition cannot be meant to include me as her betrothed—"

"On the contrary, Mr. Harlaw," Lady Wickenden said shortly,

"we will not have her excited or upset."

"By *me*, Lady Wickenden?"

"By anyone. Good day, Mr. Harlaw. Frances, Serena." She stalked off to rejoin her husband, leaving Harlaw with somewhat mixed feelings. It seemed clear that Isabella was not at home, whatever her stepdaughter said. But also that Lady Wickenden knew something he would probably rather she did not.

Encountering Bernard by the gate, he said, "I am sorry to hear of dear Isabella's fatigue."

"Are you?" Bernard said shortly. It was barely even a question, and with the utterance, he walked away quite rudely.

They suspected *he* was involved with Isabella's disappearance! Well, all to the good. They were keeping it quiet, had even induced the local nobility to back up the lie of her presence. But surely it all served Harlaw's purpose. Isabella would be delighted to marry him by Saturday night.

BERNARD WAS NOT normally a violent man by nature, but he could not trust himself not to hit Harlaw full in his smug face. Mostly for what he had done to Isabella—who had only agreed to be left alone because she was with the children and Gillie's nursemaid, and had Danny sitting at the top of the stairs. But also for showing Felicia so little respect.

And then he felt guilty for seducing Felicia himself. Was he truly any better than Harlaw? Did all men and their lusts not conspire to make her believe she was worthless, that her only happiness was in avoiding marriage, even with a man who worshiped her, who would die for her?

"Damn it, Muir, you're a hard man to track down." Bernard stopped, blinking in some surprise before the young officer who had accosted him. Carey, he recalled with an effort. Lieutenant Carey, who had joined the 44th after Waterloo and was not as well known to him as most of the other officers. "Couldn't get you at home at all yesterday."

"No, I was out most of the day. What can I do for you?"

"Can we talk somewhere more private?"

"No," said Bernard, who had no intention of leaving his sister unguarded in the presence of Harlaw, even under Wickenden's nose. "Waiting for my sister. Can't be that private, can it?"

Carey leaned closer. "It's to do with Winslow. He called you out."

Bernard struck his forehead. "Damn, I forgot! So he did."

Carey stared at him, as though torn between admiration and annoyance. "You *forgot*? Seriously?"

"Got a lot going on at the moment," Bernard said apologetically. "I'm happy to accept his apology, though."

Carey frowned, drawing himself up to his full, stiff height. "There is no apology, Muir. You insulted his sister, broke your promise. I can't understand why you would do that."

"Neither can I," Bernard said. "In fact, I didn't. And if the idiot isn't apologizing, why are you even speaking to me? If you're his second, you should be talking to Lord Wickenden."

"I know," Carey said, lapsing back into confidential conversation. "Thing is, I'm not acquainted with Wickenden. Could you possibly introduce us?"

Bernard's lips twitched. It struck him that Felicia would laugh herself silly at this farce. Except, of course, that he couldn't tell her anything about it. "You want me to introduce you, my enemy's second, to my own second, so that Geoffrey and I can attempt to blow each other's brains out like proper gentlemen?"

"Put like that, it does sound wrong. But yes, in a nutshell, old fellow."

Bernard looked over the railing and, after a moment's staring, managed to catch Wickenden's eye. He jerked his head in a summoning kind of way, and a moment later, Wickenden strolled through the gate.

"Bernard," he said. "You do like to live dangerously, do you not? I don't recall giving you permission to use me as a lackey."

"Don't imagine you ever would," Bernard said, unimpressed, though Carey looked distinctly alarmed. Wickenden had once had quite the reputation as a duelist. "This is Lieutenant Carey, who has been seconded to help Geoffrey Winslow shoot me. Carey, Lord Wickenden—who, I hope, will do his best to make you all see sense. I'm going to take Gillie home."

BERNARD WAS WASHING before Sunday dinner when a brief knock at his door heralded the arrival of Wickenden.

Bernard finished drying his face on a towel and reached for his coat.

Wickenden swung a chair into his desired position and sat astride it, leaning his arms along its back. "Carey has bought into everything Geoffrey told him."

"That's probably because Geoffrey believes it," Bernard said.

"Then what on earth has got into Genevra? Have you really done or said nothing from which she could have misunderstood an offer of marriage?"

"Absolutely nothing. She was jealous of Felicia Maitland at the garden party, as I told you, but then she seemed to agree she had no right to such jealousy. Now she's got Geoffrey involved, and I've no idea why. I'm not exactly an ambitious young girl's catch of the year."

"It depends what her ambitions are, and I'm not sure the Winslow children's were ever the same as their mama's. As for you, Bernard, trust me, you have your moments."

Bernard regarded him with some amusement. "I do?"

"Doesn't Felicia Maitland think so?"

Bernard's smile faded. "Sore point, David. No."

"Bollocks," David said. "She rode halfway round the county yesterday just to find Isabella for you."

"She won't marry me." As soon as the words were out, he felt like a child who couldn't have the toy or the cake he wanted, and hastily tried to wave it away. "Well, who would? Apart from Genevra, of course. Perhaps I could solve all this by agreeing to marry her and then watching her run?"

"You think she would?"

"She'd be a fool not to."

"But Felicia Maitland *should* marry you? I think you're more concerned with your own feelings than with those of either lady."

Bernard closed his mouth. "Probably. I still know I'd make Genevra miserable in a month—or less—because I don't love her."

"And Felicia?"

Bernard sighed. "Oh, I love Felicia. But if she loves me, the feeling is so buried under all the mire Nick Maitland heaped upon her that I doubt she could even recognize the feeling if it waved at her."

"Love waving from under the mire. An unlikely image, but one that might, unfortunately, stay with me. As for the duel mess, you may have to face each other over twenty paces. Unless you are prepared to apologize for unintentionally misleading Genevra. He might accept that."

"But I didn't do it, damn it. This has *all* come from Genevra."

"Then Tuesday at dawn."

"Not this Tuesday. There's the charity card party on Saturday evening, and I have to be there. Can't risk getting shot or arrested before then. Let's make it Saturday night after the card party. Which will also be after Lady Helen's wedding."

Wickenden's eyes began to dance. "Yes, we don't want it interfering with your social engagements. You are very cool about the whole thing, aren't you?"

"No," Bernard said. "To be honest, it's damned irritating, and I could do without it."

"I'll speak to Carey again tomorrow. Point out the disad-vantages for two old friends risking murdering each other over a misunderstanding. With luck, Geoffrey will come around. Especially if you have the chance of reconciling at the wedding. But Bernard?"

Bernard, halfway to the door, glanced back at Wickenden. He was deadly serious again.

"It doesn't make you feel better. Shooting your friends."

"I have no intention of shooting him," Bernard said ruefully. "Whatever happens."

⚜

THE VALES WERE joined for dinner by both Antonia Macy, soon to be Julius's bride, and Lord Eddleston, looking pale and romantic with his arm in a sling following the shooting at the castle. He had removed from the castle only that morning and refused to retire to bed. Touchingly, Lucy watched him like a hawk for signs of illness or exhaustion, but was induced to laugh on several occasions.

Felicia, despite her doubts about any marriage, felt theirs was hopeful. As was Julius's, but then, it was different for men. Their word was always law in a marriage.

Still, for the first time, odd thoughts and visions crept into her mind. Sharing this table with Bernard as her acknowledged suitor. Gazing at him as Antonia gazed at Julius. Neither Lucy's nor Julius's marriage would be like hers. Because neither Eddleston nor Julius were remotely like Nick.

Neither was Bernard.

I am not being fair...

But I have to protect myself. Once I am married, there is no protection.

Wasn't there? Julius would not stand by and allow any abuse of Lucy. None of them would. That they had not been there for Felicia in her troubles was a mixture of circumstances and her own secrecy. Julius and Roderick had been out of the country, as had Delilah with their father for some of the time. Cornelius had

been stewarding an estate in Yorkshire. She had no doubt that if
Eddleston behaved badly, they would all take action on Lucy's
behalf, as they would have on Felicia's—if they had known.
Felicia had begun to know Eddleston already, and she could not
imagine him ever behaving remotely like Nick.

Bernard... Bernard was simply Bernard. A sweet and passionate lover and good, loyal friend. But he was at heart a player, a
gambler, as Nick had been. And she must never forget it.

"I discovered something recently that I should probably tell
you all," she said during the soup course."

"Roderick isn't here," Lawrence pointed out.

"Then we can tell him when he comes home. It is just that
we seem to have yet another half-brother."

Julius threw down his spoon. "Oh, for the love of..."

"No, wait, I'm not sure we should blame Papa or anyone
else," Felicia said. "And I rather like the new brother."

"Who the devil is he?" Julius demanded. "And why did we
not know about him before? That, at least, is not like Sir George!"

"He is Scottish. Or, at least, he was brought up in Scotland by
a wealthy family who adopted him as their own. His name is Alan
Bryant."

"And his mother?" Delilah asked.

Felicia hesitated. "Confidentially."

"Of course," said Eddleston, and Antonia nodded as though it
went without saying.

"Miss Margaret Muir," Felicia said.

They all stared at her.

"Seriously?" Lucy said. "She is so...*spinstery.*"

"Did you get this from Bernard Muir?" Cornelius asked abruptly.

For no reason, Felicia blushed. "No. I got it from letters Miss
Muir wrote to Papa, and the fact that once Papa left Blackhaven
the last time, he never went back. And the fact that Miss Muir
spent a long holiday in Scotland around the same time, and now
goes back every year for several weeks to see her child. Alan

knows who his mother is, but he had no idea that his father was Sir George Vale. And actually, I think Margaret might have been Papa's one true love. Except she did not trust him."

Something twisted inside her. *Is that not what I am doing to Bernard? Not trusting him, sacrificing a future because of the past?* She thrust the thought aside.

"She was *different* for him," she said. "An old friend who became much more."

Julius pushed his soup plate aside. "And where is this brother now?"

"With his mother, Miss Muir. I hope. I think Waller Harlaw found out about her child and tried to hold it over her head, as it were."

They all stared at her.

"Your Nick had some dashed odd friends," Aubrey remarked.

"Harlaw was never his friend. He cheated Nick blind and therefore robbed me, too. And you, who bailed me out. I propose to make him pay. For that, for trying to blackmail Miss Muir, who is a sweet lady, and for what he did to Isabella."

"What did he do to Isabella?" Cornelius asked. Clearly, he had already connected that to her strange questions yesterday.

Felicia told them, then listened to the stunned silence.

Inevitably, the twins spoke first.

"Can we help?" Leona asked.

ON WEDNESDAY MORNING, Wickenden departed to meet Carey, hopeful that time—or Genevra's good nature—would have cooled Geoffrey Winslow's angry desire for blood. Bernard, delighted by an invitation from Felicia to take tea at Black Hill House that afternoon, had decided things were at last moving in his favor.

Until, on the doorstep as he was about to leave the Haven, he encountered Wickenden scowling.

"He won't accept so limited an apology," Wickenden reported. "Now nothing less than a full engagement will satisfy him. Even Carey thinks it's insane, like someone is whispering poison into his ear."

Bernard paused. "Harlaw doesn't call there, does he?"

"Not to my knowledge, but they're bound to meet in the town occasionally."

"Hmm. Well, if Geoffrey is being an ass… We have the right to choose the time and place. So, as discussed, let's make it midnight, Saturday night-Sunday morning, after Lady Helen's wedding and the card party. And refuse to budge. I want it all over with, David."

Tea at Black Hill was not quite the solution Bernard had hoped for. Nearly all of Felicia's family were present, and they were alternately a formidable and entertaining lot. It seemed they were all happy to help with the fall of Waller Harlaw. And while he and Felicia played cards, they discussed strategies.

He did not get the chance to see her alone. Even as he took his leave, it was Sir Julius who conducted him to the front door.

"Funnily enough," Sir Julius said, "apart from a little vengeance, I don't believe it was ever explained to me what your interest in this matter is."

"Apart from a little vengeance," Bernard said, accepting his hat from the manservant, "I have none. Except friendship."

"And this friendship will ensure you give all your winnings on Saturday to your… er…friend?"

"Or to the charities if she won't take it," Bernard said steadily. Sir Julius had quite an alarming one-eyed stare, and he knew how to use it, but Bernard would not back down, not unless or until he failed Felicia.

"Felicia is kind, by nature," Sir Julius said. "I won't sit by and see her taken advantage of again."

"Good," Bernard said, clapping his hat on his head. "Good afternoon, Sir Julius."

Chapter Seventeen

I T HAD BEEN a long week for Harlaw. His rebellious minion, Bosk, when traced to the tavern, would tell him nothing about Isabella's whereabouts or even her condition.

"How do I know you haven't murdered her?" Harlaw demanded. What would happen to her money then? Presumably it would go to her son and be managed by the bloody annoying Bernard Muir.

"You don't," Bosk said. "But you will, just as soon as you cough up the blunt. Now bugger off. Unless you *want* to be fixed with me in people's rememberings?"

Harlaw departed. He did not care for his brush with the underworld, where people, it seemed, could "out-devious" him without breaking stride. In fact, he looked forward rather desperately to never having to deal with such creatures again. It had been a mistake to draw them into the matter at all. But he had needed someone to make sure Isabella was not found that first night.

Waste of time and effort, he thought bitterly.

Apart from anything else, Isabella's disappearance had not achieved its purpose. No one was talking about it, even though it had gone far beyond the single night he had intended. He had played on her fears for her reputations, as a high stickler, a mother, and a foreigner, while knowing full well no one would really care if she anticipated her vows with her betrothed. But as her absence stretched into days, he could not help wondering why it caused no comment at all.

He saw the Wickendens, the Muirs, and the nursemaids, out and about with Isabella's son, but they stuck to the same story, that Isabella was suffering from exhaustion and was not receiving.

In his role as devoted husband-to-be, Harlaw called twice at the Muirs' residence, only to be denied access to any of the family, who were never "at home" when he called. He looked forward to dismissing all the obstructive servants, especially the old soldier who seemed to imagine he ruled the roost.

Encountered elsewhere, the family were civil but firm. Isabella was doing better but not quite ready to receive. Less understandably, he saw no signs of anxiety or worry, and yet he could have sworn they were fond of Isabella, who thought the world of her stepchildren. No wonder Bernard played such a good game of macao, with such a straight, amiable expression.

At least the matter of the duel appeared to progress in the manner he had hoped. Around male gatherings he heard the odd whisper, and when local opinion tended toward a reconciliation between Bernard and young Winslow, Harlaw sought Genevra out and suggested a more lurid tale of violent seduction. By the following evening, the duel was back on.

Of course, there were no guarantees that Bernard Muir would die at the hands of the Winslow boy. Muir might kill his opponent, or they might both muddle through, but Felicia did not approve of duels, and he had hopes this one would, at the very least, wean her from Muir's charms and give her a better appreciation of Harlaw's. So, although he had begun the scheme mainly from spite when Felicia had rejected him, he had quickly come to the conclusion that it was one of his better ideas.

Meanwhile, his hopes rested in the charitable card party at the King's Head, where he planned to win Felicia and enough readies to liberate and marry Isabella—after which, the world would be at his feet.

Accordingly, he strolled up to the inn on Saturday night, hoping Felicia would be there. It was by no means certain that any of the Vales would be present, since Major Vale had got married the day before—and to one of the Earl of Braithwaite's sisters, no less. But Felicia did seem to love cards, now that she was out from under the late Maitland's thumb, and he *had* beaten her at the castle ball. Here, with the stakes higher, anything was possible. A true gambler would stake even her virtue...

The inn was already busy. A couple of almost identical urchins sitting on the yard wall bolted inside as he approached. Perhaps they hoped to earn a penny by taking his hat. Or picking his pocket.

But it was one of the inn's maidservants who took his hat and his entry fee at the door, and directed him straight on into the inn's common coffee room.

This normally rustic, unimpressive chamber had been turned into a busy gaming salon for the evening. In fact, had it not been for the ladies' silk gowns and sparkling jewelry, he would have called it a gaming *hell*, with too many tables squashed into the available space and the volume of noise stupendous.

Much to Harlaw's amusement, the event was organized by the local vicar and his wife. Mind you, since Grant's wife was Wicked Kate of glorious memory, it perhaps was not so surprising! Blackhaven really was a curious place.

Mrs. Grant welcomed him as though to a Society ball, and explained the rules of the evening to him.

"Play according to your nature and your purse," she said gaily. "You will find tables that cater to all games and all stakes. Scores will be kept of each player's winnings, and each player will pay a tenth of those winnings to the hospital, either at the end of the evening—midnight—or whenever you choose to leave. What would you care to play first, sir?"

"I believe I shall stroll around and look before I decide," he replied, bowing again before he moved on.

He had just glimpsed the imposing, one-eyed figure of Sir

Julius Vale, standing behind his betrothed, Mrs. Macy as she played. So some of the Vales at least were here… His heart skipped a beat as he caught sight of Felicia playing loo with several other ladies, who included the doctor's wife, Lady Launceton, and, more surprisingly, Lady Helen Conway, who had just married Major Vale. And yes, he was present, too, playing faro for pennies with a few military types.

It seemed the whole town had turned out for the event. Amazing what attaching the word "charity" to an evening of vice could do.

Harlaw glanced over as some other late arrivals entered, cheerfully paying their door money to the maid before strolling into the main area. Lord and Lady Wickenden had arrived, and with them…

Blood sang in Harlaw's ears. He had to grasp the back of some stranger's chair for support. Behind the Wickendens came Bernard Muir, and on his arm, the upright and really quite dramatically beautiful Isabella.

Bosk had let her go early!

Or had she escaped?

Worse, had someone else found her and rescued her? And more to the point, what the devil had she told her family?

For several frozen moments, he had no idea what to do.

If she had seen him, she gave no sign of it, but he quickly realized that he must keep up his role of devoted betrothed. If the worst happened and she blabbed, he would just have to portray her as maddened by her experience and remain devoted in the face of all insults. One way or another, he would still marry the woman. He no longer had any other options.

Summoning a delighted smile, he squeezed between the tables and strode toward her. "My dear, how wonderful to see you out and about once more! And looking so well!"

He held out his hand as he spoke, compelling the courtesy she would never ignore.

She did not so much as glance at his hand. Instead, she looked directly into his eyes for an instant. She seemed to see straight through him.

"Oh, there is Lady Launceton," she said, smiling at a point just beyond his shoulder. "Bernard, let us go to her table."

She swept off on Muir's arm as the Wickendens walked in the opposite direction, leaving Harlaw standing alone, the heat burning up his face.

"Cut direct, old boy," Aubrey Vale murmured on his way past. "You must have some *serious* groveling ahead of you."

✆

"MAGNIFICENT," FELICIA MURMURED to Isabella as the latter sat down beside her. "That should keep him nicely on edge. As should you and I sitting so close together." She gave Isabella a smile of quite unnecessary brilliance, and Isabella, playing her part, managed a laugh that was not too shaky at all.

Bernard hovered behind them, just in case Harlaw tried to approach. But the twins were keeping a discreet eye on him, and there was Wickenden and all of Felicia's brothers to stop him before he could get anywhere near Isabella. Felicia admired her courage in coming at all, so shaken had she been by her experience.

Felicia rose the winner and paid her "tithe" to Mr. Grant. By now, Bernard was playing loo with Harlaw and others and was clearly winning. Harlaw looked very disgruntled, and as the game broke up, he glowered at Bernard paying his "tithe."

"A new pack of cards here, I think," Harlaw said loudly. He rose to his feet. "Have you come to bring me luck, Mrs. Maitland?"

"Perhaps to one of us," Felicia said, smiling at the departing players and taking one of the vacant seats.

Bernard sat back down too, and Mrs. Trent, the innkeeper's wife, looking harassed, dropped a new pack of cards on the table.

Harlaw immediately began to swipe up the old ones.

"I'll get rid of these while I stretch my legs. "May I fetch you something, Felicia?"

Her name on his lips offended her. She had to force herself not to scold him in public for the liberty she had certainly never granted him.

"No, thank you," she said icily. And as he bowed and strolled away, idly shuffling the rejected cards as he went, she met Bernard's gaze.

He leaned across the table. "Spades again?" he murmured, for this was very probably when extra cards would find their way up his sleeves and into his pocket. All the packs of cards this evening were supplied by the inn, and had the same backing.

"We are not ready to expose him," she murmured back. "We haven't won enough."

"Then it might have to be piquet, where the face cards will be vital to him."

Felicia grimaced. "He could have an entire pack in the folds of his cravat for all I know."

Bernard smiled and sat back. Over his shoulder, she saw Mr. Winslow, the squire, with his daughter Genevra. Genevra was staring at her with bitterness. And then, realizing she was observed, she smiled brightly with a curious…smugness.

As Genevra walked on, her head high, Felicia felt inexplicably uneasy. *What are you about?*

But she had no time to worry about that tonight. Harlaw was the truly dangerous enemy, and he had to be brought down for everyone's sake, not just hers or even Bernard's.

Harlaw reappeared with a bottle and fresh glasses for everyone at the table. It was an excuse to have left, for Trent had staff for such tasks. She avoided looking at Bernard.

Early in the game, she realized that Harlaw had indeed swapped cards. She had not seen it happen, but she knew that queen of spades should not have been in the game. She met Bernard's gaze at last and nodded imperceptibly. He betrayed no reaction, and she thought he already knew. Perhaps he had seen the maneuver, although Harlaw had been too quick for her eyes.

She played on, avoiding spades when she could, and winning so steadily that a frown of incomprehension began to form on Harlaw's brow.

Bernard suggested increasing the stakes, and everyone agreed. Still, Felicia won. A bead of sweat trickled down Harlaw's forehead. His frown deepened. Two of the players left and were replaced, and still she won.

At last, Harlaw could contain himself no longer.

"This is impossible!" he burst out.

"The lady has all the luck," Colonel Doverton agreed, smiling as he rose from the table and bowed. "I must cut my losses and try elsewhere."

"You should, for *no one* wins all the time," Harlaw said waspishly.

There was an uncomfortable silence, for his meaning was quite plain. Felicia held his accusing stare with as much haughty contempt as she could muster.

"I daresay you don't mean that as it sounds," Colonel Doverton said soothingly.

"It isn't natural," Harlaw said, realizing belatedly that he had a crowd of watchers who disapproved of his bad sportsmanship.

"It is for Felicia," Julius said unexpectedly. "Beats us all to flinders regularly. My father used to trot her out at embassy parties when she was a mere child in order to cut the overconfident down to size. Don't take it to heart, Harlaw—you are in excellent company, including princes and ministers and men of supposed genius."

Felicia hadn't even known that Julius was aware of these things. But there was more than amusement in his voice—there was pride. Warmth seeped through her. She was not useless. No one had ever thought of her as a mere drain on the family resources. Like the others, she had known her bad luck, that was all. And now, she was putting it right, along with everything else.

"It's mathematics," she explained.

Several men laughed, including Harlaw, for what did women know of mathematics?

But, sensing his audience, Harlaw subsided and bowed graciously. "Then give me a chance of revenge, Mrs. Maitland? A little piquet, perhaps?"

Two players, less scrutiny. And he had beaten her the last time because she let him. Bernard's gaze went quickly to hers. But then, before she could reply, a late arrival caused a stir by the door. The inn maid hurried toward the newcomers, a young man with a middle-aged lady on his arm.

Bernard sprang to his feet. "Aunt Margaret!"

Gillie and Isabella almost ran from the other side of the room to welcome Margaret home. Alan Bryant stood to one side until Bernard, releasing Margaret from his bearhug, turned and thrust out his hand to him.

Surprise seemed to paralyze Bryant for a moment. Then he smiled and grasped Bernard's hand. Felicia swallowed a lump of emotion.

"Piquet?" Harlaw repeated in her ear, far too close for comfort.

"Why not?" she said lightly, and strolled through the tables to a vacant table. "How much would you like to wager per point?"

≪≫

BERNARD DID NOT know if it was a good thing or not that Margaret had come home exactly when she did, but he was so relieved to see her, and looking so well in her own vague style, that he didn't even think before he strode up and hugged her.

"Alan says you know," she whispered.

Bernard swept her into the empty private parlor. Gillie and Isabella followed, and Alan stood hesitantly by the door as though unsure of his welcome.

"About him?" Bernard said, yanking Alan inside and closing the door. "Felicia worked it out, and Alan confirmed it. You have no need to hide from us. We would always stand by you."

Margaret blinked rapidly. "Gillie is a baroness, with all David's family to consider, to say nothing of her own children... Isabella—well, you are so strait-laced, my dear! Even card parties offended you when you first came to us!"

Isabella flushed. "Let us say I have learned a little more understanding and forgiveness since I came to Blackhaven."

"There is no shame here, Aunt Margaret," Gillie said firmly. "We will not allow it."

Bernard met Alan's gaze. "Did you persuade her to come back?"

Margaret did not give him time to answer. "Alan said you were up to something, had some plan to bring Harlaw down. I could not leave you to do it without me."

"He might hurl some vile accusations around. We all know even false gossip can stick. Alan should be aware of that and warn his family if necessary." Bernard gave a quick smile. "His other family."

Alan's eyes widened. Well, Margaret had kept his existence from Bernard and Gillie. He must have thought the reason was them rather than Margaret's own peculiar scruples.

"I already have," Alan said. "Er...what is your plan?"

"Ruin him. Win his money, prove he is a cheat, and ruin him." Bernard's breath caught. "Felicia!"

Leaving Gillie to say anything else necessary, he all but bolted back into the gaming room, searching frantically for Felicia. If Harlaw had somehow taken her as he had Isabella...

She sat at the back of the room, at one of the piquet tables, looking somehow unbearably elegant, her elbow on the table, her hand lightly against her cheek before she played. She gazed directly at her opponent, Harlaw.

Harlaw's complexion was more florid than usual. Before even seeing the cards, or the points, Bernard knew he was losing, and badly. So badly that the game was drawing quite a crowd. Well, at least she was safe among so many…

Bernard eased his way to the front of their audience. His heart skipped a beat as he realized Felicia had eschewed all subtlety. Harlaw won an occasional few points, but never enough to reverse the extraordinary total of Felicia's.

It was a master class, not only in the skills of piquet, but in the ruthlessness of gaming.

"Remember this is for charity, Mrs. Maitland," old Lady Braithwaite said with a hint of distaste that infuriated Bernard as never before. He had to bite his tongue, remain invisible, or the end game would fail.

"I will pay my charitable dues, my lady," Felicia said without raising her eyes from the cards.

Harlaw's face was now white. He tried to smile as he sat back, acknowledging total defeat. "The game is yours, madam."

"It is," Felicia agreed. "Do we stop there, or have you the desire and the means to continue?"

Harlaw laughed, an unnatural, oddly grating sound.

"That amuses you?" Felicia said. "Why? Because it is that what you said to my husband? *All my winnings against your town house?*"

Someone gasped. There was a rustle of movement, both avid and uncomfortable. Her taunt was a mistake, reminding Harlaw of his past successes. She saw it as immediately as Bernard, for her eyes flashed a hint of self-annoyance and defiance.

Harlaw sat up and snapped his fingers for brandy. The predator was back.

On the other hand, Felicia's reminder seemed to revive more sympathy for the widow whose husband had been fleeced by this same man, to the extent of making her homeless and crushed by debt. Only Bernard understood the deeper wounds, those she showed to no one.

In that moment, his heart broke, because he finally understood that whatever happened this night, he would lose. Felicia would never trust any man, let alone someone like Bernard, to whom gaming was second nature.

But he could not fall apart now. He would not let her down.

He could not dwell on her play, her beauty, her every expression. He could not even watch the cards that could still destroy her hopes. Instead, he stood by Harlaw's chair, fixing his gaze to the man's hands, to his every physical movement, however small.

The moment would come, he knew that. Harlaw had lost Isabella, as he must have been well aware. He could still attack Margaret's reputation from spite, of course, but it would do him no material good. He needed his money back *now*, if only to escape the country and try again abroad. Or just to avoid debtors' prison.

Or worse. Isabella could still charge him with abduction and false imprisonment, if she found the courage...

Concentrate, imbecile!

He had to guess the ups and downs of the game from the reactions of Harlaw and the other watchers. Hardly anyone else seemed to be playing as the whole room tried to see the ruin of a man at the hands of a woman who, as anyone who understood the game could see, clearly had the greater skill.

Harlaw benefited from odd moments of luck. But Bernard knew from the gasps of the watchers that Felicia was still pressing him hard, forcing him toward use of those extra cards inevitably still hidden somewhere on his person.

Harlaw was good. Bernard allowed him that. He had been cheating for years, and no one had ever been able to quite catch him. And that, Bernard suddenly realized, was because he used stage tricks of misdirection. He took advantage of moments when all attention was drawn elsewhere, as now, when everyone waited with bated breath for Felicia's final card.

Harlaw met her gaze, held it, smiling, taunting as she began to lay down her card. And then he moved.

A mere scratch of his wrist whisked one card into his right sleeve, and one from the left into his hand. If Bernard had blinked, he would have missed it. As it was, there was no time even to think.

He shot out his hand, grasping Harlaw's left wrist and pinning it to the table with a bump.

Everyone stared at Bernard, astonished, no doubt, by such sudden violence in a man they had assumed always amiable. Some of these people had known him all his life.

Harlaw's muscles jumped under Bernard's fingers, like an involuntary spasm, but he made no effort to throw his attacker off. He couldn't, or it would reveal the card hidden in his palm. There was stark terror behind the outrage in his eyes.

"Bernard, old boy…" someone murmured in embarrassment.

"What in the world…?"

An uncomfortable titter of laughter.

Then Felicia spoke with calm interest. "Ace of hearts?"

Bernard wrenched Harlaw's hand over. In fury, the man fought back, even curling his fingers over the concealed card. But Bernard grasped the hand firmly, palm up.

"Open your hand," Tristram Grant said quietly. "Prove him wrong."

"I will not grace such an insult with proof of its folly," Harlaw blustered. "I am a gentleman! Clearly Muir is not."

"Open your damned hand," Lord Braithwaite said with unexpected fury, and leaned over, wrenching up Harlaw's fingers.

A crumpled card lay in his palm. Grant leaned forward and picked it up, lifting his eyes slowly to Felicia's. "Ace of hearts."

"Yes, but how does she know?" Harlaw screamed. "Because *she* is the cheat! I have only been trying to catch her, expose her to you all!"

Savagely, Bernard wrenched him to his feet, his fist already swinging back. He hadn't hit anyone since foolish fights in the school playground. Harlaw tried to yank free, but quite suddenly, Sir Julius Vale grasped Bernard's arm.

"Don't hurt your knuckles," he advised. "Turn him upside down and shake him."

Chapter Eighteen

WITHOUT WARNING, FELICIA began to laugh. Revenge, anger, tragedy, all dissolved into mirth, for between them, Bernard and Julius really did turn Harlaw upside down and shake him. As the cheat yelled and struggled, cards fluttered out of his coat pocket and cuffs.

Bernard and Julius had stood up for her, believed in her, publicly. The knowledge warmed her heart and tightened her throat with tears, but all she could do was laugh.

"He took them from the discarded pack after he lost at loo," Bernard explained, giving Harlaw one last shake before he and Julius abruptly let him go with perfectly synchronized timing.

Harlaw dropped to the floor.

"Apologies, ladies and gentlemen," Julius said. "but we could not allow it to continue."

"False accusations!" Harlaw screamed from the floor. "Muir is only trying to discredit me because I know all about his whore of an aunt, and as for his stepmother…"

Bernard whitened. And all Felicia's laughter vanished, because however indirectly, she had caused this. But something very strange happened. Every one of the men and women present turned their back on Harlaw and began to talk as if he was not there.

"Of course, Mrs. Maitland wins his house now," Lady

Braithwaite said loudly to Grant. "As is only fitting in the circumstances. But what can the hospital do with a tenth of a London house?"

"Sell it," Felicia said shakily. Her gaze met Bernard's. She had wanted the money also to help him fulfil his dream of travel, his own club somewhere in Europe. But he would never accept it from her. She read that much in his eyes. He had never even been comfortable about her using her advantage in play, except against the man who had wronged her, and had now wronged his aunt and his stepmother too. She had his permission.

She turned to Mr. Grant. "The house is all yours, for the hospital. I find I do not even want his money now, beyond paying back my brothers and sisters for what he stole from me when he cheated my husband."

"Slander!" Harlaw cried from the floor.

No one so much as glanced at him at him.

"That is very generous," Grant said quietly. "And especially appreciated, as I'm sure you know after the hospital's recent troubles."

"Will his family honor debts to a woman?" Lady Wickenden wondered aloud.

"Yes," the dowager Lady Braithwaite said, so firmly that everyone looked at her, and no one doubted her.

Braithwaite bestowed an affectionate smile upon his mother. Bernard smiled at her too, and rather to Felicia's surprise, the dowager smiled back. They too were old friends.

Bernard was at the heart of this community. In many ways he *was* the heart—friendly, tolerant, kind, fun… Felicia's heart began to ache all over again. He was everything she had ever wanted from the days of her romantic girlhood, everything and more she had ever secretly hungered for in the darkness of unfulfilled and lonely nights. But she had made her decision long ago, and she knew it was the right one. She just had not expected such intense pain.

"So the money he cheated from Mrs. Maitland and her hus-

THE GAMBLER'S LAST CHANCE

band is returned," Isabella said suddenly, and she did not sound satisfied at all. "And through the hospital, he makes reparation to all he has cheated since he came to Blackhaven. But what of his other crimes?"

Bernard turned slowly to face her. Lord and Lady Wickenden stood beside her.

"What other crimes?" asked Mr. Winslow, the magistrate.

Isabella lifted her chin. "Abduction, kidnap, false imprisonment—whatever the correct charge is, I make it against him."

For the first time since they had turned their backs on him for insulting the Muirs, everyone turned to regard Harlaw.

He was on his feet now, halfway between the crowd and the inn door, and froze under the sudden attention. He could only sneer, but his voice sounded wild, almost unhinged.

"You, who led me to that disused barn to seduce me? You were the most willing, the most eager captive ever!"

"*Commoner* doesn't really come close to describing you, does it?" Bernard said, walking inexorably toward him.

Wickenden and Julius approached the door from one side, Roderick and Cornelius from the other. Harlaw's eyes flickered.

"You don't know the truth of it," he jeered. "You don't even know where she was this last week! She was with me!"

"On the contrary," Wickenden said in his soft, dangerous voice, "she was...er—with us at the Muir house from Saturday evening after Bernard and Mrs. Maitland brought her home."

"We saw her on Saturday evening, too," Lady Torridon piped up. "She did not look well, poor lady."

Lord Torridon took a threatening step forward, glaring at Harlaw. "Are you going to call my wife and everyone else a liar too? It's clear to everyone who the liar is. Besides, we have witnesses to her false imprisonment—alone—for several hours in the old barn."

"Fool!" Harlaw flung at him with mingled triumph and contempt. "Even if they didn't vanish into the criminal slime they sprang from, they would never bear witness."

Felicia said with certainty, "They will for Bernard."

Harlaw blinked at her. Everyone else stared.

"And," Alan Bryant added, "I believe you have just betrayed knowledge of said witnesses. I call that proof, Mr. Winslow."

"So do I," Winslow growled. "Seize him. Trent, be so good as to send for my men."

"No need, sir," Trent said cheerfully. "There are enough here to see him off to the gaol."

As Trent's men and a local officer manhandled the furious Harlaw out of the door, a silence descended on the players in the inn, who all looked at each other as though wondering what on earth had just happened that they should see a well-known and fashionable gentleman of excellent family hauled away to prison during a charity card party.

We won, Felicia thought numbly. *Despite the odds, we won.* She moved toward Bernard from an instinct to be near him, to feel the mood of celebration. But he did not look at her.

"Game of cards, anyone?" he said mildly, and laughter broke out around the room. Wickenden clapped him on the back, and Aubrey hauled him off by the arm to play.

Felicia smiled, yet she felt suddenly shaky, as though she were about to cry. She turned away, longing for the peace and solitude to be found at Black Hill. Perhaps she should take the twins home, though the party would finish soon anyway...

Her gaze fell on Genevra Winslow, who was watching Bernard with tears shimmering in her eyes. Felicia felt a stab of guilt, wondering all over again if she had overset Genevra's hopes. And yet those hopes would never have been fulfilled, for Bernard did not love her.

"You look at my sister," said a bitter voice beside her, and she glanced up at Geoffrey Winslow. His lips twisted. "You and Bernard Muir are the heroes of the hour—again!—and no one notices the rest of the carnage you leave so blithely in your wake!"

"I beg your pardon," Felicia said frostily. "You appear to have mistaken me for some housemaid who has failed to give satisfaction. If you would rather Harlaw were back here cheating, take it up with your father, not me. Until you are prepared to apologize, please do not trouble to address me again."

Geoffrey flushed bright red. In truth, he had no business to speak to anyone like that, let alone a lady. He had the grace to bow, though it was a jerky affair, and muttered, "I'm sorry—my feelings got the better of me, but that is no excuse for rudeness."

"There really is no reason for such feelings either," Felicia said. "I thought you and Mr. Muir were friends."

"So did I," Geoffrey said savagely, and stalked away.

Of all the people Felicia had ever met in Blackhaven, Geoffrey was the only one she had ever heard speak ill or disparagingly of Bernard Muir. And that was all very recent. Since the garden party, in fact. Since then, some devil of hate had clearly been eating Geoffrey from the inside out.

Because of Genevra's foolish jealousy?

Roderick materialized beside her, throwing his arm around her shoulder in a brief, fierce hug. "A splendid victory," he said, grinning. "Well done, Fliss."

"It was a joint effort. I could not have been sure of anyone's safety without you and the others. Thanks, Rod." It struck her that she had not seen him so relaxed since he had first come home from Waterloo, not evening during his wedding—heavens, was that only yesterday? She peered at him more closely. "Marriage is agreeing with you already."

That Roderick could blush was another revelation. "Helen is all I ever wanted. Realizing it was the challenge." He hesitated a moment, then said, "She is young, as you were when you married Maitland. I always thought you were too young."

"I was."

"Helen is not."

"Of course she is not," Felicia said bracingly, before it came to her that Roderick was not seeking reassurance. He was communicating something else entirely.

"Experience varies," he said. "One bad marriage does not damn the entire institution."

She nodded, because suddenly she could not speak.

"Take your time, Fliss, by all means. But don't throw your future away because of the past."

"I don't know what you mean," she said with dignity.

His lips quirked. "Yes, you do. I like Muir. Which is hardly important, besides the fact that so does Lucy. And the twins approve. In many ways, it seems to me, he is perfect for you."

Tears hurt her throat, tears she refused to shed. "Don't, Rod. I can't bear that *ownership* again. I can't."

Casually, he kissed the top of her head. "But can you live with the alternative?"

Missing him. Loneliness, pain... These things would all pass. Marriage was before God and forever. Vows that women took seriously and men did not.

Experience varies.

"Felicia. Last game of commerce?" Antonia Macy took her arm, and Felicia smiled because here was another upcoming marriage that she knew would be happy and honorable. Antonia and Julius, Lucy and her mad Eddleston, Roderick and Helen.

"I am so glad Julius met you again," Felicia blurted, and Antonia smiled and hugged her arm.

During the game, her mind wandered, and she found herself increasingly aware of Bernard on the other side of the room. His presence, his being, was a joy that somehow *hurt*. She rose from the table with a minor loss, and moved toward the twins, who were chattering with Miss Gaunt and her brother-in-law Lord Launceton, known locally as the mad Russian.

"Felicia."

Was that why she had left her game? In the hope that Bernard would leave his and come to her?

"I have hardly seen you all night," he said lightly. "Not even to congratulate you on the rather brilliant thrashing you gave Harlaw."

"Beating him is easy. It was you who finally caught his sleight of hand and exposed him."

"Walk with me, then, and we can congratulate each other."

Experience varies. She blocked Roderick's voice from her mind, and yet found herself walking toward the inn door by Bernard's side. Just because simply being with him made her happy.

The evening was somewhat chilly for summer, but at least it was not raining. She took Bernard's proffered arm. Would this be the last time? Or could he, would he, persuade her otherwise? Her confused heart beat too quickly. She no longer knew what she wanted.

"Isabella was rather wonderful," she said. "I wasn't sure she could stand up to him, let alone accuse him, after what she has been through. Or even if she should."

"She said your courage was her inspiration."

Felicia blinked. "*Mine?* If only she knew!"

"Knew what?"

Felicia shook her head. They strolled around the corner of the building, toward the stable yard. The silence between them was warm and exciting as it had always been.

"You mean the world to me," he said. "From the moment I met you. You always will. My one and only."

Her heart shattered all over again. "I'm sorry," she whispered. Sorry for making him suffer, for not being the woman he deserved, young and loving and innocent.

"Don't be," he said with sudden intensity. "I am not. I bless the night I met you. I treasure every moment you spent with me, every word, every caress. Felicia…"

He stopped, swinging around to face her, but she had already turned into his arms, raising her mouth to his.

His kiss was almost like coming home. Almost. But it was too deep, too desperate, too passionate. So lost was Felicia that it took her several moments to realize he was kissing her goodbye.

"I know you cannot love me, that you will never marry me," he whispered. "And yet still I am glad. Still I hope that one day, it will be different. We may never have that day, but I will always love you. Always."

He kissed her again, silencing the half-formed words, and there was only wild, overwhelming feeling. And then he tore himself free and strode off.

She stumbled after him to the corner of the building, her mouth open to call after him. Only she didn't know what to say. She had no words except *I love you*, words that had nothing to do with marriage. And without marriage, he would not take her.

He was wrong that she could not love him, and she wanted desperately to tell him so. And yet why hurt him further? Because he was right about his other belief, that she could never marry him.

His tall, vanishing figure blurred before her eyes as he strode out of the inn yard and hurried up the street. She touched her tingling lips as though to hold his kisses to her, to keep the memory of his mouth on hers forever. Dampness washed over her fingers. She tasted salt on her lips.

"If it were anyone, my love, it would be you," she whispered, and let the tears come.

She only allowed herself a few moments of weakness. Outward weakness. She knew the pain would go on, perhaps forever, but in parting, at least they preserved the love. Bernard was only three or four and twenty. He would love again, and she wished him happiness with another. Really, truly, she did. For he, more than anyone she had ever met, deserved it.

She went back inside and straight to the ladies' cloakroom, where she splashed water on her face and practiced smiling again. She hadn't done that since the early days of her humiliation, when she discovered that everyone had always known about Nick's infidelities.

Emerging from the cloakroom, she almost walked into Lord Wickenden, who, hat in hand, was heading for the front door. He paused to bow to her, with a quick smile, then hurried outside. A few paces behind him came Geoffrey Winslow and a young lieutenant from the 44th. They barely noticed her, but their faces were grim and serious, not those of young men who had just enjoyed a convivial evening of cards and were about to go on, no doubt, to further entertainment.

Perhaps they had lost. Or Geoffrey was still bearing all his foolish grudges against Bernard.

Returning to the main body of the gaming room, she was surprised to see play still in progress. No one else seemed in a hurry to leave the party. There were still games to win, dues to pay, the main scandal of the evening to gossip over.

Felicia, for once, could face no more games. It was time to pay the rest of her charitable dues, and merely watch until her family were ready to leave. The twins were taking an unhealthy interest in the game of macao unfolding in the middle of the room. Aubrey was losing at Faro.

Felicia moved toward Kate Grant. She had to squeeze behind a young girl watching the macao.

"Sorry," the girl muttered, moving aside without looking.

Felicia paused, for it was Genevra Winslow, and her eyes were full of unshed tears. Strands of thought seemed to wrap around each other and snap into place in Felicia's mind.

No one had left the party since Harlaw's exodus, except Bernard, Wickenden, Geoffrey Winslow, and one officer. Bernard and Winslow had quarreled. Bernard had said goodbye to her.

No.

No, he would not...

Brushing past the oblivious Genevra, Felicia changed directions and marched up to Aubrey's table, all but yanking him out of his seat.

"Dash it, Fliss, steady on!" he protested. "Where's the fire?"

"You tell me. Is Bernard Muir fighting a duel?"

"Hush, for God's sake," Aubrey said, clearly harassed. "You're not meant to know about such things."

"Which is why they still happen," she raged. "Is it with Geoffrey Winslow?"

He stared at her defiantly.

"You don't need to answer that. Oh, the devil, I never imagined he could be so *stupid!*"

"Not really his fault," Aubrey said. "From what I hear, Winslow rather forced it on him and refused reasonable apologies."

"Why?" she demanded. "What is it all about?"

Genevra. There was no need to ask. Genevra had escalated her claims to Bernard and somehow brought these two to a lethal quarrel.

"I don't know," Aubrey said. "And I wouldn't tell you if I could. Leave it alone, Felicia, you'll only—"

"Where is it to be?" she interrupted, in a sudden panic. "When?"

But she knew the when, didn't she? The principal players had already left the party, and she was as sure as she could be that it was not to get an early night.

"I don't know," Aubrey said. He sounded so relieved that she believed him.

Swinging away without further word, she marched back across the room to Genevra. Without pause, she linked arms with the astonished young woman and walked her briskly to the private parlor where, earlier, Bernard had greeted his aunt and cousin.

It was empty.

"I have no desire whatever to speak to you!" Genevra exclaimed, as though suddenly springing to life when Felicia closed the door. "What do you want of me now?"

"Information," Felicia replied coldly. "What did you tell your brother about Bernard Muir? That he had offered you marriage and then reneged?"

Two spots of color appeared on the girl's cheeks. "You are insulting."

"No, but I rather think you were. At the castle ball, you were in the stables with Waller Harlaw. Bernard saw you."

"Of what are you accusing me now?" gasped Genevra.

"Oh, not of an illicit love affair with Harlaw," Felicia said, allowing contempt into her voice. "Even *he* could not manage *three* women in a town the size of Blackhaven. Did he tell you these foolish accusations would win you Bernard's heart and hand? I'll bet you never told Geoffrey that part of your tragedy."

The red marks on Genevra's cheeks had spread across her entire face and neck. "Bernard is so stupid to be inveigled by your ageing charms! He deserves everything he gets!"

Felicia held her gaze. "A bullet in the stomach?" she suggested. "Or would the heart be more fitting? Either way, he'd be dead and unable to marry you. Perhaps you could wear black and get the attention due a grieving, affianced bride. Is that what you want? You want him dead?"

The blood drained from Genevra's face so quickly that she almost fell into the nearest chair. "Stop it!"

"You object to *my* brutality?" Felicia said incredulously. "You, who have lied through your teeth in order to send your brother to kill your old friend? Does it matter if it's the other way around and Bernard kills Geoffrey? Will you enjoy comforting your parents in their grief? Won't you feel even a *tad* guilty?"

"Why are you being so awful to me?" Genevra whispered, white-faced.

"*I* am being awful? Genevra, your lies endanger both of their lives! You do know that if one of them dies, the other will hang?"

A great sob erupted from the girl as she dropped her face into her hands. "Stop it! Stop it!"

"I can't stop it," Felicia said. "Only you can do that."

There was silence, apart from Genevra's shuddering breath. After several moments, she raised her tear-stained face. "It has gone too far," she said in despair. "I can't stop it now."

"You can. Geoffrey does not want to kill his friend. And despite your foolishness, I don't believe you want him to either. But that is the reality if all you will do is sit here feeling sorry for yourself while your brother and your old friend try to blow each other's brains out over your lies."

Genevra moaned and clutched her hair in both hands. "How?" she burst out. "How do I put it right?"

"Oh, for..." Felicia drew a calming breath. "You tell the truth. Now."

"But it will be too late," the girl wailed. "I think—I am afraid!—they're doing it now!"

"Where?" Felicia all but barked at her.

"I don't know! They never tell women such things!"

"But I'll bet some know all the same. Fetch your cloak and wait for me outside the front door."

"But what...what will I tell my mother?"

"Whatever you like," Felicia said brutally. "Invention has not been a problem for you up until now."

Striding from the room, she found Gillie helping Kate tally the donations and winnings.

"Where do duels happen in Blackhaven?" she demanded.

"Braithwaite Cove, as a rule," Gillie said at once. Her eyes narrowed. "Why? Oh God, Wickenden hasn't reverted—"

"Not Wickenden," Felicia said quickly. "But if you could send Dr. Lampton there, that might be best."

"If there is a duel, he will be there already. He always is, however much he rails—"

Felicia did not wait for the rest, merely snatched her cloak from the cloakroom and hurried outside.

Genevra seized her arm. "Hurry!" she pleaded. "Oh, hurry! What have I *done*?"

Chapter Nineteen

I T WAS AS if Felicia's contempt had forced scales from the younger girl's eyes, and now she was as terrified as Felicia by the results of her lies. They managed to hail a hackney in the street before they got as far as the hotel, and ordered it to take the road as far as Braithwaite Cove.

"What did you tell your mother?" Felicia asked, mainly to distract the younger woman as she sat with her hands squeezed together in her lap.

"Nothing," Genevra replied. "She didn't see me leave."

"Then we had better be quick before she notices," Felicia said wryly.

"Oh God, what if we are too late?"

"Pray we are not."

There was light coming from the beach, even before they reached the cove.

"It must be them," Genevra cried, thrusting her head out of the window. "And there's a carriage stopped here!"

Felicia rapped on the roof, and their own carriage pulled up behind. The women all but tumbled out of it.

"Wait," Felicia commanded the jarvey, already rushing to the edge of the hill that sloped down to the beach.

The scene below was perfectly clear, by the light of many lanterns set up in an oval shape along the stretch of beach only visible when the tide was out. If it had not been lit up like Vauxhall Gardens, it would not even have been visible from the castle.

Felicia recognized Lord Wickenden standing outside the oval of light in company with the same young officer who had previously been with Geoffrey. A couple of feet away from them stood Dr. Lampton, rigid with disapproval. Within the oval, two men were pacing away from each other. Each held a pistol in his right hand by his side.

"Oh God, we're too late!" Genevra cried. "They'll never stop for us now!"

Felicia did not answer, simply hurled herself down the hill. For clarity had burst into her mind with all the force of a pistol shot. She could almost hear it echoing in her brain as she slid and ran and tumbled down the hill.

Bernard could *die*. In moments. This was what she had been moving heaven and earth to prevent.

Without Bernard, her life was nothing.

Besides her love and his, what did anything else matter?

I will not let him die! I will not!

❧

BERNARD HAD WALKED to the meeting place still with the hope that Geoffrey would see the truth and come to his senses. He had the feeling that they were all still being manipulated by Waller Harlaw.

Wickenden and Dr. Lampton caught up with him on the path down to the beach.

"Do I really need to tell you this is idiocy?" Lampton fumed.

"No, but feel free to repeat it to Geoffrey," Bernard replied. "Is Carey bringing the lanterns?"

"They're here already," Wickenden said. "All we have to do is light them."

"Splendid," Lampton said. "That should bring the watch down upon us."

Bernard helped light the lanterns and spread them along the sand. In the meantime, Geoffrey and Carey arrived. Wickenden went to speak to Carey, but one sight of Geoffrey was enough to tell Bernard that there would be no reconciliation. The fool was still determined to go through with this. Though it was probably only pride now.

Well, they could all go through the motions. For Bernard, the duel, like the arrest of Harlaw, was only a minor distraction from the misery of parting from Felicia.

"He's holding firm," Wickenden said grimly. "But don't make it a killing matter, Bernard. I really doubt Geoffrey will."

Bernard was a pretty good shot. Wickenden himself had taught him at his country estate, and at Manton's shooting gallery in London. But he doubted Geoffrey's accuracy. If Bernard died, he expected it to be by accident.

The duelists met in the middle of the oval of light. Their seconds checked the pistols, and Geoffrey snatched one up. Bernard took the other and looked Geoffrey full in the face. But Geoffrey's gaze was fixed on a point above his head. He turned his back without a word.

No, no reconciliation. Lampton was right. This was a bloody stupid way to solve anything. But Bernard knew how to play his part. He turned his back to Geoffrey's and, on Wickenden's instruction, began to walk away.

By the count of twenty, Bernard had had enough. He was damned if he would play this silly game any further just to please Geoffrey or Genevra or bloody Harlaw. He turned. Geoffrey faced him and raised his pistol, his arm at full stretch, his body side-on in the classic duelist's stance.

"Bah," Bernard said. With his pistol still at his side, he strode toward Geoffrey.

"What are you doing?" Geoffrey demanded. "Get back and face me!"

Bernard kept walking. "I *am* facing you. Blow my head off if you want. I was going to *delope* anyway. But what the hell is the point? Why should I even pretend I want to kill someone I remember being born? I did not wrong you. I did not wrong Genevra. And if you can't accept that, tough! Shoot me."

Vaguely, through the sound of his own voice, he was aware of others—women's—voices. One of them sounded like Felicia, so he presumed he was going mad. He kept his gaze on Geoffrey's furious, boyish face.

And then something hurtled in front of him, blocking Geoffrey from view. He blinked. Perhaps he had already been shot and was now unconscious and dreaming, for Felicia threw herself against him.

Felicia...!

One arm closed about her because nothing else was possible. Helplessly, he held the pistol away from them both, and someone—Wickenden?—took it from his grasp.

"*I* was going to *delope*!" Geoffrey declared furiously.

Incredibly, Genevra was tugging at her brother's pistol arm and shouting at him. "Don't shoot, Geoffrey, don't! I made it all up. None of it was true. Bernard never touched me *or* offered me marriage. I lied for stupid, stupid reasons, and I am so very sorry..."

"Harlaw was whispering in her ear," Felicia said, her voice muffled in Bernard's coat.

He didn't care. It was sweet to hold her, to feel his cares and anxieties drift away into the peace only she had ever brought him.

But then she drew back, and reluctantly, he loosened his hold. Geoffrey sat down on the sand as though his legs had given way. Hastily, Carey took the pistol from his grasp.

"Oh, thank God," Geoffrey said. "I couldn't *not* meet you, Bernard. I couldn't have people calling me a coward. But I *knew* you hadn't touched Genevra."

"So you would have *deloped*, too?" Felicia said, staring from one to the other. "The pair of you put us through that for

THE GAMBLER'S LAST CHANCE

nothing?"

"It was not for nothing," Geoffrey said with an attempt at
dignity. "Though I don't expect females to understand."

Bernard released Felicia. "Oh, they understand perfectly, and
it *was* for nothing. Idiot." He stretched down his hand to
Geoffrey, who clasped it and let Bernard haul him to his feet.

"Idiot yourself," Geoffrey said shakily.

"Well done, gentlemen," Dr. Lampton said sarcastically. "I
shall bid you goodnight and go back to bed."

"Oh, will you drop Genevra and Geoffrey back at the inn on
your way?" Felicia asked. "Mrs. Winslow will be looking for
them."

"Of course," Lampton said. "Wickenden? Carey?"

"I'll walk, thank you," Wickenden replied. "Bernard? Mrs.
Maitland?"

"I am going home," Felicia said firmly. "If someone would
pass that fact on to my family at the inn, I should be grateful.
Perhaps I might have your escort, Mr. Muir?"

There was nothing he wanted more. A few moments more
alone with her before a lifetime apart.

She had come to save him. She had thrown herself into the
path of Geoffrey's pistol without even considering her own
safety. Her care for him warmed his heart, his bones, even while
fear swamped him at what could have happened to her. But he
knew better than to read any more than friendship into it. It was
all part of her kindness, her spirit, her being.

God, he loved her.

Somehow, he was in a hired carriage, and it was driving along
the coast road toward Black Hill. The warmth of her body was
next to him. Her fingers closed around his hand, and he turned
his head to look at her.

"You persuaded Genevra to tell the truth."

"It wasn't hard by then. She had already seen what kind of a
man Harlaw was, knew she was in the wrong. I think she was
trying desperately not to think of the consequences when I forced

the issue. All she needed was a dose of reality. But still, we were afraid we were too late. My heart almost stopped when you walked right into the path of his pistol."

"You *ran* into its path," Bernard pointed out.

"Geoffrey would not have shot me."

"Turned out he wouldn't have shot me either."

"Except by accident. Dr. Lampton is quite right in his condemnation of duels."

"Of course he is. He gets to sew up the results periodically." He brought their joined hands to his mouth and kissed her knuckles. "Thank you."

She nodded. Her lips trembled. "I could not have borne you to die. Such fears do focus the mind and the heart. Bernard—" Her voice broke, and she swallowed. "Will you stay with me tonight?"

There was only one answer he could give. "Yes, I will stay with you tonight." And every night, if only she would let him.

∞

THE SERVANTS HAD gone to bed, leaving a lamp burning in the entrance hall. Felicia lit a candle from it and took Bernard by the hand, leading him through the quiet house to the staircase and upward to her bedchamber.

Her heart galloped, not just because she was with him, but because everything was different this time. No clandestine intrigue conducted in the summer house. She was taking him to her bower, her bed, her trust. He must surely grasp the difference, though she could not speak to explain it.

He took the candle from her, and she closed the door, turning the key in the lock. He moved toward the bed and lit the lamp there. He looked around her private space, her haven, which she had always kept light and tidy. A landscape of Tuscan hills decorated one wall. A faded, rather exquisite tapestry, the work of

THE GAMBLER'S LAST CHANCE

her grandmother, hung on another. Apart from the bed, her furniture was sparse—a small dressing table, a wardrobe, a washstand, a small bookcase. The whole effect was pleasant, airy, uncluttered, which was how she had wanted her whole life. Could he see that and understand?

Slowly, he walked back to her. Her heart melted because he was so beautiful, so *Bernard*, so beloved...

"I've missed you," she whispered as he took her face between his hands. She placed her fingers over his and parted her lips.

"And God, I have missed you," he said, and took her mouth.

It *was* different, this time. *He* was different, savoring every moment, every touch, every scent. He removed her clothes with care, letting her divest him of his between kisses that were hot and sweet and arousing. And yet leisurely, as if they had forever.

We do have forever, she thought with wonder, and felt no anxiety, no fear, only joy. She gave herself to him with eager passion, which somehow he met even while he slowed the journey, taking control from her and making love to her with exquisite tenderness. Her whole being thrummed with pleasure, with love and hunger and need. It became her mission to make him lose himself equally in her, and he let her see the bliss of her every caress, every movement beneath him.

The delight was so intense that it was a long time before she realized what he was doing. He was not just making love. He was saying goodbye. Again.

She gasped, unable to prevent the sudden tears trickling from her eyes.

"Oh, my sweet," he whispered, kissing the dampness on her cheeks and hair. "Why do you weep?"

"Because I have hurt you." She clung to him. "I thought you knew."

"Knew what?"

"What I only realized when I thought you would die and I would really, truly lose you. I need to be with you, Bernard. I love you. Please, will you marry me?"

He stilled, staring down at her.

"Please?" she whispered.

A smile slowly dawned in his eyes, spreading across his face as he began to move once more and brought them both to joy.

⊰⊱

AT SOME POINT during the night, the door handle turned. Then she heard the whispering of the twins and fading footsteps. She smiled sleepily and tucked herself even closer to her lover, inhaling the scent of his skin.

"Every night," she whispered, imagining he was asleep. "We can do this every night."

"And every day too, if we wish," he rumbled.

"I will wish," she assured him.

He smiled and kissed her hair. "What else shall we do when we are married?"

"I've been thinking about that," she said seriously. "Do you really want to leave Blackhaven?"

"Yes," he said. Then, "Not forever, perhaps."

"Don't you think there might be room for a gentlemen's club here? One with high standards, a gaming license, and frequent ladies' nights? Or even lady members!"

He rolled her under him, the better to see, perhaps, if she were joking. Slowly, the frown cleared as his eyes grew distant. "Perhaps...membership would be strict, but not by class, only by honesty."

"You could have a more exclusive salon, with supper, perhaps."

"We could..."

We. She smiled and kissed his shoulder.

"It will cost," Bernard warned. "It may take us years to save for such a venture. Especially if we go to Europe on an extended wedding journey."

"I've been thinking about that too," Felicia admitted. "And

THE GAMBLER'S LAST CHANCE

according to some, it's cheaper to live on the Continent than here in England. Plus, we have won a great deal of money between us. Even if we give a large part of my winnings from last night to the hospital—I know you will not accept a share of it—and pay back the last of what I owe to my family, we can invest a good deal."

"I know nothing about investments," Bernard said ruefully.

"I do," Felicia said. "I can't help but absorb such matters."

Bernard flopped back onto his side. "I won a good sum last night too," he admitted. "Added to my savings, it will be enough to marry and travel with, and perhaps to learn."

"Then we shall invest the rest of mine, ready for when we come home," Felicia said. She threw her arm around his neck and closed her eyes, smiling.

She was just nodding off when Bernard said, "When will you marry me, Felicia?"

"Tomorrow," she said drowsily, and he laughed softly, folding her close as they both fell asleep.

✂

SHE OPENED HER eyes to find Bernard gazing down at her in a shaft of sunlight through the window. She smiled with happiness—and a surge of thrilling desire, for he looked all golden, tousled, and handsome.

She slid her arms around his neck and reached for his mouth.

"Fliss!" came Delilah's voice, along with a brisk knock on the door. "Are you coming to church?"

"No," Felicia replied.

Bernard frowned and nodded energetically.

"Oh! Yes!" she called. "I need to speak to the vicar. Don't wait for me!" She bounced out of bed, and Bernard smiled appreciatively.

"We had better both speak to Grant," he said. "Will we catch him before the service and get him to read the banns today?"

"My family is rather monopolizing the banns," Felicia said.

"We can be married by special license if you prefer."

"Three weeks will not hurt us," Felicia said. "I think I would like to see Julius and Lucy married before we run off to Europe. Where shall we go?"

"Wherever you like," he said, rising and padding across to the washing bowl.

She joined him, skimming a hand over his hip.

His breath caught. "Don't do that, or we shall never get to church."

THEY WERE ONLY just in time to catch Mr. Grant before he left the vestry. He blinked with surprise to see them at such an inconvenient moment, but ended by laughing and agreeing to read their banns that very day.

His surprise was nothing, though, to her family's as they emerged into the church together only a moment ahead of the vicar, and squashed onto the end of a Vale pew.

Julius raised his eyebrows at her, and she smiled.

When it came to the reading of the banns, though, all her brothers reached over to shake Bernard's hand or thump him on the back. The twins were grinning and nodding enthusiastically.

And behind them, Gillie, Margaret, and Isabella smiled with genuine delight.

Felicia tucked her hand surreptitiously into Bernard's. She was not afraid. She was eager. Her new life with Bernard would be not only exciting but happy. And in that moment, she knew that no one could ever have more joy than she.

"Four down," Cornelius murmured in her ear. "Who is next?"

"I hope it will be you," she said, and his smile was uncharacteristically soft.

Epilogue

(Three years later)

I N IMMACULATE EVENING dress, Bernard strolled through the front door of Black's, glanced with approval at the liveried doorman, and said to Felicia, "Four carriages approaching."

Felicia could not remember ever being so nervous. So much hinged on this official opening of Black's Club—not just the success of the venture but the wellbeing of all employed therein, and also the place of her husband and herself in Blackhaven's respectable society.

When they had discussed their future during their two years of travel in Europe, they had called the club "Muir's." Only when they had come home had Bernard argued against the name.

"It ties us to ownership."

"We *are* the owners. Or will be. And everyone will know it."

"Yes, but...the secret of success in Society is not to thrust unpalatable truths in its face. The world might know the club is ours and that our labor has brought it about. But a gentleman does not run such an establishment. A lady most certainly does not work there."

She had stared at him in consternation. "I thought you wanted this. We both did."

"I still do—if you do. But we must be a little smarter. We

must not tie the club too obviously to us. We have to be more like…the sponsors of Almack's. We must be the patrons, the hosts of events, without shouting, *We are the owners and this is our living.*"

Felicia had frowned over this. "It sounds very hypocritical."

"Yes. But necessary. Like after my father died, when Gillie and I made money out of gaming in the house—we only got away with it by calling them card parties. It will be more comfortable for us. And for Celia."

She knew he meant for her. But it was the thought of the children that convinced her. Their daughter was a year old when they returned to Blackhaven, and in their hearts, she came first. Little Celia must not be brought up in a gaming house. She must not be shunned as the daughter of unrespectable parents.

"So, we shall live in your house," she had said.

Isabella had gifted the house to Bernard when she decided to spend half the year in Spain and buy a larger property in England.

"And we shall be the chief patrons of…what? The Blackhaven Club?"

"Or just Black's—the opposite of White's in London."

"Perfect! And we should draw the local worthies in by persuading them to make small investments in the venture. It will do us no harm to have Braithwaite associated with the place. And maybe Julius, now that he has Black Hill back on its feet. And Colonel Benedict, perhaps?"

And so finally, here they were, on opening night, the discreet chief owners of Black's, Blackhaven's newest club, welcoming the first members and their guests to the party.

Felicia's stomach jangled with nerves as Bernard came and stood beside her in the ornate foyer. His fingers curled around hers, and she smiled.

It was odd how that still worked. One touch, and all anger, fear, and doubt were vanquished. Bernard was her rock, her companion, her friend, her ally, and her partner. Most of all, he was her husband and lover. They rose or fell together, and her trust in him was utter.

The irresponsible fun and excitement of their travels in Europe, the nights of gaming, their months incognito managing a club in Geneva—all seemed to have been leading to this moment. Felicia's investments had done extraordinarily well, so much so that she now advised her brothers and brothers-in-law, too. Her money had paid for the refurbishment of these crumbling but beautiful buildings behind the high street, on the edge of the once failing and now reviving old business sector of the town, and for the staff to run the place, from maids and doormen to housekeeper and manager. The club's safety and honesty were protected by Roderick's growing company, who would also investigate the more doubtful membership applications. So far, all their members were people known to Bernard or Felicia or their families.

"Is it bad luck to wish ourselves good luck?" Felicia wondered.

"We make our own luck," Bernard reminded her. Despite the waiting footmen and the doorman, he dipped his head and kissed her lips. Just as the first approaching silk rustled, and, strengthened by his caress, Felicia turned her smile upon Lord and Lady Braithwaite and the guests lining up behind.

"Just imagine," young Lady Braithwaite said with a twinkle, "a club where ladies are not only permitted but welcomed! What do the gentlemen think of that? Most of them go to White's and its ilk to avoid female company."

"Here at Black's, we may avoid male company if we choose," Felicia said, sweeping the fascinated ladies with her across the foyer. "Let me show you the ladies' salons... In here we may chat or read or write letters. Through there, we may dine or take tea. And here is the ladies-only gaming salon."

"Then we are completely segregated from the gentlemen?" Bernard's Aunt Margaret asked.

"Only if you wish to be," Felicia replied. "The gentlemen have a similar arrangement upstairs. In between are the mixed salons, where we shall have supper tonight—and play some cards, if you choose!"

"I do love a game of cards," Margaret confided. "It does seem quite perfect, my dear. Only…" She lowered her voice. "Will the company be respectable?"

"We have not limited membership to the gentry," Felicia admitted. "But standards of respectable behavior will always be maintained. Personally, I have found it very beneficial to talk to people of other walks of life and learn about their joys and concerns."

Lady Braithwaite looked about her, at the tasteful decoration and furniture, at the ornate ceilings and the crystal glass in her hand. "But we are not talking about the poor, are we, Felicia?"

"No. Membership costs. But the club also employs a lot of people who will grow considerably less poor with time."

"You want us to believe it is a charity?" Mrs. Winslow asked. She was still a little stiff with Felicia, having picked up Genevra's dislike of three years ago without acknowledging the younger women had become friends ever since the abortive duel.

Felicia smiled. "Hardly. Though I see no problem with us holding charitable events here."

"No, that would work very well," Mrs. Grant said. "This is very spacious. Tell me again about your grades of member-ship…"

❧

IT WAS TWO o'clock in the morning before Felicia and Bernard returned home, exhausted but still excited by the success of the evening and the buzz of ideas for the future.

Bernard, who had lived most of his life in this house, could climb the stairs without any lights, but he carried a candle for Felicia's benefit. Without any discussion they turned as one toward the nursery, and found little Celia asleep, quite undisturbed by old Dulcie's snores coming from the adjoining room.

"I can't believe how beautiful she is," Bernard said softly.

A lump formed in Felicia's throat. "I still can't quite believe she exists. I thought I was barren."

Bernard's arm crept round her waist. "I would have loved you just the same if you were. But this...this is perfect. She is perfect."

The child stirred in her sleep, emitting a huffy little sigh, but she didn't wake. She was a happy child, extremely lively during the day, which at least meant she slept soundly through the night. Though she was a little too much for the ageing Dulcie.

Felicia took Bernard's hand and drew him quietly from the room. "Perhaps we need a nursery maid," she said as they walked to their newly decorated bedchamber.

"Someone for Dulcie to boss about? Celia does run rings around her, and we will both be quite busy now that the club has opened."

"And now," Felicia said, "that Celia is likely to have a little brother or sister."

It took him a moment to realize she was not speaking generally of some possible event in the future. His sleeve button dropped from his suddenly numb fingers.

Felicia came closer and wound her arms around his neck. "Are you happy?"

The quick smile she loved flooded his face, leaving her in no doubt. "Oh, my dear, my love, I could not be happier..."

Inevitably, after much talk and sweet, gentle loving, it was very late indeed before they fell asleep. As a result, they slept in and rose to face a very busy day with much to do and to plan. And so much to be grateful for that Felicia was ecstatic.

Author's Note

I hope you enjoyed Bernard and Felicia's story!

Readers of the original *Blackhaven Brides* series will know that Bernard has been a constant presence in the town from the very first book, *The Wicked Baron*. It has been one of my great writing pleasures to see him grow throughout the series from callow youth to responsible yet still fun-loving young man.

Over the years readers have often asked me about him and if he was ever going to have his own happily ever after, but I always felt he was too young—a mere twenty-one in *The Wicked Baron*. However, since *One Night in Blackhaven* opens in 1816, three years after Bernard's first appearance on the page, I finally decided it was time. Hope you agree!

Next up (July 2024), in *The Poet's Stern Critic*, is another old friend from the original series, Lady Alice Conway. Her sweet-natured, talented younger sister Helen already found happiness in *The Soldier's Impossible Love*, but Alice, equally talented in her own way, is a much more abrasive character who will need a very special man to make her fall in love. He might just be another Vale ☺.

About the Author

Mary Lancaster lives in Scotland with her husband, three mostly grown-up kids and a small, crazy dog.

Her first literary love was historical fiction, a genre which she relishes mixing up with romance and adventure in her own writing. Her most recent books are light, fun Regency romances written for Dragonblade Publishing: *The Imperial Season* series set at the Congress of Vienna; and the popular *Blackhaven Brides* series, which is set in a fashionable English spa town frequented by the great and the bad of Regency society.

Connect with Mary on-line – she loves to hear from readers:

Email Mary: Mary@MaryLancaster.com

Website: www.MaryLancaster.com

Newsletter sign-up: http://eepurl.com/b4Xoif

Facebook: facebook.com/mary.lancaster.1656

Facebook Author Page: facebook.com/MaryLancasterNovelist

Twitter: @MaryLancNovels

Amazon Author Page:
amazon.com/Mary-Lancaster/e/B00DJ5IACI

Bookbub:
bookbub.com/profile/mary-lancaster

Milton Keynes UK
Ingram Content Group UK Ltd.
UKHW021137130524
442628UK00014B/649

9 781963 585513